Dekker's Dozen:

The Armageddon Seeds

Special Offer:

Get a free 5-book Starter Library from Christopher Schmitz FOR FREE Details found at the end of this book. Subscribers who sign up for this no-spam newsletter get free books, exclusive content, and more!

Dekker's Dozen:
The Armageddon Seeds

by
Christopher D. Schmitz

PUBLISHED BY TREESHAKER BOOKS
please visit:
http://www.authorchristopherdschmitz.com

For those fans at conventions who kept requesting new Dekker's Dozen story… even more is on the way! These characters keep me awake at night, demanding I continue telling their tales.

Contents:

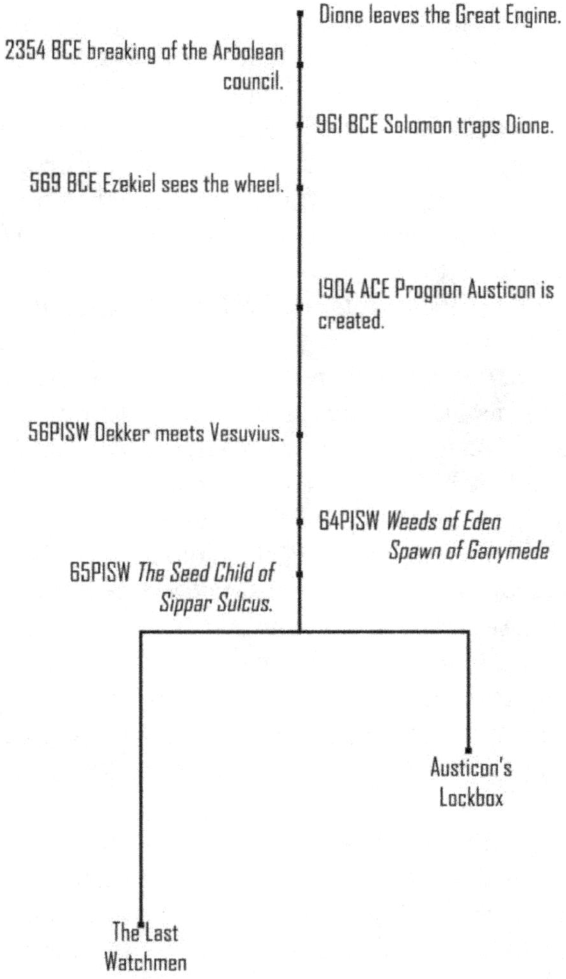
Dione leaves the Great Engine.
2354 BCE breaking of the Arbolean council.
961 BCE Solomon traps Dione.
569 BCE Ezekiel sees the wheel.
1904 ACE Prognon Austicon is created.
56PISW Dekker meets Vesuvius.
64PISW *Weeds of Eden*
Spawn of Ganymede
65PISW *The Seed Child of Sippar Sulcus.*
Austicon's Lockbox
The Last Watchmen

Author's Note:

The Dekker's Dozen series involves occasional elements of time travel that can confuse some of the events. Those familiar with *The Last Watchmen* will have encountered the minor character Ezekiel who works to preserve the fabric of reality by traveling through time via arcane technology. *A Waxing Arbolean Moon* adds some further details to the chronology and all prior to the events of *The Last Watchmen.*

The Last Watchmen represents the original time-stream as A. Its ending makes it clear that a B stream exists. Some events of *The Last Watchmen* happen in both. *A Waxing Arbolean Moon* takes place prior to the split of the time stream but also prior to the existence of chronology B. *A Waxing Arbolean Moon* and *Weeds of Eden* both happens in the A& B lines and function as prequels to both the *Last Watchmen* timeline and the new, ongoing timeline (timeline B). It may sound confusing as I'm trying not to give away spoilers for any of the stories.

I originally began writing *Weeds of Eden* as a bit of a writing exercise and wanted to demonstrate some character elements and backstory from *The Last Watchmen* while I worked with some new story outlining software for a future project. I figured some familiar and well-loved characters would be right at home for me to whip up an 8k-9k short story over a week so I could experiment with the software elements and have a product people were asking for at conventions. Yeah… ten days later I had written more than twice that, completed the short story which became the first in a series of three, and sketched notes for a follow-up novel (tentatively called Austicon's Lockbox).

Hopefully the preceding graphic helps keep the timelines organized for the reader. Because Ezekiel is pivotal to *The Last Watchmen* but not necessarily the future stories, *Weeds of Eden* is perhaps the most logical place to begin reading this series. (If you want my recommended reading order, at the time of writing this it would be: *Weeds of Eden, The Last Watchmen,* and then *A Waxing Arbolean Moon.*)

I'm super excited to get back into the Dozen's world! If you guys keep requesting stories, I'll keep writing them.

--Christopher D Schmitz

DEKKER'S DOZEN:
A WAXING
ARBOLEAN
MOON
CHRISTOPHER D.
SCHMITZ

A Waxing Arbolean Moon

Dekker's Dozen #000A
Prequel

1

Long before time...

The Divine Gardener scattered seed upon the fertile soil. All creation held significance to him, though none of the others were quite like his Earth: the blue jewel revolving around Sol.

He sowed as he pleased. Dipping his hand in a satchel pocket, he grasped seven seeds. These seeds were special, he knew. Sprinkling them, they landed in a perfect circle: the special, chosen seven. They were not yet mighty timbers, not yet chosen, but still the Gardener knew them as he knew all creation.

In time, they would choose themselves from among their peers, for who else was there to choose? The eldest, and the first to root, would elect herself chief.

The Gardener knew he could walk among the rows of this garden for only a short time. He could only wander in this way, the manner he desired, until his great freedom—life—was blasphemed, torn by the violence of humanity and freewill: a deviation in the operation of the cosmic machine that he had just begun.

He *was* the Machinist and now he was the Gardener. Soon, he would be something else.

For now, as long as he chose to spin reality into motion, the Gardener would provide their light. And he would shine there until time and motion begun, when the redness could fall and until the blasphemy at the great tree. He knew of mankind's eventual betrayal, but he loved them anyway.

2

Pre-history, N.D. ...

Dione watched from her station upon the great engine. She'd remained perched, dedicated to her astral post for what felt like time eternal—though she knew how foolish her thoughts were. Only the Machinist was eternal. Despite its power, not even the great engine was infinite.

Deep were her thoughts and far-flung her vision. Ambition had begun to well up within her. The Light-Bringer, Asmodeus, had earlier come to her with unjust words, words not accurate of her: a lexeme of flattery. She secretly enjoyed it and secretly hid the embers of her stoked pride deep within her heart.

It was different than the adulation given to her by her comrade Leviathan—the baal who longed to become her suitor—Leviathan ranked a grade below her station. But the Baal of Light? His esteem was unwarranted, desperately desired, and yet altogether welcome.

For all his beauty, perhaps the Light-Bringer was right in his private doubts against the Machinist? Asmodeus was undoubtedly canny, as well as majestically handsome; did that blind her to reality? Perhaps dissention was possible; perhaps Dione could abandon her place overseeing the machine without consequence. Could they really divert the Great Plan and enforce their own desires within the confines of the engine? Could they take control away from the Machinist?

As she speculated, something awakened inside her. A seed of malevolence birthed deep within her core, resentment for her assignment—antipathy against her place and purpose.

Asmodeus would soon call an assembly before the Machinist. He promised to present his case. She considered joining him. Perchance she could sit at his side? She coveted him just as Leviathan desired the same from her.

She brooded over those secret thoughts and kept watching over the saplings that grew within one of the distant gardens far removed from Eden. The arbolean children had only recently discovered themselves, begun to understand their own significance and sentience.

If she abandoned her post for new purposes, perhaps these secret children would be of use to her? Light-Bringer's game might need pawns, disposable pieces in a game that pitted the nature of life and reality against itself.

So many options blossomed in her mind—she was especially good with plants. She could nudge the race of star-farers towards them and grant them freedom. Dione could build a new race from their material. If Asmodeus was right, as she strongly considered him, she could be so much more than she was now. Desire welled up within her, some new sense of carnality.

It had already been decided deep within Dione's bowels; she'd already chosen. If Asmodeus asked her, she would follow him.

She could ask her associate, the would-be lover, Leviathan, to infiltrate the distant star-farers and guide them to Rico. She knew that, above all else, she could entrust *him* with this. He had already pledged himself to her for time eternal.

Dione smiled, still assuming that her thoughts remained only mere conjecture and that she still belonged to the Machinist. She did not realize it, but she had already fallen.

3

2354 B.C.E....

La'ibum left the tent where his woman nursed their newborn son, Sargon. The tribal cleric had prophesied mightily over this child and over La'ibum as well. He claimed the child was touched by destiny and La'ibum had sealed those words up, afraid that anyone knowing Sargon was a child of fate might be prompted to murder. Many might smother the babe to avert his destiny: raising up the men of Akkad into a powerful empire.

La'ibum's task was to protect his child, teach him to navigate the ways of men and keep him safe. In that task, La'ibum, chief warrior of his tribe, felt utterly confident.

He did not find his tribesmen at the central pyre. Something had drawn them away. La'ibum figured it must be a matter of primary importance if it had lured them *all* off. Nervous suspicion crept into his heart and he dashed through the settlement searching for any of his brethren.

Just beyond their camp a ring of fire burned in the sky. The women had recently traded stories about the rhinoceros-men from the fiery, floating circle. He'd thought it blind superstition until now.

The young warriors fled the light, screaming warnings and pledges to any village deities if they should deliver them. La'ibum skidded to a halt, watching a shaft of light snatch up his best warriors from among the young men. Yanking them into the sky, it pulling them into the scorching ring above, La'ibum spotted Kriegen, his best footman.

In an act of discretion, not of fear, La'ibum turned and fled. He had to think of the child; Sargon had to be protected, and he couldn't do that if he was dead.

4

The seven alien warriors loomed above the primitive, trembling men of the Akkadian village. The largest of the seven abused the captives who cowered under the massive, strong arms. Red, paint-like markings on its gnarled, root-like head set it apart from the others.

Red shook her massive head. Though humanoid, the seven could not be mistaken for homo sapiens. Larger, bulkier bodies had been transformed as they played host and avatar to the Arbolean Council, the circle of seven trees who tricked the ambitious star-travelers into joining with them; a long tusk protruded from the cranial break at their brows, and their thick, mottled skin grew xyloid scales like woody armor. The other six wore pates colored green; they watched as Red shook the dust off her horn, forcing the earthling captives to breath in the particulates that fell.

This was the second tribe they had visited. The first of them readily fell to the apothecium, although a small minority of them proved immune to infection. Those with resistant bodies had been kept confined to the spacecraft, which now hovered high above the clouds, for further study.

Their captives' initial uprising proved futile. Natural body armor and superior physical form easily overmatched the earthlings. Here, they were gods, in fact—ascension was nothing less than Red's plan.

Sisters, that is our very course of action! See those cowering ones, those immune to the apothecium? We shall train them up; form a cult for us with them dedicated to our worship! In this, we shall find a greater use for, something more than fertilizer.

Five nodded their assent. One of the green ones protested. *What of the ancient one? The gardener who once walked among us, long before we matured. Shall we consider it proper to claim a title that only He deserves? Plundering those he made after His image does not sit well with me. Is this truly the will of our council, or just that of a particular zealous sister?*

Red drew herself up and squared off with Green. She struck her sister to the ground and continued to beat her until Green fell limp. *How long have you envied me, weakling? I've watched you jealously eye my red crown centuries now, at every turn you have advocated dissention! We were given ultimate freedom from our stations—who do you think engineered that but the gardener! He granted us this magnificent mobility and you seek effacement rather than glory? Here then, become the least of we sisters!* Red snapped the horn from Green's head, breaking it cleanly; she tossed the wooden chunk aside. The sisters could feel intense pain ripple through their psionic bond. Red wrapped her powerful arms around the wounded one's head, flexed, and stretched until she broke the avatar's spine.

Red pointed to another sister. *See to the education of our cultus. These ones are special, reserved for our worship, meant to preserve and protect our seed and legacy through the ages. They are granted immunity to the blooming. Have them watch our new captives germinate through death and become drones. Then, as benevolent lords, we may release our reverent ones back to their homes where they will worship us!*

5

2353 B.C.E....

The desperation in La'ibum's voice convinced enough of the warring tribesmen to assemble and unified force against the god-like intruders. His tribal seer had guaranteed victory with the proper sacrifice to the village Baal. La'ibum had sent his own wife to die upon the altar in order to guarantee the outcome; such was his resolve towards protecting his son.

Ur-Zababa, the young upstart, heard of the Akkadian's determination and sent a contingent of his own men from Kish in support. The men rallied around La'ibum who led the rally against these foreign invaders. Moving secretly through the night, the Akkadians and Kishites surrounded a mustering army within the valley. Several villages had already fallen to the sky-borne ones in the past months, and their numbers promised to continue spreading unless a resistance arose to stop them.

Day broke and La'ibum signaled the attack with a horn blast; warriors charged into the valley. The six alien giants, clad only in their armored skin, stood naked where they lorded over their minions: mindless, slobbering imitations of the Akkadian peoples. They too had grown sharp spires and skin like that of a rhinoceros; their eyes burned hollow and vacant. Despite that, La'ibum recognized Kriegen on the distant battle line. La'ibum's resolve hardened all the more until a giant metal craft dropped out of the sky.

Like a god of death the giant metallic fish floated above the valley where it fired bolts of holy fire and lightning into the human armies. Dirt and flesh erupted as the pandemonium broke their ranks. Both Akkadian and Kishite fled back up the valley.

One of his own tribesmen shouted at La'ibum as he passed, "Your cleric was mistaken! There is no Baal who can give us the power to defeat this threat!"

La'ibum fell to his knees, defying the Baals and all gods of this world. Desperately, he invoked any higher power and cried out to the one who must have made the Baals—for surely even they must have had a master. He pleaded with this unknown maker and asked for a deliverer—a hero—he would even forsake the bonds to all his old tribal gods for the sake of his child, Sargon!

He looked up amid the anarchy and spotted a strange man cloaked in foreign clothes. "Are you the hero?" he demanded. The foreigner appeared calm despite the surrounding anarchy of the retreat; they obviously spoke different tongues. "Are you the hero?" La'ibum shouted again, as if increased volume would somehow penetrate a language barrier.

"I am Ezekiel," the stranger replied, barely managing the rehearsed Akkadian words.

As the fish-god's lightning magic tore through his fleeing comrades, the hero calmly pointed an odd metal tube at it. The tool erupted with dazzling light, concentrating the power of gods much stronger than the fish-thing's. It intensified into a light beam and the arcane shaft slammed into the sky-fish. The monstrosity spun and lilted until it slammed into the earthy valley where it belched smoke and fire. A landslide half-buried it in stony rubble.

Smiling, the hero slung his weapon on a leash and opened his purse. As the frenzied throng of rhinoceros-men charged towards them, a buzzing cloud of beetles poured from the hero's bag. The insectoid plague ignored the men and began feasting upon the enemy only. They first cloud devoured the eyes and horns of the foreigners, and then they chewed from the outside-in, leaving behind pulpy sacks of skin before the beetles settled down, eventually falling dormant as if they'd died.

La'ibum turned from the incredible scene and searched frantically for the hero from his new god. He needed to thank the him and pledge his life and obedience to him. He would devote his whole tribe to the hero's worship. But the hero could not be found

6

961 B.C.E.…

"A most excellent gift, my dearest Benaiah!" Solomon clapped his hands with glee, gleefully prancing around his lavish, private chamber. Benaiah, the king's captain, had seized the demon king Asmodeus and forced the blazing behemoth to bend a knee before King Solomon. "Truly, your gift is the best I've received upon this wedding."

"Indeed," Benaiah stated as he glared into the eyes of the humiliated demon, "as I served your father before you as one of his Mighty Men, so I will follow you—even through the pits of Sheol if necessary." Benaiah returned Solomon's precious ring to him. Borrowing the precious Ring of Aandaleeb from the king, even for a moment, was a demonstration of complete trust.

Solomon grinned and turned to Asmodeus who still kneeled, bound to the floor. Only months prior the demon had disguised him and taken Solomon's place atop the royal throne while Solomon wandered the deserts. He thought he and his lover Naamah, the Ammonite princess, would die as a result of Asmodeus's trickery. "That this gift comes to me at my wedding to Naamah is especially delightful."

Narrowing his eyes, he turned to the chief of demons. Solomon made a demand. He consulted his personal notes and scrolls the wisest of his sages had collected on his behalf and made sure he performed the rites accurately. A lack of caution with these powers could prove disastrous. "Asmodeus, I invoke power over your name and demand you grant my petition."

The beast chuffed indignantly, but resigned himself with a nod. "What is your request?"

"My beloved Naamah misses her gardens. I'm sure you know how beautiful the plants grow east of the Jordan. You will summon for me a Baal whom I may seal within this lead vessel, a demon who can commune with plants and spur their growth. It will be a wedding gift to my Naamah."

He growled, but the demon answered. "You must open the earthen chest and make your mark within it to bind her there. Baal Dione will answer a call if you invoke her in my name. Tell her I will be attending the royal wedding. She *will come* at my bidding, thinking her time has finally arrived; but do not let her escape. She will be a vengeful thing—capable of destroying life on a grand scale."

Solomon began preparations for the summoning. "You may go now, Asmodeus, until I need you again… I bind you to my service, still."

King Asmodeus bowed low. His eyes narrowed to slits. "This contest is far from over,

King Solomon; someday, either your wisdom or your god will fail you. *And then,* I *will be the vengeful thing.*"

7

938 B.C.E.…

Solomon sat near Benaiah's bedside. The warrior's sweat had soaked through his sheets despite the cool night air. Benaiah looked as healthy and young as ever, a byproduct of his king's mystic dabblery. Solomon waved a scribe into the room. "Tell me what you saw in this vision of yours!"

"I saw horrible things yet to come, a tree—burning red—the stripping of her green sister's leaves and an army of metal demons fighting a war against briar bushes. Men are caught between them in this war, tricked by six old women and a djinn! The whole world burns—man, woman, and child. None escape." Benaiah gave the story in great detail, point by point, with great clarity of narrative.

Solomon's skin faded ashen as his friend described a vision that could have only come from the divine. When Benaiah finished, the king instructed his scribe further. "You must make an addendum to this scroll. Take down my words."

He described the method, the key to wielding his magic ring's powers and how his artifact, a celestial gadget, drew upon great power. "This ring, my seal, might be of critical importance to preventing this war." He turned to the scribe and rolled up the scroll, "Have an artisan inscribe warnings upon Naamah's chest—the one she keeps in her garden. It must never again be opened now that I am parted from the ring!"

Solomon turned to Benaiah. "You must prevent this thing from happening. Form a secret corps of loyal men to watch over your words and ways. They must hold safe the power to protect *life* in the face of such horror. God Yahweh will see this thing through if He wills it!"

Benaiah nodded as the king thrust into clammy hands his royal sword and the Ring of Aandaleeb. "I shall keep them safe all my life, my lord, as will my children and all who take our oath."

8

569 B.C.E....

Ezekiel walked down a trail outside the hills of Anathoth. The brass serpent medallion jangled on the chain around his neck. He wore it as a constant reminder of the exile—the past wandering of his people and the powers he served: the almighty God of fallen Israel.

A rumbling in the distance caught his ear and he turned to locate source. He found it there again, a burning portal, a gateway to the spinning chariot wheels of the divine engine.

The voice was the same as previous encounters: the voice of the great machinist. Within the orb of intense light, spinning like a wheel, it called to Ezekiel.

With his senses overwhelmed, the exiled prophet stepped through the mysterious doorway and slipped off the dimension reserved for mortals. Ezekiel bowed low and waited upon the majestic.

"A NEW TASK IS SET BEFORE YOU," the voice boomed like thunder. "YOU HAVE FAITHFULLY STEWARDED MY WORDS AND SERVED AS MY MOUTH. YET NOW I HAVE NEED OF A HAND."

Ezekiel dared not look directly into the source of light. "I am yours to direct."

"WALK AROUND, COME BEHIND MY THRONE. I WILL GIVE YOU THE TOOLS NECESSARY

FOR YOUR MISSION. CAST THROUGH TIME AS THE EMISSARY OF THE WHEEL, YOU WILL VISIT FOREIGN TIMES AND PLACES. WHEN YOU LOOK INTO THE ETHER, PAY ATTENTION TO THE RED STRAND—IT WILL GUIDE YOU. THE INVENTOR, HERO OF ALEXANDRIA, WILL GIVE YOU A DEVICE NECESSARY TO THE TASK; I HAVE GIVEN HIM THE DIVINE KNOWLEDGE AND SKILLS FOR ITS CONSTRUCTION."

"Alexandria?"

"CAST YOUR EYES THROUGH THE MACHINE. DO YOU SEE IT?"

Through the mirror of liquid silver, infinity seemed to spread out before him, planes of time and existence confined within the nether of nonexistence. Facets of reality spun upon the wheels: places, times, life interlinked and tied by silk stands blowing within the ether. Fine cords of silver occasionally intertwined with those of bright vermillion.

"ALEXANDRIA WILL NOT YET EXIST FOR MANY GENERATIONS. I WILL SEND YOU TO HIM AND HE WILL SEND YOU ON A QUEST. YOU MUST GO AND OBSERVE A GREAT MANY THINGS—FIRST WITNESS THE END OF TIME. THERE IN THE NOTHINGNESS YOU WILL LEARN WHAT MUST BE DONE TO PROTECT THE MACHINE, TO KEEP THE WHEEL IN ROTATION. DO YOU UNDERSTAND?"

"I confess, I do not!" Ezekiel cried.

"AND YOU WILL NOT UNTIL YOU'VE BEEN PLUNGED THROUGH ETHER AND ENERGY. NOW ENTER BEHIND THE THRONE AND BEGIN YOUR JOURNEY. BUT FIRST, LOOK THROUGH THE MIRROR AND SEE THE END—THE BREAK IN THE CRIMSON CORD. KNOW THE CHOKING NOTHINGNESS OF EVIL'S VICTORY AND UNDERSTAND WHY SUCH A THING MUST NOT BE ALLOWED."

9

1904 A.C.E....

The archaeologist could feel it taking over, the dark presence in his mind. It crept around through his thoughts and memories, affirming his desires. It tried to disguise itself as a natural part of his own psyche, but the researcher knew something was wrong with his mind. He'd read enough of Pierre Janet and Richard Hodgson to suspect that his recent fugues might be part of something larger.

The fact that he couldn't quite remember his name after emerging from his last apneatic haze should have concerned him—except that he felt physically better than ever. The great feeling helped him downplay any concern for his unhealthy mental state.

He momentarily considered traveling to Zurich. The Germans had made great strides in fields of psychology, but the blackouts he'd experienced ever since unearthing an ancient pithos couldn't be related to ancient gods or the supernatural. While there had been many dire warnings of curses etched upon the lead cask, he'd never been one to give credence to superstition.

After his latest, long blackout, the archaeologist found a note left upon his dresser. It contained a map and an address; it had been signed by one Prognon Austicon. He'd hoped it a good indicator that there was a mere physical explanation for his mental problems—perhaps a vitamin deficiency or something. Perhaps this Austicon was a physician or an observer with insight to the recent gaps in his memories.

Arriving at the address, he rang the bell and an elderly woman met him at the door. She welcomed him in and bid him into the sitting room without even asking his name. Five other women also met him there.

"Excuse me, have you been expecting me?" he asked, surprised by their demeanor.

"Why yes," the first lady stated. "You told us that you would bring the map if we would initiate you. As much as we chafe against such a phallic consideration, we *must* have the location of the arbolean star-craft."

He grinned, sure these ladies were putting him on. "That's where this map leads?"

"That is what you claimed."

"I did? Just who do you think I am?"

The old women stared at him. "You are Prognon Austicon."

10

2416 A.C.E.…

"Doctor Dyson?" the young woman interrupted the middle-eastern engineer in his laboratory. "Our benefactor is here. You said to show him in immediately."

"Yes, thank you."

The female lab assistant escorted a dapper, silver-haired man into the lab. He kissed her hand in farewell, making her blush. He turned and introduced himself. "A pleasure, Doctor Dyson. I am Prognon Austicon."

"We want to thank you for your continued funding, Mister Austicon. I thought it prudent to show you some of our progress with AI and robotics, especially given the timetable for our budget and funding concerns."

"Understood," Austicon stated before Dyson launched into a full demonstration of their achievements in practical robotics.

He indicated a workbench containing several types of prosthetics and biological enhancements; a chart showed projections for upcoming tests. "This here," he motioned Austicon to a computer display, "is our greatest achievement. It will revolutionize the way computer software operates in the future."

"And why is that?" He noticed a number of units creating real-time backups of the software; it networked only with itself, cut off from the world; a minor explosive device blinked upon the processor unit's housing.

"Because this unit has achieved singularity!" Dyson grinned. "It has become self-aware."

"And the explosives?"

"There has always been great fear that self-aware software could become dangerous, murderous even in the interests of self-preservation. These backup drives preserve the coding, rolled back in three different stages in case the deterrent becomes necessary to activate. That way, the software can be salvaged and steps to remedy the software can be initiated."

Austicon smiled. "I don't think you will have any problems securing my continued funding."

"I hope not," Dyson said excitedly. "However, the technology might still be decades away from use. It would be unwise until the proper failsafes are developed, Asimovian inhibitors, for example. The next step is to develop solid, yet versatile logic algorithms in order to enforce the necessary thought restrictions within the software context."

Austicon nodded, though he'd clearly lost further interest in the topic of fail-safes. He picked up a mechanized prosthetic. "So, given the trajectory of the research and technology, is it possible to implant the AI and utilize partial mechanization in order to create hybrid units. Cyborgs?"

"I suppose, but to what end? I believe full mechanization is the future. It will create safer conditions for future workers in hostile environments. We can send in invulnerable forces to handle hostile situations without risk to humanoid life."

"Potentially, yes. But financial costs might prohibit it. Also—one cannot overlook the fact that enhancement could improve the quality of life of many individuals… the disabled, mentally defunct, that sort of thing, not to mention the possibility of restoring those with genetic defects or brain trauma to their families utilizing AI?"

"I suppose the cyborg version might be cheaper for some commercial uses. Is the value of life the thing we are trying to preserve?"

Austicon grinned. "Values change and shift with each generation. Suppose one holds to a lesser view of human life? Think of the potential market there."

11

0036 P.I.S.W....

The media mobbed the young soldier. Flash LEDs burst and flared. They'd given him a hero's welcome. The people, the citizens of the MEA, desperately needed something ad someone to believe in. And this brilliant, young soldier had become that man: an icon.

Bad news had become an unhealthy staple during the Mechnar Contra, and the populace had withered under it. There was no doubt that Harry Briggs was a bonafide hero, not some media stunt—although the cameras certainly did love him.

Pushing him along in a flow of paparazzi, reporters hurled questions and requested interviews from the man whose bravery had ended the six year battle with the resurgent mechanized race. The mechnar threat reappeared thirty years after the end of the Intergalactic Singularity War, when the machines made their first bid for power. Under Brigg's tactical leadership, the threat appeared to have finally subsided. Briggs's heroic actions had been so final and resolute that the potential for another, unforeseen attack was remote.

"Is it true that they are going to give you command of a new battleship?" one reporter shouted the rumor.

Briggs chuckled and stopped to explain how he was a ground commander, not a space commander. Through the whole interview, however, he could not take his eyes off the pretty, Japanese reporter to his left. Her name badge identified her as Muramasa.

12

0043 P.I.S.W....

Austicon raged at the head of the long table inside the Druze stronghold. He paced as he vented his frustration upon the diplomat who had failed to block a trade agreement with the main shipping conglomerates.

"There was no way it could be legally done… I could not make it happen," he defended weakly. "There was just no way to negotiate those contract conditions for Halabella Corp."

"Since when have we worried about the legality of issues? This was *your* task to accomplish and you have failed us." Austicon pulled a disruptor from his side. "See, this action isn't legal, either!" The laser burst flashed, erupting a hole of light through the negotiator's skull. He fell to the floor, dead.

Austicon turned to those at his table. "You waited centuries for your great, foretold leader. I've finally come only to be met with failure after failure over these past hundred years! I will go and show you how to strike from the shadows, how to subjugate your enemies and wage secret wars. After today, you will forever be *my army* and do as *I say* with unquestioning loyalty—even if I command you to lie down and die! There will remain no doubt as to who leads this group. Some of you doubt I am your prophet, the foretold

Anagogue—I tell you I'm more than that. *I am a god!* And to prove it I will destroy entire planets and relocate entire species."

Their furious leader whirled around and stormed from the clandestine meeting. He had murder on his mind, and his allegiance to those ancient timbers provided him with a perfect means to that end.

13

0044 P.I.S.W.…

The Pheema panicked. An agent of nonviolence, the Krenzin religious leader had always thought he was prepared to lay down his life. Glancing at the pools of blood leaking from his body guards, he no longer felt so sure.

Swallowing hard against the wicked blade against his throat, the felinoid alien considered his options. He could beg; as a person of stature and position, he could afford to barter.

His assailant's wild eyes gleamed with mirth. He enjoyed killing.

The Pheema assumed martyrdom had found him. He'd been chased from the great diplomatic hall during a parliamentary recess and cornered here in this distant alley. But now, the assassin might release him?

"You must flee—but only you," the murder insisted. "These are the coordinates you must go to."

Confused, The Pheema asked why.

"Chiefly because I told you to—and if you don't I will kill your entire species—but I'm feeling cheery today and will leave it with this: your presence is requested by my friends. So stay here and die as I plunge your home-world into chaos, or be thrust into a position of unimaginable power. You could be a key player in a cosmic game of thrones, should you so choose. It matters little to me, but it is my duty as the Left Hand of the Verdant Seven to give you their invitation. Only go alone," he repeated his warning.

With another smile the assailant made a show of clicking the button on a remote detonator. The ground rocked as the parliamentary hall exploded in the distance. A fireball rushed up through the air, capped, and curled down to form a mushroom cloud.

The Pheema fled, but paused to watch his attacker.

The Left Hand set up a recording device and overrode the media transmission signals with his own. The terrorist broadcasted live. He cackled into the camera and boasted of his evil accomplishment. Prognon Austicon took full credit for the parliament's destruction. "And it does not stop there," he laughed. "Even now your environment has been seeded with a biological invader that will slowly eradicate all life on this planet. It cannot be deterred, it cannot be stopped. Like my wrath, it is vicious and eternal—your ecosystem will be dead in a matter of days."

14

0045 P.I.S.W....

General Harry Briggs sat opposite his late wife's brother. Briggs and Muramasa watched their respective children play in the yard outside. The red-haired Vivian tumbled over her cousin Shin as they played a game of tag.

The General nodded to the set of swords that sat mounted on his mantle nearby. "I used those the other day," he confessed.

"How so?"

"My campaign for the office of Chief Magnate has not gone so well. Certain individuals have fought me at every turn by… let's call them people of influence. Some of them live in the shadows and use their power only to acquire more power."

"And this is a surprise? I never thought you so naive," Muramasa chided. "You still have a couple years to make your bid for Chief Magnate."

"I fear it's not enough. Humanity, people, have changed. The Krenzin philosophy has poisoned us... made us weak."

"And you think violence is the answer?"

"Not always, but it must always remain an option. If the Mechnar Contra happened right now, Earth would fall. Sometimes, one cannot act with diplomacy—sometimes situations call for violence."

"But the mechnar race is gone."

"And newer, more terrible forces have replaced them," Briggs sighed. "Yesterday a man came to me. *The* man, Prognon Austicon. He claimed he could guarantee me favor with the shadow players who've tried to steer me out or buy me for years." Briggs grinned and took a sip of black coffee.

Muramasa sipped his tea and smiled back. "The sword?"

"I cut his ear off! The monster threatened my Vivian. Nobody goes after my girl."

Muramasa grinned. "And is this conflict resolved then? Can such ever be when a men such as Austicon court you?"

Briggs couldn't reply. In silence, the fathers watched their children play. Both understood that the General's career and life had fallen into serious jeopardy.

15

0051 P.I.S.W....

Jude Knight embraced his only son and then hung his decorative amulet around the young man's neck. "Give this to her tomorrow, on your wedding night. I'm sure you know how special it is. Her people also share a certain history with the artifact. Surely she will understand its value."

Jude beamed as his son checked it out in the mirror. Dekker fingered the dent at the brass serpent's edge where it had once deflected an assassin's bullet.

"Did I ever tell you story of how I decided what to name you?"

Dekker nodded. Barely twenty, he'd proven to be an impressive scholar.

His son had absorbed a vast array of knowledge from Jude's closest friends: Diacharia, Harry Briggs, and Doc Johnson. He'd also hoped to send him to learn under Yitzchak ben Khan, but that would be impossible after Dekker's marriage to Aleel. If Jerusalem was anything, it was not open-minded.

Jude sighed, content despite it all. He accepted that Dekker's destiny was something other than what his father had planned for him. That did not make it worse—only different.

"You know as well as I do the danger of these secret wars," Jude said. He smiled, "If it weren't so, you might have never met Aleel. But I want to also give you this." Jude placed the reliquary, his namesake hero's weapon, into Dekker's hands.

"But, I'm not a fighter," Dekker protested at first.

"I know," Jude replied. "But you must learn to fight. Protection demands it. Some fights need to be fought, and we are protectors of something sacred—never forget that. Never desire conflict, but neither run from it. You know as well as I do how the Red Tree assassins pursued us. I have a friend, Harry's brother, actually brother in law…" Jude paused a moment in respect for the dead. "His name is Muramasa. I've known him for even longer than General Briggs. Not right now, but sometime, you should consider training under him. Diacharia may have taught me *when*, but Muramasa taught me *how* to fight. Marrying Aleel might demand you know some of that. This marriage will only incite our enemies and stir a frenzy against the Watchmen."

Recognizing the apology in his son's eyes, Jude waived it off. "I'm not saying that it is necessarily a bad thing—not all conflict is evil."

Dekker nodded and hefted the ancient gun.

"Let me show you how to use it should things ever get so bad that they force you to invoke such awesome, destructive powers."

16

0056 P.I.S.W....

Sweat dripped off her brow and into her teenage eyes. Vivian blinked against the stinging and wiped her face while she placed her bokken on the shelf. She bowed to her uncle and sensei, Master Muramasa.

Muramasa chuckled. "The way you fight, we might call you Vesuvius, like the volcano. You're explosive, and very surprising."

She joined her uncle at the window overlooking the courtyard below. A group of people went through a series of motions and exercises. Physical fitness programs kept the dojo operational; while the market for defense classes had withered, fitness training and enlightened paths such as t'ai chi ch'uan remained in as high demand as ever.

"Who is that, there?" she asked, pointing.

A handsome young man laughed as he spoke with Shin at the edge of the courtyard. Her cousin obviously enjoyed the stranger's company.

"He is the son of a very old, very dear friend, Vesuvius," Muramasa teased.

She watched him for a few moments and blushed when her uncle caught her staring. There were not many other people who looked like her in the immediate geography. Their region was quite traditional and she had very few friends who she shared non-asian traits with. Her fiery red hair, pale skin, and physique came from her father and she often longed to be near someone more similar.

It was less scandalous in these days that she did not have any of her people's blood. The egg implanted in her Japanese mother had to be genetically engineered for viability and had lost most of her people's DA markers in the process. She never resented her birth, but she'd always felt somewhat anomalous. Almost an adult, now, she'd become increasingly self-conscious of her appearance over the last couple years.

Shin tossed a wooden sword to Dekker and they squared up to spar. Vesuvius watched with rapt interest as they crossed them on the courtyard below. Shin was one of the best in the world in the art of the sword. Dekker seemed to hold his own, although his moves had very little to do with traditional techniques.

After Shin had toyed with him a few rounds, Dekker abandoned what little training he possessed. Using his greater upper body strength, he crossed blades and whirled his bokken in a large arc, spinning the swords in several large, widening loops. At the peak of the widest loop, Dekker delivered a palm strike to the butt of the sword, popping it high into the sky. It fell neatly into Dekker's free hand and the resourceful fighter pointed both blades at Shin, grinning.

Muramasa laughed. "He is a resourceful one, if nothing else." He beckoned her to leave the room with him. "But Dekker is a sad man, lately. His story is like yours: he has lost much. Maybe you can cheer him up? Like you, I sense that he has a touch of destiny on his life and I think you two will get along… allow me introduce you," Muramasa said.

17

Now…

A fell breeze rattled the leaves of the Arbolean Council. They intuitively felt the summer of their plans rise to their apex. The time had come to set their long campaign back into motion.

The seed child had sprouted and been returned to them by agents of the Left Hand. It only required fertile soil and patient tending.

Again the arboleans would invade Earth, this time, though, they would employ more subterfuge than force. Technology and guile were their new tools, honed and practiced through the eons. These past few millennia they had waited patiently for the proper timing, and that moment had finally arrived with the germination of their new seed. Osix.

DEKKER'S DOZEN:
WEEDS OF EDEN
NO. 0.33 A/B
CHRISTOPHER D.
SCHMITZ

Weeds of Eden

Dekker's Dozen #000.33 A&B
0064 P.I.S.W....

1

Despite the hangar bay yawning wide open, someone knocked on the front door. A sign hanging above the steel barricade simply read Licensed Investigators.

"I'm comin," Rock hollered as he shuffled through the groups Earth-side Headquarters belonging to the Dekker's Dozen. The spacious facility more than met their needs and occupied a sizable chunk of expensive real estate at the edge of Reef City. Of course, it looked more like a dump than a respectable business... which it wasn't.

Rock flung the door open and found an unfamiliar Asian man standing in the doorway. He clutched the straps of a duffel bag in one fist and looked up at the massive warrior who dwarfed him.

"You are licensed Investigators?" He spoke with a slight far Eastern accent.

Rock nodded curtly at the polite term given to those in the mercenary profession.

"Is this where I would locate one Vivian 'Vesuvius' Briggs?"

Raising an eyebrow, Rock asked, "Who are you? Walk-in clients aren't something we typically get in our profession. I'll call for Dekker. He's in charge of all client negotiations."

"Nevermind," the stranger mumbled. "There she is."

Beyond the hallway Rock had ushered their guest into, the fire-haired woman walked past the doorway where it spilled into the hangar. She strolled through the bay where the Dozen's ship, the *Rickshaw Crusader*, remained parked.

He took a step forward and Rock put one massive paw up to block his entrance. "Hold up a second, friend," he warned. "You're going to hafta wait here until we know a little more about you as a precaution. Sometimes we tend to make enemies..."

Quick as a flash the smaller man ducked beneath Rock's guard and slipped past him. He dropped the duffel bag but clutched a katana in his hand. He charged forward, howling. "Briggs!"

Vesuvius whirled to lock eyes with the intruder who rushed at her with a drawn weapon. She leapt backwards and out of the path of his blade. "Everybody stand down," she shouted to the other mercenaries who had already rushed to her defense. "This guy's mine!" She snatched a nearby length of pipe and wielded it like a staff, blocking and parrying the man's keen edge.

The intruder stutter-stepped and used the motion to add further power to his next blow. His edged weapon sliced cleanly through the pipe, splitting it into two lengths.

Vesuvius pressed him, doubly wielding her blunt segments and creating a space cushion. She chucked the pieces of pipe at the invader and leapt into a somersault. Rolling to her feet, she snatched her sword which leaned against a nearby box of parts Doc Johnson had shipped them from his moon-side salvage yard.

Tossing aside the saya that sheathed her own katana, Vesuvius brandished her own blade. One of the world's top-ranked sword-fighters, she grinned at the stranger while motioning him forward. "Now we can dance properly," Vesuvius growled.

2

"We're shutting it all down," Jace screamed into his megaphone. He waved towards the heavy machinery and to the radiation-proof cargo haulers. "All of it! The work stops until the corporation comes to the table."

A chorus of cheers agreed with him.

Jace Strengen looked out over the growing crowd of sickly looking miners who had gathered at the central part of the domed mining town of Outpost 7 on Io. Jupiter's moon had been terra-formed well enough to split the oxygen and other elements into a relatively breathable concoction that passed for an atmosphere. However, the community still relied on the dome to protect them from radiation storms and to gather and properly distribute the geothermal heat sloughed off by the planet's volcanic activity. Its gravity wells also provided them with enough sense of grounding to keep them comfortable--inside the city limits at least.

Most of the operations within the city had ground to a complete stop under Jace's direction. Stoppages had begun in the other outpost cities under his direction, as well. Jace led the union for Io's workers.

"The reports have come back verified as true," he broadcast to the sea of workers. "Halabella will continue to get richer and our men and women who work the mines will continue to get sicker... the transport tubes leading to the workstations--the very place where the protective gear is located at--those tubes are not properly shielded against all of that radioactive substrate that local ops President Jai so desperately wants us to harvest."

A cloud of boos and hissing rose up from the mob at his name. Jai Janus was a private businessman and owned controlling shares of the Jupiter subsidiary of Halabella. Locally, the corporation harvested and refined material for the radioactive cores that powered the Thumper Drive systems: transit technology for Faster Than Light travel initiated by nuclear detonation. The products dug out of Jupiter's moon and refined on its surface were far cheaper than the Earth-side fuel alternatives... but they hadn't come without a hidden price tag. The local populace had been ravaged by recent bouts of radiation poisoning.

"Until Jai sits down to negotiate with us, not one worker sets foot back in those mines. The rail tubes are leeching poison!"

The worker's assents nearly shook the buildings around them.

Jace grinned at the frenzied mob as they stomped the ground and shouted angry protest slogans. He knew that every place on Io remained mostly safe but, the tubes where the monorails traveled were a completely different story.

The Geiger counter readings were not strong; the leeching materials were not refined and only posed a threat to those with regular exposure. Jace was a skilled negotiator and he knew he could get the people what they needed to remain safe... and for him to earn his sizable paycheck from the union's head office.

Jai's brother was Chief Magnate of the Mother Earth Aggregate and an election was coming soon. If Miko Janus wanted to remain head of the MEA, Jai would cave--if he didn't, the union would throw all of its support behind his opposition... and there were lots of voters in the union.

3

Vesuvius ducked around the landing pads that supported the bulk of the *Rickshaw Crusader* and defensively used the ship's mass in order to out-maneuver her assailant. Most of her comrades stood nearby, watching the duel while nervously gripping their weapons in case the intruder had any other mischief in mind.

He swung and chopped like a whirlwind. Vesuvius ducked underneath the sharpened edge, nearly losing some hair in the process.

She stepped back, losing ground step after step. Behind her, Dekker Knight ambled across the second-level catwalk from the business office that overlooked the hangar bay and descended the stairs. Nibbs looked over at him and adjusted his glasses.

"I've never seen anybody push her back like this before," Nibbs stiffened. "Except you, of course."

Dekker nodded measuredly.

"Do you think he can beat her? What if he does?" Nibbs asked with a hint of worry in his voice. The attacker punctuated the threat with a deadly slash that Vesuvius rolled under backwards.

"Is that Shin?" Guy called out from the catwalk overhead. "It is!" he howled, dropping down to their level.

Shin and Vesuvius didn't stop their duel--or even look sidelong at Guy and Dekker.

Nibbs looked at Guy with expectation.

"Shin Muramasa is Viv's cousin," Dekker explained. "He trained with Vesuvius and I when we were younger."

Guy elbowed Dekker, his long-time friend, in the ribs. "Well, *they* were younger."

The rest of the gathered Dozen holstered their weapons.

"Wow," Rock whistled as Vesuvius reeled. "I don't think I've ever seen anyone actually beat her."

Shin slashed. She ducked and parried. Her cousin blocked and thrust forward with his body, knocking her flat. "And you're not gonna see it today, either," she snapped at Rock. She didn’t take her eyes from Shin who pointed the tip of his blade to her neck, signaling she ought to surrender.

Vesuvius nodded to him with mischief in her eyes. He traced her blade down his body and found its tip less than a millimeter from his crotch.

Shin reeled, staggering with surprise. She hooked his foot with the tip of her toe as he stumbled backwards and Vesuvius laid him out on his back.

Leaping to her feet Vesuvius kicked his blade away and pointed her katana at her cousin.

Shin began laughing and Vesuvius reached down and hauled him to his feet. Arm in arm they walked back towards the group, faces and necks flush and sweaty.

"You've got a strange family," Nibbs remarked.

4

Prognon Austicon leaned back on his stool. The air smelled musty in the subterranean research facility far beneath the surface, like soil and old books.

Shelves lined the walls and rows of tables displayed artifacts and aquariums filled with plant life beneath grow lamps. No outside light sources pierced the veil of darkness as the ancient archaeologist stepped from microscope to microscope, noting his findings.

He grinned as he jotted notes in his journal. A loud knock boomed at the thick, metal door.

Austicon looked from face to face in the low light. All eyes turned to him. He was the galaxy's most wanted and stayed well protected. His team of sentries positioned throughout the tunnels snaking beneath the Mars Museum would have radioed ahead if they had cleared any guest for entry.

The man stiffened and his silver locks fell around his shoulders. What passed for a smile twisted upon his face. It had been a while since he'd spared the time to engage in physical violence. A smirk tugged at the edges of his lips--he did miss the way that made him feel alive.

Someone on the other side of the heavy door pushed it open. An elderly woman in a faded yellow cloak walked into the room; the edges of her cloak bore the distinct red taint of Martian soil where it had dragged upon the ground. A trio of bloody bodies lay crumpled against the wall in the hallway beyond her.

The burgeoning grin on Austicon's face faded away. She glowered at him. "I can hardly believe that you made an agent of Dodona travel all the way out here in order to make contact."

"I made you do nothing," Austicon growled.

"You killed everyone else we sent," she chided like an old schoolteacher.

"Maybe I did not want to talk."

Eyes watched them from the dark. Prognon Austicon's faithful adherents shrank back as they noted the exchange. His wrath was famous and none wanted to be caught in the crossfire.

"You do not need to talk," she said evenly, but sternly, "but *you will listen.* The Red Tree has need of you."

5

Dekker held the door open for his friends. Shin and Vesuvius stepped through and into the dingy pub and followed him to the back where they took a seat.

"You sure know how to pick em," Shin joked, running a finger along the edge of the room divider. He wiped the grime on his pants leg as Dekker waived to a waitress.

"Only the best for those closest to me," he smirked.

"You Investigators really live the high life, don't you? Fancy wine and dining, special weapons privileges, hobnobbing with the rich and famous."

Vesuvius shrugged. "So much glitz and glamour," she laughed. "And not all of our weapons are legal."

"Or even reported to the MEA," Dekker winked.

Shin turned over the menu in his hand. He blinked at the trilingual entries and tried to make sense of it. "Anything you recommend?"

"Anything but the fish," Dekker muttered.

Vesuvius scanned the listings. Everything was fish. A smile tugged at the edge of her lips and she playfully curled a lock of red hair around her forefinger.

Shin probed again, "So business is good? It's been a couple years since you guys incorporated and neither of you has been back to visit since... I know Master Muramasa misses you both, though I'm sure your company keeps you busy."

"It's hard to stay on top of it--being the best in the business," Vesuvius grinned wryly.

"The best in the business, huh? What makes you the best, little sister?" the Asian man bumped his shoulder playfully against hers. For all practical purposes it had been true--she'd gone to live with Shin and his family during her teenage years after the tragic, politically motivated murder. "Maybe there's still some friends of General Harry Briggs floating around on the MEA cabinet?"

She only offered a thin-lipped courtesy smile in return.

"Not likely," Dekker said. "We're not in the black nearly far enough for my comfort. It tends to be like that when we turn down jobs we think are less than savory."

A mousy waitress slipped past the table, sliding a plate full of glasses into the center and a trio of tiny glasses filled with saké. She left the bottle with them.

Shin bobbed his head. "So it's not money that makes you successful, then, old friend... what is it?"

Dekker rummaged through his dark hair with a free hand as if looking for an answer. "I dunno--relationships. Friends... keeping a crew that's like family, a ship topped off with fuel, and the fact that none of my men have died despite all the danger we've been through."

Shin grinned and looked sidelong at Vesuvius, about to enlist her help in ribbing their friend for not saying "men or women." Something in the way she watched Dekker changed his mind. Her eyes twinkled as she watched him talk.

"That's a pretty good answer," Shin said instead, raising his shot glass in salute. "Here's the next question." He held up three digits. "How many fingers am I holding up? I just want to make sure you can count".

Vesuvius nearly choked on her drink. She knew what he meant; they'd had this conversation long ago, privately.

"Were you drinking this saké when you chose the name? Because you realize there are thirteen people on your crew, right?"

Dekker shrugged while Vesuvius rolled her eyes. "Paragon of self-control, this one," she winked. "I don't know that I've *ever* actually seen him drunk."

"High constitution," he simply explained. "And I can count just fine."

"But like, only to five," Shin teased.

"Trigger just asked him about this yesterday, in fact," Vesuvius chuckled. "He's kind of superstitious and freaked out a little at the number thirteen."

Shin lifted another glass, "Well if this doesn't keep panning out, you can open a laser-cooked pastry shop and call it Dekker's Baker's Dozen."

Dekker grinned and poured himself another saké.

"Whoa," Vesuvius cautioned. "Slow down, chief. You've already had like, a dozen of those."

Dekker smiled and shook his head with a chuckle. "I think I'm remembering why we don't all hang out more often."

"Then let *her* come and talk to me if the Red Tree finds me in such high demand," Austicon spat.

The old woman looked down her nose at him, barely acknowledging his tantrum. "You are bound to the circle, eldest, and you will play your role." She handed Austicon a packet filled with photos and information. "There is a target we have identified for disposal."

He flipped through the pages. "Anyone can do this job. I only kill individuals for pleasure. There is no sport in this kill."

"You do not need to enjoy it," the woman hissed. "But you must make sure it goes according to plan. A new plant child is born... a seedling of New Eden. Our sources have confirmed its genetics--it is somehow Arbolean. You will kill Jai Janus and collect the child from his possessions."

"Fine," Austicon snapped.

Her stern gaze remained upon the hardened killer. "This is a surgical strike, Austicon. In and out. Do not make a production out of this; it is work, not play."

Austicon glared at her. "I will complete my mission, priestess," he said, "but I will do it *my way*."

She held her gaze. "You have your orders. If you don't follow them and you are captured *we will not come to your aid*. Eliminate Jai and deliver the helpless seed to the holy ones. *You have your orders*." The old woman turned her back on him and shambled out the way she had come. She paused momentarily at the portal, "and for both our sakes, next time we send you a messenger, don't kill him."

8

Fuming, Austicon desperately wanted to murder her--but he knew that he could not... not yet, anyways. *He was bound to the circle, as was she.*

The research lab fell quiet. Too silent--his team had witnessed the entire exchange; the woman had made him look weak in front of them. Austicon retrieved a high powered handgun from a desk drawer and shot his nearest man in the head, splattering blood all over the villain's face. *Oh, how I missed the violence.*

Chaos erupted as his devotees panicked and tried to flee--but the only door was where the priestess had exited. Each clamoring for the door, they lined up his shots perfectly, allowing him to easily murder anyone who had witnessed the conversation.

Silence resumed moments later. Austicon picked up a communicator and clicked it on. "Leviathan. Arrange a meeting with our pirate friends. We have a new objective on Io."

Leviathan did not respond, but Austicon knew he'd heard him. Leviathan was always listening. More than any other creature in existence, Leviathan loved him.

He clicked his communicator again. "And gather the Druze. I'll satisfy the old crone, but we'll do this *my way*."

Prognon Austicon grinned wickedly and turned a body over with his foot. Imagining the face of his longtime enemy, Dekker Knight, he gleefully pumped the remaining bullets into the nearest body.

9

Dekker galloped down the stairs and towards his team where they'd assembled. Shin mingled with some of his crew as their leader waved the work order.

"Got us a job, everyone. Pays well, too, for what it is. It's a simple transport."

"Mustache" Sam, an old soldier who'd been with Dekker since day one piped up. "What's the catch?" He curled the edge of famous mustache and spoke in a steady drawl.

Dekker bit his lower lip. "Some of us may not like the passenger: a Krenzin negotiator sent to mediate a miners strike on Io's Halabella outpost." He glanced sidelong at his business partner, Vesuvius.

Jamba brightened up at the news. Io had some decent, independent casinos established to entertain the miners. Typically, the most dangerous part of the job was boredom, when it wasn't bullets, at least.

Vesuvius bristled and pursed her lips at the info, but kept otherwise silent. Her hatred of the felinoid alien race was widely known and given for good reasons.

Dekker continued, "Sorry to drop our work on you, Shin, but duty calls. It won't be a long mission, though, and you're free to..."

"I'd love to join you," he interrupted. "I don't get off-world much and this is the perfect opportunity to see the world's greatest team of Investigators at work." He grinned.

Mustache chuckled behind him. "Hey kid, those guys are on the *other* side of Reef City. You must've made a wrong turn."

"Sorry about the Krenzin thing, guys," Dekker said as he walked closer. "I don't understand why Halabella Corp keeps hiring them," he lied. It wasn't difficult to find the political motivation on the corp's behalf. The cat-like race had made a mess of the Mother Earth Aggregate's politics ever since their inclusion and emigration to Earth. Even worse, their ideologies had ruined Dekker's life long before he met Shin and the Muramasas. "Skids up in two hours."

Part bounty hunter, part mercenary, part armed tour guide, Investigators didn't always get to choose what kind of jobs they would be offered--and they needed to work. Many other crews never distinguished between distasteful and evil and that gave the profession a bad name.

"At least it's not immoral work," Trigger shrugged. He winked with an eye branded by a long, vertical scar. "Everyone knows that's why I joined this crew--had enough of the kind of work that keeps me up at night. Ferrying a kitty-cat around... how hard could that be?"

Dekker threw an arm around Vesuvius. "You gonna be okay with this?"

She stiffened. "Just don't expect me to make small talk."

"Yeah..." Dekker trailed off, thinking of his own vendetta against them, *of the ones he lost...* of her. "I don't blame you. Not at all."

Vesuvius kept a blank face and walked off. "Let's just get paid and get on with it."

Shin watched her go and kept his voice low. "I see you still haven't told her about... you know who?"

Dekker shook his head. He hadn't even told Guy.

Shin paused until everyone else had drifted well beyond earshot. "You know how she feels about you, right?"

Dekker shrugged slightly. "I think so."

His friend shook his head. "If you only *think so* then you really don't. But I get it--your father was the last Watchman and the Watchmen had a ton of secrets... just don't get so used to keeping them that you forget about everyone else." He clapped Dekker on the arm.

"You're a real pain in the rear, you know that--just like your old man?"

Shin shrugged and grinned. Master Muramasa had never hidden his desire to see the two together. "Yeah well... what goes around comes around," he called out as he walked away to find his cousin.

"You're still mad about the time I ruined your wedding? She was an assassin who was hired to kill you!"

Shin shouted back with a laugh, "Don't judge our love!" He flashed his friend a grin and then turned a corner leaving Dekker alone with only his thoughts and a preflight checklist.

10

"Come in," Prognon Austicon slid the door open to make way for the stout, ash-skinned alien. "Glad you could arrive so soon. Time is of the essence."

The Shivan pirate captain stepped over the cold bodies of Austicon's guards who still littered the entry.

"My apologies, Gr'Narl. I haven't had time to tidy up." Austicon beckoned the shorter alien over to the hookah set in the comfort area of his subterranean quarters.

The couch creaked under Gr'Narl's weight. Shivan's were notoriously heavy with heavy muscle and dense bone mass developed by the species native to a high gravity planet. "Blood doesn't bother me," he growled with his low, guttural voice, "especially not when there is incentive in it for the Gr clan."

Austicon reached for the hookah pipe and took a deep draw. "There is indeed, Gr'Narl. And so much more."

Gr'Narl's pate shifted back, wrinkling the skin on either side of his jet black widow's peak as if he had arched his eyebrows. "What is the job?"

"A simple transport smuggle, as far as your end goes."

"The cargo?"

Austicon smiled and took another drag, bubbling the water in the hookah's base.

"*You* are the cargo," Gr'Narl smiled and took the pipe on his side of the smoking apparatus.

"I just need to get dirt-side at Io."

Gr'Narl bobbed his head. "We can hide your body scans from the sensors and smuggle you past the orbital security hub."

"There's one more thing, old friend," Austicon said. "I seem to have made the old women angry as of late."

"Intergalactic genocide will do that, you know."

Austicon continued unabated. "Spread the word. In the event that anything goes wrong, any of my colleagues who rescue me from capture will get my lockbox."

Gr'Narl's eyes widened. Pirates living on the fringe traded stories about Austicon's lockbox. Consensus gave it mythical treasure status. Nobody really knew what it was, but it was common knowledge that he destroyed an entire planet during the Intergalactic Singularity War in order to obtain it. With the MEA and allied planets preoccupied with the xenocidal Mechnar threat, Austicon had free range to eradicate everything on Phobos 12. Hidden from the MEA core by the LDN1774 "Dark Tentacle" nebula, none remained alive willing to share specific information beyond it being "glorious." Nothing remained of Phobos 12 in Austicon's aftermath.

"You will give me the lockbox," Gr'Narl clarified, "If I free you should you ever become incarcerated?"

Austicon nodded slowly. "If I've been locked away longer than a year, then yes. It is a standing offer."

Gr'Narl sneered. "I think someone might help you get locked away if the lockbox is on the line. I think it wise if you keep the offer close to the vest."

"No!" he snapped. Austicon regained his composure and smoothed his clothes and hair. "It is an open contract."

The Shivan shrugged. "Okay, but I think it will make life more difficult for you."

Austicon sat back in his chair. "Excellent. When do we leave for Io?"

Gr'Narl shrugged. "Whenever you're ready. It's not a long trip; we'll just need to secure an invoice for delivery and some disposable cargo first. It won't take long."

Austicon sucked in a lungful of hookah smoke and then let it out in one massive blast like a dragon breathing fire. He stood. "I am ready now."

Gr'Narl rose and followed him. "You've hired me before, so you know the quality of my work," the flat-topped alien probed. "Gimme the inside track. What is the lockbox?"

The villain looked down his nose at the space pirate. "It's glorious."

11

"Entering District Nine's airspace, now," Matty reported to Dekker who sat in the copilot's seat aboard the *Rickshaw Crusader*.

Dekker nodded. Matty was their best pilot, so the *Crusader* fell into his lap. The leader stood and threw his trademark duster over his shoulders as he left the cockpit.

"We should be at Greenhome Central any minute," Matty assured him.

"Perfect. I'll go grab the cargo."

Vesuvius watched Dekker leave but made no movements to follow him.

Moments later, their ship descended over the bright green terra-formed island in the middle of the Pacific. Gigantic, artistic alien structures surrounded the landing pad that their VTOL thrusters set them down upon.

Dekker tried not to grimace as the landing ramp opened before him giving him a view of The Pheema's grounds. "Crap," he muttered as he sauntered down the entry. If he'd have known the job was for someone in the alien religious leader's inner circle he might have declined it on principle.

He met the furry humanoid on the grassy tarmac and nodded his head towards the ship. Dekker tried to hurry the process along for Vivian's sake. "Let's go then. We've got a time line to keep."

The alien cocked his head. "No formalities?" He bowed. "My name is Zarbeth."

"You don't want to be late, do you Zarbeth?"

Tight-lipped, his whiskers drooped and he followed Dekker into the ship which climbed skyward as soon as the ramp closed.

"I didn't realize The Pheema and the Krenzin religious leaders had such a vested interest in the success of the corporations," Dekker mused.

"As you know, our people are always concerned about peace above all other interests." Zarbeth's face soured when he spotted the pistols tucked beneath Dekker's coat. "I did not realize this was an armed escort--I might have made other arrangements," his voice hinted at disdain.

Dekker squinted. "I'm guessing you didn't make the travel plans. Maybe someone thinks your mission is too important to send you off-world where things can easily get hostile. Maybe the situation on Io is more dangerous than you realize."

"Hardly," Zarbeth countered. "I am merely moderating a discussion between Halabella Corps and the head of the miner's union. It is in the interest of the MEA, *my people's home*, to prevent a shortage of Polonium necessary for starship fuel."

Dekker stomped the floor. "Only the capital class ships use those polonium drive rods. This ship is only a class B," he said.

"And any ship older than twenty-six P.I.S.W." he clarified. "I'm not here to argue, Mr. Dekker Knight."

"Just Dekker."

"The Krenzin merely want to prevent the financial instability that will result from a costly spike in interstellar fuel."

"Yeah," Dekker said. "I can see how that might cause an upset in the upcoming election cycle. Where does the Krenzin stand in the political race? You guys like Miko Janus's chance for reelection?"

Zarbeth narrowed his eyes. "What are you implying, Investigator?"

"I don't get paid to imply anything. I'm just an escort." Dekker leaned into the hall and caught the pilot's attention.

"Maybe you should just stick to escorting," Zarbeth's voice verged on anger.

"Maybe you're right," he digressed as he reached up and grabbed onto a ledge while pointing to an empty crash couch on the other side of the ships great room. "You should sit down and buckle up."

Dekker leaned forward before Zarbeth could take a step forward. "Matty, time to square the circle."

"Yes, boss." Matty punched the button and lit the FTL drives for a micro-jump. The ship bucked momentarily, spinning Zarbeth to the ground right in front of his seat.

As soon as the inertial compensators caught up with the momentum, the alien slid into his seat and massaged his bruised knee. He glared at his host while suffering in silence.

Matty's voice crackled along the intercom. "All crew and guests, we should arrive at Io's transfer station in thirty minutes... plan your card games accordingly."

12

Joliver, Tina, and Julio stayed in lockstep with the other students. They followed Mr. Beck, their teacher, through the streets of Halabella's Io station.

Tina rubbed her bare arms and shivered. Outpost 7 felt chilly to her--and far from an impressive place compared to other places she'd traveled in her short life.

"We just got here, how can you be cold? It's like, a million degrees warmer here than on Europa." Julio rolled his eyes as Joliver offered her his zippered sweatshirt.

Mr. Beck warned the trio of thirteen-year-olds to quiet down with a finger laid across his lips and a stern glare. Their geology teacher was *really* into the tour.

Tina smiled at Joliver and accepted his spare layer of clothing. She was a newcomer to their region of the solar system and was much less acclimated.

"Don't mind him," Joliver bobbed his head towards Julio. "He's a good guy... my best friend for like, ten years. I'm sure he just feels a little..."

Mr. Beck shushed them again and skulked away from the tour guide to chastise his students. "I shouldn't hear a peep out of you three, you got it?"

They all nodded, fearful of the extra essay assignments that he might administer as punishment for misbehaving. His essay papers were famously brutal and dreaded almost more than expulsion. The students clammed up; it was far too early in the field trip to fall under the teacher's scrutiny.

"Good. I shouldn't see or hear a peep out of you three for the rest of the trip. Not a peep. If your peeping makes me look over this way... we'll have an unpleasant conversation."

Mr. Beck returned to his post near the tour guide.

Julio shook his head and made sure to keep his voice down while he talked out the side of his mouth. "Geez. How many times can a guy use 'peep' in a sentence?" They hung back an extra couple of steps to help avoid the watchful eye of their teacher who, luckily, found another student that required his attention.

They mostly kept pace with their group while the Halabella Corporation's PR guy droned on and on about how they harvest the radioactive polonium from beneath the planet's crust and send it off to local refineries where machines compressed it into the one-meter rods used to initiate FTL travel in many types of starships. He began talking about planetary tidal heating and geyser plumes when he lost the last scrap of attention the teenagers could spare him.

None of them had any particular interest in geology--unlike Mr. Beck who seemed to have developed odd, romantic attachments to their fact-spewing guide. Julio was mostly interested in media and current events and Joliver was interested in Tina.

They shambled onward, as bored as hibernating Scythian worms, when Julio perked up. "Do you guys see that man?"

Joliver and Tina glanced at the shifty character peeking out from around some heavy equipment at the edge of the operations site. Joliver shrugged. "He's just some old dude."

"You don't recognize him?" Julio insisted, "That guy looks exactly like Prognon Austicon--from the news wire!"

They looked again as the smiling man stepped out of the shadows and walked casually across the yard and towards them. He veered away as he drew nearer the doors leading towards the business hub.

"Pssh. You're crazy," Joliver said.

"No," Tina disagreed after watching their target for a few moments. "I think he's right!"

Julio beamed.

"You think the galaxy's most wanted man just walked past our school's tour group?"

She nodded her head very seriously.

"Guys," Julio whispered. "Let's follow him."

Joliver stiffened like he'd been electrified by their crazy idea. "I don't want to get stuck with a stupid Beck assignment! You guys are nuts."

"Do you really want to stay on this boring field trip?" Tina winked playfully. "We can just say that we got lost--we can't get quizzed on something we don't know anything about anyway, can we? Trust me; we'll be fine as long as we stick to a group alibi."

Joliver grimaced and bit his lip stubbornly.

His friends shrugged and started drifting slowly away towards the direction where the dangerous criminal went. They ignored his protests.

"Guys. Guys? Guys--wait up!"

13

"I'd much prefer to land on Io," Matty said into the com unit as they crawled nearer the moon at sub-orbital speed.

"Negative," the channel crackled. "I don't care about your licensure or who you have on board," the uppity officer aboard the orbital security hub squawked. "Everyone goes through the transit hub. Report to OSH3 to transfer your travelers to the surface.

"But your rules don't make sense," Matty argued. "No ship this size could pose any kind of threat. We've got a stock Ein-Warp tachypomp drive system--there's no way our FTL systems pose a threat of igniting any polonium stores." He neglected to mention all the custom work Doc Johnson and Fryberger did to modify their systems the last time it was in for repairs at Darkside Station.

"Report to OSH3," the voice repeated. As if to punctuate the statement the MEA's class E sentry ship pulled closer to monitor the situation. Its transponder identified it as the *Vigilance*.

"It's not worth the argument," Vesuvius sighed from the copilot seat. "Just get us over to the transit hub so that we can ferry down and get this job over with."

Matty nodded and shifted course. "Reporting to OSH3," he responded on the com.

"Acknowledged." The capital ship slowed course and hung in orbit nearby, rather than pursuing. It *looked* more threatening than it was--MEA military ships were a joke amongst Investigators and any of the shadier classes they sometimes consorted with. MEA military rarely ever took action, let alone fire their massive weapons.

The political red tape tying up the galactic navy over the past few decades is what gave rise to the Investigator profession. People still needed soldiers willing to pull a trigger when necessary but the intergalactic government had so hamstrung its forces that jobs of necessity fell to the much-villainized private sector.

The *Rickshaw Crusader* pulled nearer the ring-shaped station where a shuttle-craft would take them to the surface. A cluster of various corporate and private ships of all makes hung nearby; the largest was a class D Shivan vessel. That didn't seem unusual as the heavy-g species had been prospecting Jupiter's resources for decades, though not much else in the local solar system particularly interested them.

Matty did a double take on the ships.

Vesuvius leaned forward, trying to glimpse whatever had gotten his attention.

"Hey, Dekker--you might want to see this," Matty called.

Dekker approached from the hall where he babysat their passenger.

Matty pointed to another class B frigate only slightly larger than the *Crusader*. "See the symbol painted on the hull?"

Their leader bobbed his head solemnly. "I see it," Dekker kept staring. "I dunno if that's a Druze marking or just graffiti," he commented. "There's lots of paint on that thing--but good eyes. It looks to me more like a refurbed ship bought from one of those scrappers on the wrong side of District Three... but let's keep an eye on it all the same."

Shin, occupying one of the four seats in the cockpit looked at him sidelong and then stood to get a glimpse of the markings. "Did you say Druze?"

Dekker nodded.

Shin shot him an inquisitive look. "Aren't they usually hanging around Prognon Austicon?"

"Yeah," Matty interjected excitedly. "They think he's some kind of messiah or something."

"They used to be a religious offshoot of an old religion," Dekker explained, "at least a millennium ago. Somehow Austicon corrupted them from within around the time that the MEA began entertaining laws prohibiting faith groups aside from those allied with the Krenzin. They fed the hysteria and started the Secret Wars until the MEA outlawed all religions."

Shin raised an eyebrow. "Aren't the Secret Wars still happening?"

Dekker holstered a pistol. "Yeah. To some degree. The MEA's religious edicts are about as effective as their ban on weapons."

Vesuvius watched the distant ship. "You don't think Austicon is here, do you? Chief Magnate Janus's brother Jai could make an appealing target."

Dekker stared out of the cockpit for a long moment. "No; I don't think he's here. Jai Janus is too small of a fish for Austicon to fry--especially with such a high bounty on his head and with a face that's so well known."

Matty stayed at the helm but Vesuvius and Shin followed Dekker towards the mess where they would prep for transport. Vesuvius asked, "But what if he *is* on Io?"

Dekker's hand rested on the grip of his pistol. "Then I finally get to settle a score with the madman who's been killing my people since before I was born."

14

Prognon Austicon set down the black bag of tools he'd commandeered from the supply room in the warehouse district. He closed the door behind him and locked it before retrieving the laser drill and affixing it to the wall.

He set the depth and activated the device. Checking the hole's bore and tunnel, he burned the last few micrometers away and snaked a thin spy cable through the hole. Austicon paired its feed to his viewing screen as he fit the audio buds into his ears.

Jai Janus sat at his desk and spoke to a man the assassin did not recognize.

"...because I'm being blackmailed by a group of women--very powerful women."

The stranger asked, "Doesn't it always come down to a woman?"

Halabella's officer shook his head. "Far too often. But I'm not planning on giving in. The Pheema sent one of his negotiators in to mediate the dispute with the union... provided Jace Strengen makes it to the meeting."

"What are you saying?" Jai's guest leaned forward conspiratorially. *"Did your brother put a hit on Jace for you?"*

Jai looked away.

Austicon looked past Jai and zoomed in on his desk. Hovering in a stasis pod as a paperweight hung his secondary objective. The seed had only begun to germinate and looked otherwise like a miniature sugar beet. Its case had been etched with an arbolean signature but a label on the glass read: *unknown species--new flora discovered 0064PISW: Ganymede, Sippar Sulcus Mt.*

Heat burned in his gut. Austicon was not a particularly nostalgic soul, but denigrating such a unique life-form to serve as a mere bauble irked him. Only *he* was allowed such a freedom.

An alert chirped on Jai's desk. "The Krenzin mediator will be arriving shortly."

The nameless contact across from Director Janus closed his paper note file. The tab labeled it with a single word: *Satyr*. He tucked it into his briefcase and the two men left the room.

15

Mustache stood at the airlock but remained in the ship. He and Matty would keep the *Rickshaw Crusader* in orbit while the other members of the Dozen escorted their Krenzin passenger to his meeting.

Dekker stood apart from his crew. He had been flagged and detained by station security. He wore a scowl while the unarmed security officers flanked him.

"Unless you can explain the exact nature of the weapon..." the first officer scanned the ancient mechanism that hung over Dekker's shoulder by a strap.

"Well, not even then," the second one interjected.

"I've never seen anything like it," the first said.

"And you never will again," Dekker stated.

"Well, we can't let you bring it aboard," a third barked.

Dekker's scowl twisted further. The Reliquary was a mysterious gun of ancient, possibly arcane, origins and had been handed down to him by his father, and the old Watchman priest Diacharia before him.

The Dozen watched from the other side of the security checkpoint, surrounding Zarbeth who

Guy petted. Zarbeth gave the Dozen's designated prankster a dirty look, but Guy pretended not to notice.

Dekker didn't want to be caught without the incredible weapon if Prognon Austicon was in fact here. However, he couldn't press the issue without hurting his company's reputation and risk losing future contracts.

"Fine," Dekker finally said. "It's just a simple escort mission, after all. I can leave the heavy weaponry on the *Crusader*."

He put his prized item into Mustache's hands. "Be careful with that."

Mustache nodded with a cavalier wink. He'd seen it fired before and knew firsthand how much destruction it could cause.

Dekker looked at the security officers expectantly and they waved him through. He joined his crew and they took Zarbeth to the ferry and then shuttled down to the surface of Io.

The transport curved a broad arc as it descended towards the biggest of the domed cities. Set on a preprogrammed route, the dropship flew through the pneumatic travel locks that gave it access to Outpost 7, Halabella's primary station on the Io moon.

Relatively silent, the crew walked Zarbeth from the transit station to the local conference center where the meetings were scheduled. They tromped through the downtown section of Outpost

7 and eyes instinctively turned to the group of armed mercenaries.

The Krenzin shot Guy a disturbed look. "I will allow the local security team to bring me to the orbital transit dock. I'll alert you when I arrive."

"Suit yourself," Vesuvius interjected before Dekker could respond with any amount of diplomacy. Guy made eye contact with him and pretended to pet an imaginary cat.

Scowling, the alien mediator parted company and entered the government center. Guy shrugged and made a heart-breaking motion with his hands.

With Zarbeth deposited safely into the hands of the local constabulary forces, the Investigators broke off to see what kind of local color was available. The Krenzin gave Dekker a paging device to signal when his sessions concluded and he required a ride home.

Dekker dropped it into a pocket and returned to his friends. He hooked an arm over Shin and another over Vesuvius; Guy followed in tow as a third wheel. They meandered back the way they had come and spotted several of their comrades interacting with local vendors or checking out the stores.

Down a crooked alley, he pointed to a blinking, neon sign. "The Rusty Lizard? That looks like a decent place. You guys want to grab a bite?"

Shin looked at the dive reluctantly.

"A gastro-intestinally risky hive of scum and villainy? Of course you'd pick this place," Vesuvius commented.

Shin's stomach rumbled, though he wasn't sure if it was from fear or hunger. "Sure. I guess I came for an adventure, right?"

Guy hung back and turned to a nearby video display advertising a miner recruitment service. It looped information about how the polonium rods were excavated, refined, and developed into the highly regulated thermonuclear fuel. The recording featured clips of detonations and controlled subsurface blasts.

Vesuvius called back, "Are you coming, Guy?"

"Nah," he said, watching the screen. "You know me. I love my explosions... except for the kind that follow Dekker's restaurant choices."

The trio shrugged and ducked into the Rusty Lizard. "He might have made the wiser choice," Vesuvius noted. "Last time, Dekker made him try chicken paws."

"Hey," Dekker defended, adjusting his coat to keep his guns concealed. "The menu claimed they were a delicacy."

16

Austicon slinked through the laser-bored tunnels that made up Outpost 7's substructure. The impressive size and layout of the facilities were a credit to the automated design bots that crafted such places on the harsh, terraformed environments such as Jupiter's satellites. The towering ceilings and spacious feel made it seem almost like the sub-level was actually aboveground.

He finally found the thing he was looking for: a nondescript warehouse surrounded with heavy-duty fencing. Austicon walked up to the military-grade security kiosk while he rummaged through his black bag of tricks.

Retrieving a high-tech cube that dangled wires and cables like an octopoid mechnar, the assassin activated the unit and set it on the security interface. The hacker unit flew into motion, sampling data and inserting probes into the necessary ports to bypass any locks, copy and loop any feeds, and prevent detection. After a brief crackle and burst of light, a wisp of smoke rose from the electronic panel and the luminaries around the warehouse deadened.

Austicon turned at the sound of approaching footsteps. He took a blaster rifle from his satchel and leveled it towards the direction of the sounds.

A few seconds later Leviathan and a group of Druze emerged from the shadows. One of them turned back to activate and drop a metallic ball and orient its infrared detection sensor.

Half a dozen of his loyal worshipers knelt. Leviathan, a skinny humanoid creature who was more machine than man at this stage in his life, wore a formfitting black jumpsuit and something that looked like a welding mask.

Austicon grinned as his most loyal friend bowed. The mask half opened, partly revealing his gnarled and twisted beauty and lidless eyes. It repulsed any mortals who might see him, but Austicon and Leviathan had known each other since long before taking such crude forms.

"Do you have your half of the device?" Austicon dangled a set of wires attached to sensor probes.

Leviathan stood and unzipped his suit, revealing his pallid, naked flesh. He broke a few stitches and peeled back his skin to reveal a surgical pocket built into his lithe body. Pulling out the cylindrical, electronic device, Leviathan held it out before him like an offering.

"Excellent," Austicon hissed, motioning them towards him. They obediently joined their leader who gave them each a weapon from the sack. "Now we are ready for the fun to begin."

He pressed a button on the octopoid hacking unit and the immense cargo door of the warehouse opened of its own accord. The activity drew out a heavy detail of security officers armed with retractable batons. Their eyes widened when they locked eyes with their assailants and spotted the illegal firearms they held.

The Druze mowed them down with a hail of bullets and charged into the opening ensuring a swift and complete take-over. Another crew of Druze arrived with a hovering load-lifter that carried heavy mining machinery taken from a different warehouse. They immediately began their drilling operation.

Austicon finished assembling his contraption as he entered the storehouse. It had been stuffed full from floor to rafters with polonium pods that were charged and ready for distribution.

One of the Druze hollered instructions to his work crew and checked his timepiece. "We're on schedule, my lord," he reported to Leviathan, refusing to even look Austicon in the face. "It will take very little effort to open a channel into the fault lines, as instructed."

Leviathan nodded solemnly and his minion returned to his task.

With a maniacal grin, Austicon looked from his device to the mammoth stockpile of nuclear materials as he rubbed shoulders with Leviathan. "I've destroyed planets with chemicals and toxins, but this... this one is special." He looked to his silent general. "I've always wanted to blow up a moon."

17

Guy finished unsuccessfully haggling with a street vendor near the alley hiding the door to the Rusty Lizard. He momentarily considered joining his friends; his gut tightened with a rumble of protest.

Looking back towards the larger market area Guy watched the flow of traffic for a few minutes. A mining shift change must've just taken place. Bone-weary workers clad in Halabella uniforms meandered through the regular crowd of the marketplace.

A pack of uniformed men walked through the flow of traffic. Eyes forward, their gait had a certain purpose and intent destination. Everything about them rang untrue in Guy's heart. The Investigator glanced back to the other workers. Their skin was pallid and their shuffling steps were barely more than an amble.

Guy walked into the crowd and tailed the subtly different team of miners. He plotted an intercept path through the moving marketplace and nearly brushed up against one as he cut a path across the area.

His gut did another somersault. At the edge of the man's hairline, near his nape, a patch of skin bore a distinct Druze tattoo. Guy risked a glance across at the other workers as they passed by. They each had similar markings.

After pausing at a booth and pretending to look at a seller's wares, Guy pulled out his communicator. He turned and followed the impostors at a healthy distance while activating his com. "Hey, team. I found the Druze. I'm tailing them now." He noted and reported a small location plaque attached to the hallway giving an address marker.

Seconds later, Trigger and Rock dropped into step behind Guy.

"Nice of you guys to join me."

"Well, we happened to be in the area," Rock noted.

"Yeah," Trigger teased, "shopping for smocks."

Guy just looked at them for a moment. It sounded too weird to be false.

They kept walking in silence as they followed the terrorists from a distance. Guy put the com near his face. "Are the rest of you guys coming or what?"

He counted the clicks for confirmation as the rest of the planetside Dozen responded. Guy, Rock, and Trigger continued their stealthy pursuit.

"Well what am I supposed to wear?" Rock finally defended with a stern whisper. "Sometimes I like to paint, alright?"

18

Leviathan watched Prognon Austicon complete the detonation apparatus and affix it to a collection of polonium fuel rods. Beneath the mask that obscured his hideous visage he smiled with his lipless mouth.

He reached out with his psychic senses and checked the workers' progress with the laser drills. They'd already bored a massive tunnel into the floor, angling their cut through the bedrock and toward the planetary faults.

Satisfied that the project remained on schedule Leviathan emerged from the stockpile. He left the warehouse operations in order to meet his secondary team. His master still had another objective to meet in order to please the Red Tree.

His soldiers met him in the immense antechamber-style room that housed the warehouse district in the sublevels below Outpost 7. He checked his timepiece and stood in the central path to wait. Seconds passed and a voice yelled out, "Hey! You can't be here!"

Leviathan turned his masked face to the security officer who approached, peace baton in hand. The helmed assassin pointed a gun-like, vacuum tube apparatus at the guard and fired a tight beam of electricity.

The beam burned through the air and hit the officer in the chest. His torso flashed with a stroke of lightning and scorched most his upper body away. What remained of the man collapsed in a heap on the floor and silence returned.

Within a few moments, a group of his loyal Druze rounded the corner and approached. Footsteps echoed past them at another hallway and Leviathan turned to find another group of cultic infiltrators who had taken another path.

The job was important to Austicon's Arbolean friends and so it was important to Leviathan.

Gathering at the foot of the general, the assassins bowed low before the thing that they revered as a high priest. He beckoned for them to stand and led the deadly processional towards the larger collection of terrorists.

19

Guy, Trigger, and Rock ducked around the corner of the hallway and hunkered down behind a pile of loading machinery used to transport the materials stored in any of the nearby pods to some nearby shipping facility.

"You'd better hurry. The gang's all here!"

"Be there any second," Dekker reported.

"Good. That weird masked guy is here with Austicon, along with at least a dozen Druze. I'd hate for you to be late to the party--it looks like they're cooking up something big." Guy let a few moments of silence pass before opening the channel again. "You don't suppose any of them brought a pinata, do you? I like pinatas."

Austicon stood outside a storage pod which boasted higher than normal security. All of that had obviously been bypassed.

After a few more moments Dekker, Vesuvius, and Shin joined them where they hunkered around the edge of equipment.

"Check your three," a voice whispered.

Looking to their right they spotted the rest of their crew. Ahmed, the team's primary medic, gave them a discreet wave and pointed to the direction of their enemies.

Dekker nodded and used his hands to flash them a head count of the Druze that they could see. Pointing towards Prognon Austicon he held a pistol at the ready and used a hand to count down the attack. *Three... two... one...*

20

Julio leaned back into the cab of the doorless load hauler they'd hid inside and tried to make himself smaller. He crossed his lips with a finger, signaling Joliver and Tina to keep quiet.

The other two teens huddled together on the passenger seat and tried to keep their breathing quiet. Simply inhaling and exhaling sounded deafening and their breaths fogged up the interior of the forward glassine screen with a white sheen.

They stiffened, hearing footsteps of a nearby security guard as they grew louder with his approach, and then they softened as he passed without so much as a glance in their direction. He moved with an intentional pace, heading directly towards the storage sections where they'd been watching Prognon Austicon and his creepy henchman perform some kind of mining operation.

"Oh good," Julio whispered as the officer passed them and hollered out to the bad guys. "Someone's going to put a stop to him. I think they're trying to steal the polonium... if they're drilling a hole down that way, they're probably opening a hole up to ship it out on the rail system."

A jolt of lightning crackled through the air and incinerated the guard. The teens shrank down as low as they could and Tina clamped a hand over her own mouth to keep herself from screaming. Terror was evident in her eyes and her breathing came in ragged, chortling shivers. This was no game of hide and seek--if they were discovered they would die.

Julio slowly began to rise for a better look. Joliver shook his head to wordlessly warn him against it, but Julio crept up slowly and peeked over the dash of the machine. He jerked back to floorboards when the nightmarish, masked assassin looked directly towards him.

They suddenly felt surrounded by the echoing of footsteps. A group of Halabella miners trotted forward and passed by them.

Finally convinced that their cover remained intact, the three students sat back up and surveyed the scene. The miners met up with Austicon and his other minions.

Several minutes passed as they watched the most wanted criminal in the galaxy converse with his soldiers--likely assigning them duties or figuring out how to load and steal the radioactive fuel. Suddenly gunfire rang out.

Lasers flashed and Austicon's men scattered like roaches as they returned fire. A trio of them fell in the opening salvo as they rushed for cover.

Ducking back down, the teens huddled together, certain they'd be killed in the battle as blaster fire sizzled the air around them and burnt the oxygen with an ozone smell. "I told you we should have stayed back!" Joliver insisted.

Looking backwards they spotted a team of men working forward using barricades and cover fire to advance on the enemy.

"These guys look like Investigators," Julio said with hope in his voice.

"My dad says Investigators are just glorified murderers," Tina whispered.

"Well, as long as they're murdering the right people," Julio hissed and ducked as a blast ricocheted off of the nearby retaining wall near their hiding spot.

"Whatever. I don't even care," Joliver said. "But can we please just get out of here while we're still alive?"

21

"Ah crap!" Mustache yelled down the corridor to the cockpit.

The sounds of battle poured through the open comm channel down on the surface and played on the speaker system. Mustache's heavy feet clanked on the metal grating as he tromped through the ship.

Matty yelled over his shoulder, "What's the problem down there?"

Mustache was supposed to be at the gunnery controls but flopped into the copilot's chair instead. He held up a three-dimensional holographic display of the planet; topographical features like tectonic plates, planetary hydrothermal vents, and Halabella's mineral and special interests overlaid the shimmering sphere. "Prognon Austicon is down there with a bunch of armed Druze psychos."

"Yeah--so? That's just another week for us."

"So what is Austicon known for--really nasty stuff, right? Like... it's always the worst case scenario for this guy."

Matty stared at him blankly, waiting for the other shoe to drop.

Mustache clicked a few buttons and the moons geological fault lines changed color and glowed brightly.

Matty raised an eyebrow and Mustache fidgeted with the map again.

Some of the dots representing the mining operations glowed brightly and overlaid with a nuclear danger warning. The largest of them sat right on the glimmering fault line.

"Oh crap," Matty agreed. He snapped up the com unit and howled into it. "Guys! Dekker--we think we know why Austicon is there. You must be near some really big nuclear bomb or something?"

Guy broke onto the channel, barely audible over the crisp crackling of gunfire. "Almost! There's a giant warehouse full of everything you'd want to make a bomb big enough to blow up a planet... what are you saying?"

Matty blinked. "Well... I think you..."

"Ah crap! He's gonna blow up the planet?"

"There's some crazy geological features just below your location. If he's got access to diverting the blast into it, he could theoretically crack it and blow the entire planet to pieces... like driving a wedge into a log."

"Divert it with, like, a bunch of heavy mining equipment that's bored a giant hole into the planet?"

"That'd do it."

"Oh man--and my counselor wonders why I get so stressed out," Guy responded.

"You don't see a counselor."

"Fine... my massage therapist. But leave Greta out of it."

The *Rickshaw Crusader*_shuddered and bucked, suddenly coming under fire. Both heads snapped up to attention and spotted the Druze ship moving towards them with guns blazing.

Matty stayed calm and maneuvered the *Crusader*_to react to the threat while Mustache sprinted back to man the guns, caroming off the halls as the ship twisted through a series of spins and dives.

"Greta?" Matty asked nonchalantly. "I'll be sure to pass on my condolences after the inevitable."

"That hurts me," Guy retorted with mock outrage.

"Well, she sounds super cute. Plus, you're all gonna die down there... and you know... we're gonna not die cuz we're in space."

"She's crazy hairy, like three-hundred pounds of Scandinavian muscle and my uncle Jerry's jawline. She's perfect for you; I know you've got a type."

Shin broke into the chatter. "How have all stayed alive this long?"

"Good question," Matty laughed nervously over the urgent beeping from his HUD. "I'll let you know if I survive all these missiles our new best friends just launched."

22

Dekker ducked below a mechanical boom arm and rolled behind a pallet of hydraulic parts, firing as he went and killing two of the Druze warriors who charged towards his position. He reloaded his guns and peeked back into the alleyway that spilled into the larger opening.

Austicon's masked henchman taunted them from the hall's mouth, holding a jagged sword in each hand; he blocked passage to his master who stood thirty meters behind him, laying down suppressing fire against the other Investigators on the other side of the industrial sub-level. Beyond the sneering mass murderer, half a dozen of Dekker's friends continued engaging the Druze fighters.

Dekker arched an eyebrow. The hair stood on the back of his neck as he stared down the black, faceless figure who paced menacingly.

Trigger leaned out from behind an abused concrete mixer where he backed Dekker up. "It's time we grabbed this bounty!" He surged forward and barreled headlong down the corridor, blaster firing.

"Trigger! No," Dekker shouted too late.

Austicon's general blocked shot after shot with his spinning, whirling swords. He moved with uncanny speed and agility--no living thing could move that way! Only a few stray shots burned superficial wounds through his skin that leaked something appearing to be dust; he finally backpedaled in retreat as the Investigator closed the gap.

Trigger's leg crossed an infrared tripwire. The metallic ball emitting it erupted in bursts of flame and shrapnel.

Dekker recoiled from the heat but turned back as soon as possible. His eyes searched in vain for his impetuous comrade, but nothing was left but shredded boots and a blackened smear.

The murderous thing that bled sand hissed and laughed with a noise that sounded more like a death rattle than mirth.

Dekker locked eyes on it and heard footsteps behind.

"We've got this one," Vesuvius said. Shin nodded his curt agreement.

Dekker looked at Rock who nodded, silently agreeing to watch his flank.

"Bounty's dead or alive?" Rock asked.

"We've never lost anyone before," Dekker stated, glancing back to Trigger's corpse. "Let's kill Prognon Austicon."

The two parties stared each other down for a second that stretched out as long as their animosity. Finally, they both sprang into action and all at once.

Sprinting forward the masked man darted into the broad hall. Vesuvius and Shin leapt into the engagement with swords drawn.

They traded strikes, high and low as the assassin blocked and countered each as if he somehow knew it was coming.

Dekker and Rock clambered up a stack of crates and onto a roof terrace that overlooked the battle just below. They provided cover fire for each other as they took shots at Austicon and ducked below the lethal return fire.

Austicon retreated slowly towards the greater body of his men which the other dozen had pinned down from the other side. Finally, he ducked under the fire of Dekker's dual hand cannons and snatched up a black bag he'd left near the security kiosk before diving behind the cover of the terminal.

Shin and Vesuvius beat back their enemy. On second glance, they realized he was tactically retreating, moving one step at a time--trying to draw closer to his master, even though he showed no real difficulty in handling the sword wielders.

Before Dekker could come up with a way to use any of that to his advantage Austicon stepped back into view with a shoulder cannon hoisted over his shoulder. His evil cackle fouled the air as he aimed at Dekker and yanked the activation lever. It hummed and cycled up for a split second--just enough time for Dekker and Rock to throw themselves from the catwalk.

They tumbled to the ground as the violet beam cut through the building ledge where Dekker had been. The blast scattered rubble and smoking bits all across the industrial district. Dekker and Rock rolled to the floor with bone-jarring force and came to their senses just in time to see their enemy drop the heavy device; its battery had been depleted anyways.

Austicon turned and ran for a hallway between the two groups of Investigators.

The masked sword wielder knocked Shin's sword wide, sending him to chase after it. Vesuvius howled and slashed with a deadly combination few could anticipate--except for him. He bobbed backwards and spun with a whirlwind kick that sent her sprawling near Shin.

Without hesitation the thing turned and fled, seeking out his master.

Dekker and Rock caught up with the two as they sheathed their blades and drew guns again. Within a few seconds, they mopped up the remaining Druze with flanking fire.

Regrouping as a team Dekker glanced back to the charred area where parts of Trigger's body laid. He wanted to see Austicon dead more than he'd ever wanted anything else. While scrambling to count heads and make sure they were whole, he heard Guy's voice from the polonium warehouse behind them.

"Um... guys? We've got a big problem."

23

Prognon Austicon slipped through a set of doors and dashed through a hallway and into an empty industrial cryogenics facility. The high ceiling overhead allowed for plenty of room to fit the immense pieces of machinery.

He glanced around, looking for the perfect hiding spot to hatch his devious plot from. Luckily for the regular crew, there was no work scheduled for today so Austicon wouldn't have to murder them all.

The assassin grinned. He knew that very thought was why Dekker Knight would follow him. Dekker's father, Jude, had been the same way before Austicon killed him... along with the woman Dekker loved.

Rushing over to a giant, clear cryogenics tube, he slapped the release button and opened the access hatch to the pod. Gun at the ready, he looked back and spotted Leviathan entering the plant.

His masked general rushed over to him. "Today I get to avenge myself for what started thousands of years ago with the Ring of Aandaleeb... when my name was different--when we were separated for so long." Austicon smiled. Some inner need burned within him and the closest thing to peace he could ever know washed over him at the prospect. "What started with Solomon and Benaiah ends with Dekker Knight."

Austicon turned to crawl into the freezing pod. "He will get close as he searches for me and I will finally kill him!"

Leviathan removed his mask. Worry permeated his face as his eyes locked on his beloved.

Austicon shot him a comforting look and took his face in his hands. He tenderly kissed the creature's forehead. "Do not worry about me--I will have plenty of time to escape before the polonium bomb fractures the planet."

Leviathan melted into the embrace but didn't relent. He projected his words into Austicon's mind. *The Circle will be upset if you leave your objectives unfinished--you still have tasks to perform.*

"Then do them for me," the master ordered.

Leviathan bowed low and then snapped to attention. Austicon turned, too: noise in the hallway just beyond the door. *Someone is coming!*

Austicon glanced one more time at his lovesick servant and crawled into the pod. Leviathan nodded obediently, reaffixed his mask, and darted out the back.

The pod's hatch hissed slowly and Austicon leaned back in gentle repose, gun at the ready. Within a few moments, he would finally mount the first step in acquiring everything he ever wanted--a step he struggled to attain since the dawn of time and one that began with the death of the last Watchman.

24

"Yargh!" Mustache howled into the headset speaker as he fired from the *Rickshaw Crusader's* gunnery turret. He poured on as much blaster fire as he could.

Matty twisted the *Crusader* into a roll as he tried to evade the missiles and Mustache struggled to track the angles through the extreme movements. Of their enemy's ten missiles, he'd only managed to pick off a couple of them.

The Dozen's ship raced through the orbital space and weaved through the civilian traffic hanging above the planet. "We've got to get away from the station," Matty explained over the intercom. "We need to minimize casualties if this goes south!"

"Why does the south always get the blame," Mustache mused as he picked off another missile. "I mean, it seems like an unfair characterization."

Matty grimaced and grunted as he spun the ship into a tight roll right before the rockets could tag them. Ballistic death streaked past them trailing streams of propellant. The *Crusader* throttled up and sped towards a large, stationary asteroid as the missiles turned around and automatically reengaged.

"Don't forget," Matty hissed, "that the Dozen's HQ is below Earth's equator line. Technically *we're* south."

"Fair point," Mustache drawled as he spun the turret to face the opposite direction. "See that transport up ahead? Bob just underneath it and keep us steady!" Mustache whirled back around to reengage the projectiles. He glanced to the side and caught the Druze ship closing on them from another vector.

"Copy!"

The *Crusader* aimed straight for the long ship's broadside as it crossed paths en route to the asteroid. "That things just an automated drone, right?"

"Um. Yes," Mustache promised. It certainly looked like the kind of robotic freight haulers the asteroid miners had long used to ferry raw materials.

Matty howled, "You're sure?"

The unmanned ship loomed on the pilot's screen, filling it. The missiles closed in from the back, streaking closer with dogged persistence.

"Yes." Mustache lied. "One hundred percent!"

At the last second, the *Rickshaw Crusader* dipped below the unprotected freighter and skimmed its underside with the Investigator's shields. It popped back up on the other side just as Mustache poured fire into the hauling craft.

As the missiles attempted the same maneuver, the transport exploded into a cloud of debris. The missiles erupted with an angry, fireball that the vacuum of space quickly squelched.

With the threat of missiles gone, Matty spun their ship into a tight barrel roll as the Druze craft opened fire. He arched around to give Mustache a clean shot at the aggressors when the *Rickshaw Crusader* suddenly went limp. Emergency lights lit up the panels and the ship listed, dead in the water.

Thick blue beams of crippling EMP energy blasted the nearby Druze ship as well. They too began to drift, crippled by the MEA peace-keeping frigate that suddenly loomed over both of them.

Vigilance had practiced their precision targeting for the most part. Matty flipped the switches on his console to enable the audio coming from the peacekeepers.

"...in violation of MEA intergalactic laws specifically prohibiting..." Matty flipped it back off and concentrated on getting their systems back online. He could hear Mustache down the corridor also trying to find and reactivate whatever breakers might have blown and replaced any coils burned out by the *Vigilance's* EMP pulse weapons.

"What've we still got?" he shouted to Matty.

"Communications, internal systems including life support, and shields. No weapons or propulsion."

Matty looked back to the screen where an MEA officer stood, silently lecturing them and likely stressing protocol and clearances for such kinds of hostilities. Suddenly, the screen's feed shook and the officer whirled in panic. On screen turning klaxon lights flared and illuminated the *Vigilance's* command bridge.

Someone else had attacked the MEA sentry ship.

25

Joliver, Tina, and Julio crept through the halls. They'd gone for better cover at the far edge of warehouse district while the gunfight still raged nearby.

Julio asked, "Any luck with that thing, Tina?"

She shook her head. "They keep putting me on hold for the next available security member. Something else must have everybody's attention."

Joliver imagined there might be some sort of civil unrest in the main section of Outpost 7. He guessed it might make their teacher do a quick head count and moaned. "Mr. Beck is gonna kill us," he sighed.

Suddenly Austicon rushed past them and walked through the nearby doors. Julio crouched down to keep out of sight. "He can't kill a group of heroes who just apprehended the most powerful criminal in the galaxy, can he?"

Joliver squinted, confused. He looked back at the Investigators who fought Austicon's henchmen. "Why would he kill these guys, even if he could?"

Julio and Tina stared at their friend.

"Ooooh! You mean us?" Joliver cringed. "I think I've had enough adventuring already."

"Don't be such a sissy," Julio said. "Let's follow him."

Joliver hedged.

Tina nodded to agree with Julio. "I'm already on hold with the constables. We just have to follow and report his location once we get in contact with a real person."

Joliver nodded reluctantly. "You guys are killing me, ya know? Quite possibly in a very real and literal sense."

His friends shrugged. Mischief glinted in their eyes, inspired by teenage delusions of grandeur.

They glanced back to see the mercenaries flanking the last couple holdouts. Full of butterflies and jitters they pushed open the doorway and plunged into the hallway to track the most dangerous man to ever exist.

26

"We've got to follow him and make him pay," Rock said.

"I saw which way Austicon went," Dekker responded. "If we follow, we shouldn't encounter more of those tripwire bombs that killed Trigger."

They had regrouped just outside of the polonium storehouse. Nibbs had disabled the octopoid device and hacked into the security feeds, learning that assistance from the local security or constables was unlikely. Austicon's device filed a number of false alarms all across the upper levels of Outpost 7.

"I don't think any of you understand the level of scariness in that room." Guy thumbed a digit backwards. "Isn't anybody else bothered by this?"

"You're the bomb guy. Defuse it," Jamba joked.

Dekker watched Guy's reaction. The explosives junky just stared; his eye twitched.

"I know you all want to go catch Prognon Austicon and leave me here to deactivate this--but it's freaky-level bad in there."

"Nibbs?" Dekker asked their tech chief.

"Yeah. It's probably worse than he says. Terrifying. I'd like to request that I not be here when we start messing with the moon-killing scary-bomb?"

Dekker kept his eyes locked on the distance, not wanting to look away for fear that it might mean Austicon escaped. Finally, he turned back to his friend. "Who do you need?"

"Nibbs for sure..."

"Crap," Nibbs joked.

"...and at least four others in case this is a second to worst-case situation."

Shin asked, "What's the *worst* case?"

"We're all dead, plus everyone in suborbital space over this hemisphere, so it won't matter."

Dekker nodded. "Take who you need... the rest of you are with me."

27

Joliver was the tallest of the teens and so he peeked through the window. The others tried to crouch against the wall of the long, open corridor as if that would afford them any amount of cover.

"What do you see?"

"Shh!" Joliver shushed Julio. "Creepy mask guy is talking with Austicon. It's some kind of cryogenics facility. It looks like they freeze stuff here for transportation."

The trio stood exposed in the hallway. If anyone walked in and found them there they would be in a world of trouble... possibly a lethal dose, depending on who it was.

"Is there anywhere to hide behind those doors?"

Joliver shook his head. "Not without being spotted by a psychotic killer."

Julio frowned. He didn't want to give up on the chase, but their location didn't afford anywhere to hide.

"Guys? What about this?" Tina pointed up towards the ceiling where a single ladder rung dangled. An adjacent sign labeled it as the emergency catwalk access.

Julio jumped to try and reach it but came up short. "Joliver?"

The taller teen leapt and snatched the handle. His weight dragged a ladder downward with a rusty, screeching noise that stopped them all dead in their tracks; their breath caught in their lungs and they waited for Austicon to emerge and kill them all.

After a few seconds of silence, no pursuit came and they examined the access. When the ladder came down, a hatch had opened simultaneously.

Julio scrambled upwards and into the dark. A few moments later he poked his head back down. "This way. I found the perfect hiding spot."

The others crawled up and onto a maintenance platform that hung suspended from the ceiling inside the cryostation. They pulled the ladder up and closed the hatch behind them.

Creeping as silently as possible, they barely dared look at the two assassins who discussed their plans below. Joliver looked down to the com in Tina's hand and suddenly had a terrible thought: *what if the constables finally answer?*

With a look of panic, he pointed at it and raised his eyebrows, silently sharing his concern. Julio tapped him back and pointed up again. Another ladder, this one shorter and mounted to the wall, accessed a control room for the facility.

They climbed it and entered the spacious cubicle quickly and stealthily. Computers and other equipment rested on the nearby desks and consoles.

Julio, Tina, and Joliver peeked through the large pane of industrial glass. It provided the perfect vantage to keep an eye on their bounty.

Tina glared at the communicator. "Now, if only I can get someone to respond!"

28

The Shivan pirate ship swooped down upon the *Vigilance* and unloaded its full arsenal upon the larger vessel. A small complement of missiles took out the weapons on the MEA's sentry ship.

As intruders continued to beat on it with a battery of heavy laser fire, the ship shuddered and flamed. Plumes of gas and vapor leaked from damaged sections of the hull and the *Vigilance* powered up its engines to try and escape a further beating.

"No, no, no!" Matty screamed at the MEA cruiser as it tried to extricate itself from the deadly situation. They'd hobbled the Investigators and then pulled out, leaving them to die. Matty rushed through the ship, trying to find and repair any fried circuits as fast as possible in order to restore weapons and propulsion systems--or even just one of them.

The *Rickshaw Crusader* shook and jolted as their much larger enemy turned its attention back to them and began firing.

Mustache and Matty traded nervous glances as they worked feverishly on restoring the systems. Thankfully, several retrofitted, black market upgrades on their ship meant the shields would likely fare better than the *Vigilance's*... for a time.

"How long do you think we got?" Mustache asked between bouts of vicious shuddering.

Matty grimaced with a nervous, sour smile. "Probably not long enough. It's gonna take at least thirty minutes to get us running again and we're sitting ducks out here!"

"That's a very nonspecific amount of minutes."

"I give us maybe twenty minutes at most. Unless someone comes to help, we're toast."

"You think it's time to try something crazy?"

Matty nodded grudgingly. "It might be."

"Good." Mustache shot Matty a playful look. "Cuz I've got a crazy idea. Do we have power to the airlocks?"

The Shivan vessel dropped in close like a confident predator, hovering just beyond the listing *Crusader* like an animal ready to strike a killing blow.

Matty flipped a triggered breaker. "We do now, but are you sure about this?"

Mustache bit his lower lip and shrugged as he started pulling on a spacesuit. "Trust me."

29

Guy muttered as he worked with the detonation systems the Druze had set up. He traced the wires back to the detonation control unit which blinked with a timer that ticked down with uncaring diligence.

"Crap, crap, *crap!*"

"Is it really that bad?" Ahmed asked.

"Bombs--even big ones--don't normally scare me," Guy said under his breath. "But this thing? This terrifies me."

Nibbs looked over the unit and agreed with Guy. "We can't deactivate this thing without setting it off."

Ahmed and Jamba traded nervous looks and glanced at the dwindling clock. "Crap."

Dirk and Corgan grabbed communicators and tried to contact the authorities and start an evacuation. All the lines were either busy or down. Corgan finally got through and waited on hold. He looked at the clock ashen-faced; there was no time for them to get anybody off-world. Even the *Crusader* wouldn't have enough time to get them out before it would detonate.

Ahmed teetered on the edge of the giant hole the Druze had opened up. It delved deep into the crust and bored deep into the meat of the planet like a gaping wound.

Dirk wandered through the polonium stores. Only a few pallets had been wired up by the connected dongles. Once they erupted, they would start a chain reaction capable of blasting high enough to take out even OSH3, the nearest transport hub orbiting above them.

He leaned close to the connection where the cables affixed to the radioactive fuel rods and gingerly touched the union. Guy winced and motioned for Dirk to step back. The bombs were delicate and an accidental disconnect would set the whole thing off.

Dirk stepped back like he was walking on eggshells.

"If we can't disable it... what other options do we have?"

Guy and Nibbs looked over the equipment already parked within the warehouse and then traded optimistic glances. Nibbs opened his portable computer and began hacking into Halabella's systems.

Pointing his friends to the nearby machinery Guy asked, "Do any of you guys know how to operate these pieces of equipment?"

30

"This had better work!" Matty's voice crackled in the monitor built into Mustache's helmet. "The Druze ship has just powered back up--so you're only going to get one shot at this before we're dead."

The Shivan vessel continued to hammer away at the *Rickshaw Crusader's* shields. Beyond the pirate craft, the Druze ship's stabilizing thrusters came on line and reoriented the ship to the standard plane with the others.

"Druze weapons are hot and they're closing!"

Mustache stood at the edge of the cargo hold with the doors open. Magnetic boots kept his feet clamped to the floor and a tether floated through the zero-g environment just in case the gravboots failed.

"We won't last two minutes once they add their fire to that Class D," Matty insisted.

"Hold onto your horses. I've got to get this just right... whether we live or not, this is the only chance I'm likely ever gonna get to try this."

Without power, the *Crusader* rolled slightly and slowly, like a fish turning belly up. Mustache stood in the opening, grazing the edge of nothingness with his spacesuit.

Nothing separated him from the sizzling, crackling sparks of energy as the enemies hammered away on their ship except for a meter of space and a shimmering shield less than an atom thick. At the top of his view, the pirate frigate came into view; it was close enough that he could see the stumpy pilot sitting at the controls. Mustache resisted the urge to flinch as its barrage of lethal energy crashed against the barely-holding shields like violent tides.

Seconds later he spotted the Druze ship. The *Rickshaw Crusader* continued the slow roll which changed his viewing angle, like the two enemy ships were solar and lunar bodies beginning to eclipse.

Mustache smiled and waved at the Shivan pilot. "Gotcha."

He yanked the Reliquary, Dekker's Prize weapon, from behind his back and aimed the ancient device at the enemies which had lined up perfectly. He wasn't sure exactly how to aim the meter-long engraved cylinder mounted to a pistol grip, but he felt certain he could make due by pointing it. Mustache pulled the trigger.

Sigils along the barrel illuminated and a boom like thunder rattled the walls of the cargo hold. The weapon kicked like a mule and a massive blast shot from the business end, firing an emerald beam of arcane energy nearly three meters thick and wreathed with white lightning. It rocked the Investigator back on his mag-locked heels and threatened to tear him from the deck and smash him against the walls of the *Crusader*.

Mustache's knees barely held as he stiffened to keep from tipping backwards under the thrust of the weapon. He howled in excitement when the deadly beam streaked through both of the enemy ships.

The blast ripped open a seam on the pirate vessel and dashed the Druze craft to fiery pieces. Enemy bulkheads systematically failed and slagged chunks of armor plating floated adrift, blasted free from their home; air and steam hissed into the void of the Shivan ship as it began to split apart under the stress of catastrophic failure.

As quickly as it started, it ended. The etched symbols quieted and the arcane shaft of light dissipated.

Flames danced within the breach of the Shivan ship. Nothing remained of the Druze spacecraft except for busted pieces of scrap. The pirates' vehicle flickered with electrical surges and then went silent as it dropped escape pods that rocketed to the surface.

With the hold secured Matty and Mustache returned to the cockpit to check the status of their friends. Mustache called up a message from Nibbs while Matty checked diagnostics and located the rest of the system errors.

"We'll get it back up and running after about twenty more minutes. Hopefully the others don't need an expeditious evac or anything in the meanwhile."

Mustache frowned. "That's too bad."

Matty shot him a look and his friend showed him a photo beamed to the ship's logging system. A timer rigged to a polonium bomb network read nineteen minutes and thirty-four seconds and a text blurb said: *get to safety! Crusader is in the blast radius.*

Springing to his feet Matty rushed to the reset locations and began opening access panels. "If we push it, we'll make it--get to work!"

Mustache shook his head. "This was sent about eight minutes ago."

Matty's face fell, crestfallen. His friend shrugged and rummaged through a storage cabinet until he found a jar of the home-brewed booze Guy often kept on hand. A handwritten label identified its contents as "engine parts cleaner."

Mustache took a big gulp, winced, and handed it to Matty. "No part going out sober."

The pilot nodded and took a big gulp of his own. He sighed with defeat. "Can't argue with that logic."

31

Julio watched from the darkened control room. The masked man left through a door at the far end of the facility and Prognon Austicon crawled into a freezing pod to hide.

"Now's our chance," Julio whispered. He activated one of the hibernating computers and pulled up the operations software, a relatively simple program. "Which cryo bay is he in?"

Joliver stood on his toes and tried to spot any identifying markers. The bank of tubes facing them, opposite of Austicon's hidden location, had a number painted on it. "I can't see it. It must be on the front of the pod."

Julio gulped a big chest full of air and then surrendered the seat at the monitor. He crept towards the door.

"What are you doing?" Joliver hissed.

"I'm gonna get that number." He ducked through the door and crawled onto the catwalk.

The other two watch Joliver sneak across the suspended gridwork panels like a wraith.

Tina slid into the seat and pressed a few keys with her free hand. In her other hand, she still held the communicator. "Wait a second," she put down the com and her fingers flew across the keyboard. "We can't do anything, anyways. There's a manual safety lock activated."

Joliver looked through the glass and watched his friend sneak further across the suspension walkway and crouch down to make himself smaller as he moved into a position visible to the enemy's pod. Julio flashed him a number with hand signs.

"Seventeen," Joliver said, spotting the safety release lever on the wall halfway between Julio and the control room door.

"I got it," Tina said, trying to activate the pod. The screen flashed and a warning popped up each time she tried to activate the freezing cycle. "No good. I'll try and override it." Her fingers tapped the keys with a steady cadence.

Joliver pointed to the safety switch on the wall. Julio scrunched up his face to show his confusion. He shook his head. Joliver pointed more insistently.

"It's not happening from here," Tina reported. She opened a few other dialog windows and tried to hack her way around. "It's not a software lock. The switch is a hardware component--until it's flipped we can't activate *any* of the pods."

Joliver pointed again, more insistently. He made a lever pulling action, trying to communicate via charades.

Julio still didn't understand and began creeping back towards his friends to try and understand Joliver's message. Julio stumbled as he tried to rise from his crouch; his foot kicked a suspension joint and rattled the cables with a loud, metallic shiver.

He looked back down to the pod just as Prognon Austicon looked up. Their eyes met and the killer sneered and raised his gun. Julio froze--his heart plummeted in his chest.

Suddenly, loud footsteps rang through the room as Joliver tramped across the catwalk, sprinting across the suspended walkway. He leapt forward and grabbed a lever on the wall and yanked the toggle into a downward position. "Now, Tina!" he yelled. "Do it now!"

Austicon hesitated and turned to try and find the teen whose voice shattered the silence. He twisted and craned his neck around to find the boy. Austicon snapped his weapon up to aim when the pod suddenly turned white with a frosty blast of cryogenic gas, freezing the villain solid, locking a look of surprise on his face.

Tina's com began squawking. "This is the Outpost 7 constabulary office. Sorry about the wait. What's the nature of your emergency?"

32

Dekker, Vesuvius, and Shin, stealthily worked through the hallway alongside Murtaugh and Rock as they all hurried through the doors of the cryostation. They cased the room with practiced skill, each covering the flanks of the others.

They stayed away from the center of the room where they would be most vulnerable as the team systematically checked the entire place. After clearing the edges they moved towards the middle.

Something caught Vesuvius's eye and she walked forward to scout it out. A few moments later she whistled. "Dekker, you'd better come get a look at this."

Dekker and the others followed the sound of her voice. They found her near one of the cryopods in the center aisle. Unlike the rest of the units, the glassine encasement nearest her had frosted white.

Wiping away the icy fog, Dekker peered into the tube. Prognon Austicon had been caught inside, flash frozen and perfectly preserved in cryogenic stasis.

Dekker, Vesuvius, and Shin could barely react to such a strange turn. The three had been chasing the criminal for much longer than any of the others.

"Well it looks like our jobs just got a lot easier," Murtaugh quipped.

Rock checked his timepiece and looked back towards the exit where Guy and the others worked to defuse the planet killing bomb. "I guess things will be easy for about another ten minutes or so. Then they're gonna get real chaotic for a few seconds and be over entirely... unless Guy and Nibbs figure something out."

Shin and Vesuvius watched Dekker as he hovered near the glass. He wordlessly worked his mouth, having a private conversation with the helpless prisoner. Dekker may have holstered his weapons, but his hands twitched as they hovered millimeters from their grips.

Vesuvius looked him over, wondering what he might do. Nobody would blame him for taking the shot. Everyone knew Dekker and Austicon had bad blood between them, even if none knew their true, dark history.

Dekker didn't break eye contact with the figure on the other side of the glass. Austicon's frozen, opened eyeballs seemed to look right through him. "Does anybody know if a cryoed body stays conscious?"

Nobody knew the answer for sure.

"I *have* heard that the brain remains awake for five to ten minutes before it fully shuts down," Murtaugh mentioned. "But I've never been iced, so I can't say for certain."

Dekker used his thumb to write backwards letters in the crystalline frost so that his prisoner could read them. *ALEEL*. He made his fingers shaped into a kind of gun and pointed it at Austicon's face; he squeezed his thumb like the gun fired.

"Here's hoping," Dekker muttered.

Vesuvius pulled her com to her mouth. "Guy, how's it coming? Are we all gonna die, or can I make dinner plans?"

33

Guy snatched his com. "Dinner will soooo be on you if I can pull this off," he quipped. "Just don't let Dekker pick the restaurant. He tried to take me to eat Ahzoolien decapod once."

He dropped the com right after the joke and directed traffic. "This is all gonna hinge on you," Guy said to Nibbs.

Nibbs didn't look up. He stared at his computer and tapped away.

Guy didn't press him further. They hadn't had enough time to do the math and had to feel it out.

He walked around the heavy laser drilling equipment and peeked over the edge of the hole that they'd expanded and checked that the rest of his crew down below was out of the way. "Are you guys ready?"

Corgan flashed him a thumbs up. They'd cleared as much rubble as possible from the rail system so that the underground transport could still make it through the sub level of the tunnel below them.

"Here it comes!" Guy yelled unnecessarily. The train's approach rumbled through the tunnel and shook free even more debris from the laser-cut aperture.

Nibbs pressed a key and the wheels of the tube car locked. It skidded to a halt leaving the middle trucks exposed to Guy's hole.

Guy took careful aim with the laser cutter and peeled away the roof of the monorail. Corgan, Jamba, and Dirk climbed out of the hole on the far side and grabbed the load lifters.

Ahmed spread industrial grade agglutinatives across the fuel cells and solidified the polonium rod clusters so that none of the delicate sensors could get jostled during transport. He finished spraying the last of the bubbling aerosol adhesive and covered over the timer and detonator computer with barely more than five minutes remaining. "Finished," he yelled.

Guy peeled off the last segment of steel and shoved the laser aside. "Ready!" he hurried out of the way as Corgan, Jamba, and Dirk lifted the pallets with the loaders. As a team, they pushed the massive bomb cluster towards the hole as fast as they could manage and flung the whole thing into the pit where it lodged into the train.

"Go, go, go!" Guy howled, yanking the laser back into place as the others moved the polonium stores away from the wall as fast as possible.

Nibbs hit the button, blasting the deadly rail convoy as far away as possible, before joining in to help with another load lifter. Guy cut through the floor and segments of walls to collapse the pocket.

Guy waved the boring beam in wide swaths, collapsing enormous chunks of stone and concrete into the rail tunnel. He nearly brought down the polonium warehouse over their heads as he mowed through the hardened surfaces like a knife through cheese.

He risked a glance at his watch while sweat beaded on his brow. He had to seal the hole as tightly as possible. The rest of his crew ran from the warehouse and Guy began backpedaling towards the entrance.

With only seconds left he cut more of the ceiling away to bury the polonium in the rubble and further buffer it from any of the blast leakage.

Right on time, the floor buckled and shifted as Austicon's bomb erupted in the distance, miles away from sublevels of Halabella's Outpost 7. The air filled with deafening, cracking sounds. Dust rained from overhead and the entire Ioan tectonic plate seemed to rumble with tenuous unease.

Structures around Guy and his team began to crumble and sections of ceiling broke free. Everyone scattered and leapt for cover, trying to evade the falling skies.

Finally, the vibrations settled.

Guy touched himself to check that he was still conscious and alive. He jumped into the air, pumping his fists, howling with victory.

Leaving the collapsed pile of rubble with a broad grin on his face, he shouted to find his comrades. "Someone owes me dinner!" Guy strode confidently through the central section and then stopped in his tracks. His grin faltered and drooped.

The Dozen's medic, Ahmed, worked feverishly on Dirk who'd been caught beneath a pile of rubble. Jamba, Corgan, and Nibbs used a hunk of metal to lever the collapsed masonry off of their friend. Guy ran forward to help Ahmed drag Dirk to safety.

Ahmed scowled as he looked over their friend. "It doesn't look good," he mumbled and struggled with his belt to make a tourniquet.

Groggy from the pain, Dirk chuckled. "Hey, doc. Keep yer pants on til you've bought me a drink, at least."

Ahmed forced a plastic smile for his patient's sake. "He'll be fine," he said, but he caught the eyes of his fellow Investigators and shook his head to admit that he'd lied.

34

Dekker and the others huddled close, near the petrified body of Prognon Austicon. Vesuvius stood closer to him than the others and her thigh touched his, transmitting intense heat and distracting him.

"We checked all the pods and still don't know where the creepy mask guy went," Rock noted.

Dekker nodded. "We can cross that bridge when we come to it. For now, let's get Austicon into custody so we can finally bring him to justice."

Shin put a hand on his friend's shoulder. "MEA custody and justice, or yours?"

Dekker bit his lip and entertained notions of killing the enemy who had done such unspeakable evil to him over the years. "Let's just get him onto the *Crusader* for now. I don't trust the bureaucracy of the MEA constables—even if they did happen to get the trial right, they'll probably screw it up before they ever get that far."

His teammates agreed with his logic—though none would complain about missing their cut of the obscene bounty if they put a bullet through Austicon's brainpan. The reward for dead delivery would be significantly less, but the galaxy might be better off for it.

Before anyone could disconnect the stasis pod and prep it for transport the doors flew open. The Investigators had guns and swords drawn and ready in a flash.

"Lower your weapons," commanded a constable holding a retractable baton. Nearly a dozen other men followed on his heels, similarly armed. Shielding the brave officers were three teenagers who practically pulled the men along.

"I said lower them," he called over the heads of the strong-willed kids.

Dekker and Vesuvius traded glances. If they didn't decide to voluntarily disarm these men could not force them.

Vesuvius looked at the three youth and her face softened. She sheathed her blade and raised an eyebrow at their leader. It was time for Dekker to decide.

He dropped his pistols into their thigh holsters and sighed. The constables rushed forwards and checked over the cryopod.

"It's him, see," the shorter of the two boys exclaimed. "We caught Prognon Austicon. Will we get the reward?"

"Of course we'll get the reward," the other teenager interjected, looking to the lead officer for some kind of verification. The constable nodded vigorously, likely plotting to somehow interject his own name into the capture narrative.

Dekker wordlessly worked his mouth when his com crackled. Guy's voice broke radio silence. "Dirk's not doing well--the blast kinda dropped a building on him. How far away are you guys? If we don't get him to a hospital right away he's probably gonna lose his arm."

He fingered the transmit button. "We caught Austicon."

"What? That's awesome; we'll never have money problems again!"

"We aren't gonna get paid for it," Dekker responded.

A nosey peacekeeper looked Dekker up and down with a scrutinizing stare. His gaze lingered on the pistols at the Investigator's sides and he narrowed his eyes to slits. Projectile weapons were outlawed in MEA territories and only energy-based weapons could be permitted by those lucky enough to acquire even that.

"Ah crap," Guy hissed. "Don't tell me those idiots in the MEA have him already! They couldn't keep track of their own..."

Dekker switched it off before Guy dug too deep of a hole.

The officer used his weapon to point at Dekker's guns. "Aren't those things illegal?"

Dekker bit his lip, searching for some kind of excuse. The chief officer's com erupted with an emergency alert.

"Available units please respond. We have a murder in the government center. Jai Janus and Jace Strengen have both been murdered."

The officer looked at Dekker and his face fell. He hesitated only a moment and then pointed to half of his men. "You guys watch these kids and get that criminal's stasis pod locked in storage--with the highest security possible!" he ordered.

He turned to leave and engage in what would undoubtedly become a political nightmare. Firing over his shoulder he warned Dekker, "Get out of my city. I'm gonna have enough paperwork the way it is."

Dekker nodded. His pager chirped and reported that Zarbeth waited for them on OSH3. He and his crew hung their heads and exited the cryo facility empty-handed.

Leviathan tossed the contents of President Janus's desk onto the ground. He rummaged through the trash and file cabinets of the company president.

Austicon's favorite creature knew the Red Tree's prize had been somewhere in Janus's office. He'd seen it through his master's eyes and borrowed the memory.

Leviathan finished trashing the office. Finally certain that the arbolean seed wasn't present, he realized that there might be surveillance somewhere outside Janus's office that could help him determine where the item had disappeared to.

His com chirped and he wiped Jai Janus's blood from his hands before opening the channel.

The Shivan pirates alerted him that they'd made groundfall and would commandeer a transport. They would arrive at a shipping dock shortly.

Leviathan needed to catch that ride.

He took one more look around and then ducked through the door.

There would always be another opportunity to locate the item so fervently desired by the old women.

Leviathan paused in the shadows as he crept through the back hallways of Outpost 7. A guard stationed at a security outpost listened to a news feed. The broadcast reported the suspected presence of Prognon Austicon.

If the assassin still had lips he would've frowned. The Watchman had stopped another one of his master's plans.

He cocked his head and got to work. All mistakes could be corrected in due time. Leviathan pulled a knife from his boot. Only a single guard stood between Leviathan and his freedom. He could eventually correct the mistake and reclaim his master.

The guard looked up at a ship that suddenly docked without clearance and Leviathan crept up behind him.

35

Zarbeth walked towards the exit ramp as the *Rickshaw Crusader* descended towards the lawn of the Pheema's compound. He glanced back to look at the injured Investigator who had his right side bandaged with his arm tightly immobilized.

Guy waved excitedly to the Krenzin.

He turned his back on the mercenaries and exited the ship. It barely touched down before climbing skyward again on its VTOL thrusters.

Zarbeth shuddered, happy to be away from Guy, and headed into the building where his nose detected a familiar smells of trace ammonia and dander. He walked directly for the Pheema's office.

The Pheema stood when his servant entered. "Do you have it?"

Zarbeth locked the door behind him and then rummaged through his robes. Finally, he withdrew the pod which contained the seedling. "The child of New Eden, Holy One," Zarbeth reported. His fingers traced the strange markings etched into the glass.

"Excellent," the Pheema hissed as he drew a molecular disrupter. "We must make sure that no one ever suspects the Right Hand of the theft."

"I understand," Zarbeth kneeled and bowed.

The Pheema raised an eyebrow and pursed his whiskers. Zarbeth seemed a true believer. Unquestionably loyal minions were worth their weight in gold, and then some.

"Your silence is assured?"

Zarbeth bobbed his head. "You have it, my lord."

The Pheema hid the disrupter back within his robes. "Excellent. Tell me everything."

36

Dekker shuffled back and forth on his heels, trying not to pace. Shin and Vesuvius leaned against the wall of the waiting room and watched the news feeds.

The redhead's gaze shifted between the talking heads and Dekker. More than happy to push an agenda heralding increased peace in the galaxy, footage of Austicon's retrieval played on an endless loop.

Finally, a doctor met them in the waiting room. Dr. McBain was human, but the lapel pin affixed to his breast identified him as a member of the Krenzin led Peace For All Races group; it was little more than the nonKrenzin arm of the felinoid race's religion. Dekker rolled his eyes when he spotted the PFAR logo.

"I'm afraid your friend is in bad shape," Dr. McBain lamented. "We *did* have to take his arm, and he's not out of the woods yet, though I do expect that he will make a recovery... such as it may be for people in your line of work." His eyes tried to hide their disdain for the mercenaries—anything touched by Krenzin ideology opposed violence by any means or from any source.

Dekker nodded and the doctor continued.

"Have you all ever considered another line of employment? You could each end up suffering a similar fate, you know... or worse."

Dekker gave the doctor a stink-eyed look and then left the hospital. His friends followed him.

"As if we each haven't each counted the cost before every mission," he seethed.

Vesuvius put a hand on his chest to calm him down.

They took a walk back home on the streets of Reef City, taking the long way around.

"Maybe we can grab a bite to eat?" Shin suggested. "It is my last night before I must return to Master Muramasa."

Dekker shrugged, still irked by the casualties—even though Austicon was finally out of the picture. "I don't really feel like going out," Dekker admitted.

"Perfect," Vesuvius interjected. "We'll order in... besides, if we don't feed Guy he's going to whine about saving an entire planet and not even getting a free lunch out of it."

Dekker folded his arms, knowing she was right. He nodded and Vesuvius hung back a few paces as she called for a delivery.

"What should I tell Master Muramasa?" Shin asked his friend.

Dekker raised an eyebrow. "About what?"

Shin looked back towards his cousin.

"Oh. Yeah."

Chuckling, Shin shook his head. "You see so much at times--and yet you're so blind to some things. The world was meant to be a certain way, Dekker Knight... Prognon Austicon is never meant to be a part of it--and you and Vesuvius were meant to be together. My father has always believed this."

Dekker offered his friend a half-grin. "I guess I can be pretty inept at times... but maybe now with Austicon behind me."

"Hopefully," agreed Shin, "you can finally stop being so blind and finally come back into the light?"

Vesuvius caught up with them. "I got Guy something extra special. What are we talking about?"

"Just how stupid your business partner can sometimes be," Shin teased.

"Yeah." Vesuvius's eyes twinkled. "He can be pretty thick."

The delivery vehicle pulled up about the same time as the trio of friends walked into their base of operations. Dekker paid the driver with the company account and ushered the caterer inside; the Dozen ordered there often and each of the boxes was marked with a name.

He and the delivery driver were greeted with cheers as they entered carrying stacks of food sealed in biodegradable cartons. Shin pulled a pair of chopsticks from the cache of napkins, salt, and sundries.

"Hey!" Guy yelled "Why does my plate have tentacles on it? Eww! They just moved."

Dekker took a mental snapshot and watched as his crew enjoyed one of those rare family moments. Each stood and shared his or her favorite memory of Trigger and Dirk. Guy crossed out the tentacle boxed name and swapped plates with Mustache.

Austicon was gone and Dekker had truly turned a page in his life. The new chapter had come at great cost, but it had finally arrived.

After watching a few moments longer, finally, Dekker stepped back and retreated, retiring to his chambers.

He climbed the stairs near the barracks section of their HQ and found Vesuvius loitering by his door. Dekker walked towards her.

Putting a hand around her waist he pulled her close. Dekker spun her and traded places so he was closer to his door and then released her.

"We've been dancing around this for, like, two years now," she said. "When are we going to do something *truly* risky, you and me?"

He sighed. "There are some things about me," Dekker stated, "Things that I'm not open to sharing right away. I... I might need some time, Vivian."

Vesuvius smiled and leaned in for a kiss. She wrapped her arm around his neck and head and entwined her fingers in his hair. He kissed her back and squeezed her close to himself.

She exhaled heavily, almost with a moan, and bit the lobe of his lip.

"I do want to share these things with you."

Kissing his neck, she confessed between gasps of air, "You don't know how long I've been waiting for you to finally take a hint."

Dekker kissed her again. "I want to tell you my first secret--one of the things that define me on such a deep level that I'm afraid to let even those truly close to me know." He pressed his lips to her neck. "I'd love to tell you over breakfast?"

"I'd love to get breakfast with you," a lascivious glimmer burned in her eyes. "But I'd rather that you told me right now."

He reached behind his back and pressed his thumb to the door scanner and unlocked his apartment. "The first thing about me that you should know..." he shoved her two steps backwards and stepped into his dormer before closing and locking the door. "I'm very old-fashioned."

Vesuvius pounded on his door with a closed fist. "Hey! Hey--let me in. Dekker, this isn't funny."

"Sorry," the door muffled his voice. "Old-fashioned."

She pounded on the door some more.

"I'll see you in the morning for breakfast? I cook some amazing eggs," Dekker promised.

"Hey!" Vesuvius hammered on the door another couple seconds before sheepishly spotting Guy who watched the entire ordeal. She clenched her fists and began walking to her own residence.

Guy grinned.

Vesuvius glowered at him. "Did *you* know about this?"

"What? That Dekker is kind of an old-fashioned prude? *Everyone* knows that. He's, like, my grandmother's spirit animal."

Vesuvius shoved him into the wall before storming off. She screamed, "I'll see you in the morning for breakfast!" Vesuvius flung her door opened and howled, not caring who heard anymore. "You're frittatas had better be freaking amazing!"

On the deck below, Shin grinned and paid the ante to take another card. He smiled at some of his other new friends. Everyone heard the incident... and none would ever dare speak about it in front of their fiery teammate.

He raised Jamba by two chips. Master Muramasa would be pleased to hear Dekker and Vesuvius were off to such a passionate start.

DEKKER'S DOZEN:
SPAWN
OF
GANYMEDE
CHRISTOPHER D.
SCHMITZ

Spawn of Ganymede

Dekker's Dozen #000.66 A&B
0065 P.I.S.W....

1

The ground bucked and heaved momentarily, making Kheefal hold his breath. He traded nervous looks with the other humans clustered nearby under the dome that maintained the environment on the Io moon. All eyes turned to the dome and searched for sings of integrity failure. After a few terse seconds the quake subsided and it seemed the community was in the clear. Warning sirens still blared, but the tension bled away like vapor in a leaky airlock.

Kheefal quickened his pace, hoping the secondary tremors would deflect enough attention to cover his tracks. Corporate espionage and thievery carried significant risks, and he'd learned the value of the precious moments following any solid diversion.

Inside the government center, he pulled out tools to jimmy the lock but found the handle and jam were already busted. Cautiously, Kheefal pushed the door ajar and stepped inside.

Blood drenched everything in the businessman's office.

Frantically, Kheefal rummaged through the contents of Jai Janus's office. Trade secrets and confidential documents lay strewn about. Kheefal ignored them… ignored the mangled body laid out across the floor in twisted repose.

Kheefal, an Investigator in his own right, shuddered to think what could have ripped the throat from such a well-known figure. The glorified mercenary was no stranger to violence, but it seemed a terrible way to go.

A warning siren in the distance alerted him that he only had seconds left to make a safe exit before the local constables arrived.

Scowling, Kheefal knew the thing he'd been hired to retrieve had already been stolen; his mission was a nonstarter. He kicked over a file cabinet in disgust and then pulled a tiny collection of hair samples from his pouch and sprinkled them around the room as he made an exit, masking his presence with tiny filaments from an entirely different species. The Arduel race was known for shedding hair when stressed, making them a perfect scapegoat.

Kheefal didn't expect that the security officers stationed on Io were thorough enough to find anything linking him to Janus's murder, but Jai's brother Miko was Chief Magnate of the entire Mother Earth Aggregate. Surely, the MEA would send a qualified team to investigate and Kheefal didn't take chances. He hadn't gotten this far ahead in life by acting reckless.

He slipped from the murder scene and turned right. Down a short hall he found a security kiosk that had been left unmanned. *Where did all the local troops go,* he wondered? He hadn't seen a single one since shortly after arriving in the loading dock with his forged paperwork.

Kheefal shrugged and swiped the hard copy of the surveillance data from Janus's office. He tapped in a few commands and confirmed the warning message. Seconds later, the drives erased themselves, scrubbing all evidence of his presence. He could watch the remaining recorded video once he was safely away and on his ship. Surely the drives would tell him who murdered Jai Janus and stole the mining executive's paperweight.

Slipping the data drive into a pocket, Kheefal snuck away. He crossed the threshold and into the streets of Outpost 7. People meandered about their business and picked up after the quake. A strange concoction of upper class, blue collars, and slum dwellers mingled on the streets. It looked like every other backwater planet he'd been to.

Kheefal snorted and pressed a finger to his nose, shooting a grey lump of slime from his sinus that had formed from the fine dust of the mining town. He kept his eyes ahead and descended a stairwell that lead to the commercial and industrial tunnels.

After a quick scan of his falsified credentials, he accessed the industrial tubes and hurried towards the loading dock where he'd left his ship. Hairs on the back of his neck and arms bristled as he stalked closer. Something wasn't right; maybe the sounds were wrong or maybe his old grandma was right about latent precog abilities, but his gut discerned a problem.

Kheefal pulled his concealed blaster from where he'd wrapped it against his chest. He crept along the curving walls of the subterranean tunnel and tightened his knuckles on the grip.

A pool of blood widened around the security officer's limp forearm. He couldn't see much else.

Kheefal led with his firearm and hurled himself around the edge of the security checkpoint. Light flashed behind his eyes and a bone cracking roundhouse leveled him, sending his gun skittering lost into the distance and bowling him over.

Looking up from the concrete, punch-drunk, Kheefal tried to get his bearings. A lone assassin took on half a dozen strong dockworkers dressed in Halabella browns. He whirled and struck like a ballet dancer performing choreographed moves.

Wearing all black, the skinny humanoid only paused momentarily when the radio lying next to the dead security officer at Kheefal's right squawked a report. MEA constables had taken the galaxy's most wanted criminal, Prognon Austicon, into custody.

The toughs managed to land a few blows during the report, and then the creature in the black, faceless mask counter attacked.

Several more workers poured from the loading zone and rushed the invader. *He's only one man—surely they can take him?*

Suddenly, a small crew of stumpy Shivans plowed through the rows of crates and stacked cargo with blasters blazing. Tattoos and badly stitched insignias indicated allegiances to various pirate guilds.

The invaders cut down the dock workers, most of whom had no weapons. Taking one look at the assassin, their body language clearly communicated a camaraderie. Sneering, the lead Shivan with a high widows peak ordered his men into the waiting freight hauler and took off before their comrade could get aboard. "One less share for the Lockbox!" he growled as the loading ramp closed.

Kheefal sprang to his feet to attack alongside the remaining three workers.

The thing sidestepped him, grabbed the nearest worker, and broke his neck. Howling, the other two turned to flee. It jabbed one with a nerve strike, crumpling him limp and then snatched the disabled man's pocket knife.

With scary precision, he flung the knife and buried it in the base of the fleeing man's head where vertebrae met skull. Then, he nonchalantly collapsed the windpipe of the crippled knife-owner as Kheefal finally righted himself and spat blood from his split lip.

Kheefal assumed a defensive stance. Adrenaline coursed through his veins. He didn't know if he could beat this thing… whatever it was… but he felt quite sure it was not going to let him leave without a fight.

The masked creature engaged him, throwing punches that seemed to arrive split seconds before Kheefal could get his guard up. Punches and kicks seemed to come in the exact angle and styles that he was unprepared for. None were incredibly fast—but each found their mark and connected with kinetic precision.

It's like this thing knows what I'm doing before I do!

His enemy seemed to chortle with glee at the very thought. Sending him sprawling backwards with a flurry of punches and a warning kick that cut through the air, the creature stood a few paces away as if Kheefal's presence did little to threaten him.

The Investigator suddenly winced as if the light hurt his brain and he stutter-stepped groggily. A momentary fit smashed his grey matter, and he half-closed his eyes against the sudden photosensitivity. A full-blown migraine seemed to seize him at the most inopportune time.

As suddenly as it seemed to have come on, it passed and Kheefal relaxed. The black intruder turned and fled, running towards Kheefal's ship.

"Hey," he grunted. His enemy didn't respond. "Hey!"

The humanoid sprinted towards his prize.

"Hey! That's my ship!" Kheefal bellowed, starting after him. Before he could close the gap, the thing punched in an access code and darted up the landing ramp.

Dumbfounded at how the enemy knew his access code, Kheefal stood in the center of the loading bay, surrounded by bodies, and watched the other creature steal his ship. He dug a hand into his pocket as his Class A craft left without him and wrapped his fingers around the data drive he'd swiped from the murder scene.

At least I've still got this, he comforted himself.

2

"I'm tellin ya, I'm gettin too old for this nonsense," Sam, who everybody called Mustache, said. His legs poked out from beneath the *Rickshaw Crusader*. Grease and smears of carbon scoring painted his jumpsuit. He spat a bunch of crumbling dust and metal shavings from his lips as detritus rained down from above and lodged in his bristled cookie duster. "Gaah," he complained as he shook out his famous whiskers.

Guy, Rock, and Matty nearly dropped the piece of armor plating as Mustache tried to clear his face. Their older peer shot his hands back up and stabilized the plate as Matty turned tools and tightened the plating back against the bulkhead.

"Nonsense," Rock mumbled back. "You been here since the beginning. You can't be thinking retirement. That's like splitting up the family."

A few moments passed in silence as the others nodded.

Guy broke the quiet. "If we're a family, can I be the Daddy?" he laughed.

The rest broke into chuckles.

"More like the redheaded step-child," Mustache quipped.

"Hey. Don't you know that Redheads are almost extinct," Guy defended. "Of course you know. You were still around when recessive genes were invented, Grandpa."

"Don't you make me get my belt," Mustache laughed.

"It's a weird family," Guy laughed as they all pushed out from underneath the heavily modified B Class space transport.

"Yeah... well..." Mustache glanced sidelong at the *Crusader*. The blast marks and beaten plating made it look more like it should be scrapped than flown. "If we don't get that ship fixed soon we'll *all* be retiring. Quickly and violently."

Dekker walked over to his crew. "What are we talking about?"

"Nothing, Daddy," Guy joked.

Dekker raised an eyebrow, shook his head and asked the same question of the more mature members of his team.

"I don't think it's going to hold together much longer without some repairs," Matty said.

Dekker looked to Mustache. Sam had been with him a long time and brought experience to the table that couldn't be taught in a class.

"She needs an overhaul," Mustache nodded.

Dekker sighed. "I was afraid of that. It's not in the budget..."

“Well, it better get there,” Mustache said as he raked out his salt and pepper dirt squirrel. “It ain’t gonna last much longer the way she sits.”

Dekker exhaled through his nose and bobbed his head. “I’ll make an appointment at Darkside Station.”

3

Quade plunged through the thick foliage and spat the bitter taste of leaves and bark from his mouth as branches whipped him in the face. Fear and endorphins let him shrug off the pain as he plowed through both trees and nettles.

His heart pounded in his ears—nearly louder than the growls of the creature behind him. It snarled as it crashed through the bracken thicket.

Quade pushed himself further into the night.

Why? Why did I ever sign up to move to this god-forsaken planet? He berated himself silently, questioning his wasted life which was filled with cursed decisions, even his momentary self-reflection: distracted, Quade's foot caught a root, and he tumbled to ground.

The moist dirt felt slick and smelled like moldering peat. He scrambled through a copse of fungal plants and slimy undergrowth that had taken over swaths of land in recent months. He lifted his head from the gnarled plumage where he'd landed face-first; even in the dark he could see a spore cloud hanging thick in the surrounding air.

His gut sank. Whatever this plant was, it had been making the people in his community sick. Quade knew he'd was infected once before and somehow survived, but his hope for some kind of immunity wasn't important at the moment. Another predatory roar rumbled behind him and Quade hoped that he'd survive the spores again—he'd already proved himself symptom free for over two weeks since his last brush with the toxic flora.

Quade scrambled to his feet and his eyes caught sight of a light up ahead. Some kind of beacon shone vertically from the ground. He sprinted towards it, hoping that it promised some kind of protection.

As he grew nearer, the light took shape. It wasn't a beacon, but an opening in the ground, some kind of hidden hatch. Quade had heard rumors that many buried tunnels existed from the first failed attempt to colonize the planet Galilee many years ago. He dashed towards it, barely able to breathe in the thick, dank air.

The beast that hunted him suddenly crashed into the trail right behind him. Quade yelped a string of profanities and doubled down, coaxing every bit of speed from his legs that he could muster.

A man's figure took shape in the light ahead. "Quickly! This way," he shouted. "Do not let the grrz get you!"

With the creature right on his heels, Quade leapt for the hole just as his savior slammed the hatch shut behind him.

Quade laid for several minutes sucking in great, ragged gasps of air. Finally, he looked up at the man. "Th-thank you," he said.

The man wore a lab coat and a sparse five o'clock shadow. "Well, that might be a bit premature," he said with a thin-lipped smile.

Quade cocked his head and his rescuer pulled an electroshock taser from his waistband.

With a cold expression, the stranger blasted Quade with enough electricity to knock him unconscious.

4

Kheefal sat in the back of his dingy storage locker and rummaged through the package he'd received. He unwrapped a shiny, fabricated medallion. Normally, he conducted most of his business face to face or through TransNet communications. Still, he needed a place to conduct business operations and normally needed storage for items such as his ship.

With a scowl, Kheefal glared at the empty bay next door where he normally berthed his Class A spacecraft. He'd been without transportation now for several months, but he finally had a stroke of good luck. An old contact of his with a background in information trades had been able to secure the decryption codes for the security feeds he'd swiped a few months ago when he'd visited Io.

After placing the engineered token, a tiny metal decrypting disk, into the key slot of his data pad, Kheefal hit the play button and the feed unlocked. He impatiently scrolled ahead towards the end and watched himself searching for his target.

Kheefal backed the video stream up. The black, masked figure who'd murdered a score of men and women at the Io hangar trashed the room. Janus and Strengen lay dead on the floor with pools of blood growing around them.

The investigator stretched his neck and cracked his joints while he stared at the mysterious enemy. Kheefal had never lost a fight in his life. He didn't count this one as a loss since the fight never ended, but whatever this creature was, Kheefal felt certain that it would have killed him if not for its hasty retreat.

He bit his lip and rewound the data further yet. In a comically morbid scene, Jace Strengen and Jai Janus leapt back to their feet, sucking blood back into their wounds, and returned to their seats as the masked assassin walked backwards out of the room and closed the door.

Minutes passed as Janus and Strengen discussed things that had seemed so important at the time... before they knew that these would be their final words. Kheefal jumped backwards some more.

There had been another figure in the room. A Krenzin sat at the desk with them and the item, a glassine cylinder containing an exotic seed remained on Janus's desk as a paperweight.

Kheefal let the video play as his mind began to wander momentarily. He paused it and did a double take. The seed was gone.

He rewound the feed again, anxiously until the seed reappeared. *The Krenzin*, he mentally spat and advanced the video file.

The Krenzin leaned to his side, and the seed sat on the desk. He shifted with the camera to his back and it disappeared.

Kheefal backed it up frame by frame until he came to the right spot. Forwards: it disappeared. Backwards: it remained.

He advanced until he had a good shot of the felinoid creature's face and activated recognition software. It scanned his target's features and then kicked out a report.

"Zarbeth?" he read the ident file aloud. "Gotcha."

5

Doc Johnson, the madcap scrapper who owned and operated Darkside Station on Earth's Moon, offered Dekker an old glass jar filled with clear fluid.

Dekker put up his hands. "No, thank you. I'm not that stupid."

"I am," Guy piped up. He intercepted the drink and took a reluctant gulp, nearly going cross-eyed from its effects. He gasped and wheezed in its aftermath and drew a chorus of laughter from the Investigators and other scrappers in Doc's employ.

"There, now. Was that so hard?" he asked. "Even *Guy* took a slug of it."

Dekker shrugged and slapped Guy on the shoulder. "He's my emotional support animal. It's his duty to get in the way of any potential decisions like that one." Dekker tapped himself on the scalp. "Gotta keep a clear head and whatnot."

Doc arched an eyebrow and rested his hands on his hips. "Heh. Alrighty, lets see how yer buddy handles my 'deinhibitor juice.' Guy, tell me about all of Dekker's bad decisions, lately." He flashed Dekker a mischievous glare.

Guy didn't notice as Dekker tried to flash him a warning look. Guy's cheeks had already flushed; an intense warmth spread across his face and neck. His eyelids seemed to open at different speeds with brows arching to different heights as if controlled by feuding marionette strings.

He slurred his speech. "Well, I got some stories for ya," Guy's voice warbled.

Dekker took the jar away as Guy reached for another drink. He sniffed it and wrinkled his nose. "This smells like it could kill a grubark."

Doc winked. "I got a whole pack of dead grubarks out back in fact."

"Dead?" Guy's face blanched. He whispered wide-eyed, "Am I gonna die?"

The old scrapper nodded his head gravely. "I'm afraid so. It's the end of the line for you, my friend." He put a hand over his heart.

Shock and drunken heartbreak riddled Guy's face.

Fryberger, Doc's partner, entered carrying a box of parts. He scowled disapprovingly at the inebriated Investigator. "Don't go tormenting that poor boy with the Leerium." He shook his head. "Doc's just messing with you, Guy.

You'll be fine in about twenty minutes. It's a hard drunk, but it wears off quickly."

Doc and the others belly-laughed at Guy's near-death-experience. A few seconds into the laughter, Guy also laughed. Nervously. As if he had no idea what was so funny.

The old salvage worker nudged Dekker playfully. "Alright, Guy. This stuff numbs a person's inhibitions so hard that it's practically a truth serum."

"An unreliable one," Fryberger called over his shoulder.

"What's Dekker's biggest, darkest secret?"

Dekker crossed his arms and grinned. "As if you think I'm stupid enough to let any of these idiots know my darkest inner-workings."

Guy cut him off and pointed a finger. "He's too scared of commitment to seal the deal with Vesuvius. She's been chasin him *hard*, and for years, and he's barely done more'n held the poor girl's hand."

A pang of nervous emotion rippled through Dekker. He shot Guy an alarmed look.

The drunk cracked up with laughter at how spot on he'd landed.

“’At’s why she’s down at BOA doin research for th’next job.” He hiccuped. “She’s mad bout Dekker shutting her down again. He said somethin bout moving too fast.” Guy slumped, clearly losing the battle against the fuzziness in his brain.

Doc shot Dekker a confused look. “That’s funny,” he chuffed. “I never figured you for the sort who played it this safe. Always thought you were more of a risk taker.”

“Remind me why I come here again?” Dekker stiffened his jaw. Suffering minor indignations for the owners’ amusement had always been part of the price built into Doc Johnson’s work.

Doc merely shrugged. Dekker and him went way back, far enough that the inventor-turned scrap-yard manager earned the right to rib him a little.

“Well,” Doc asked Guy, “has he done *anything* right lately?”

Guy nodded. “Got us a decent job with us on the rebound from that missed payday…”

“Ah. I heard about that one… some kind of mix-up on Io.”

Nodding with a goofy, lopsided smile, Guy said, “Yeah. Austicon woulda been a big paycheck… I hear those kids are gonna make a mint. But the *Crusader* took a hella-ova… hullihfa… haliv… it took a beating. Shivan pirates and the MEA *both* tried to smash her. Ya know. You do quality work. You should start a business…" He sniffed at the air like a man between sleep and wakefulness.

Dekker took over before Guy could ramble aimlessly. "Your latest shield tweaks performed as well as promised," he said. "It didn't stop the EMP, but you never promised it would… it *did*, however, keep the boat alive despite the pirates and the Druze hammering away on her when she was dead in the water."

Doc nodded with furrowed brows, taking the info as both compliment and request. "I imagine you'll need some armor replaced and a bunch of other upgrades, plus a full diagnostic to make sure nothing's still burned out?"

Dekker nodded and handed him a list. "Anything more than this that you can think of?"

Doc pursed his lips as he ran down the items. "Gonna take some time. This is a lot of work."

Shrugging, Dekker said, "Yeah, but who else is going to let you monkey with their ship. You've got something of a reputation for coloring outside the lines. Matty here is the only pilot who seems capable of piloting anything you've re-engineered."

"That's because I actually read the manuals," Matty hollered from the back.

"He, he," Doc chuckled. "You might be the only one."

"How long?" Dekker asked."

Doc shrugged. "Thirty days?"

Dekker frowned and bobbed his head to Guy, "That job he mentioned is in ten. We have a job taking us to Galilee, over in the Trappist system. Medical mission for the expansion world."

"Aye. I know the one." Doc reassessed the list and stroked his chin. "I can get it done in ten if you do me a favor while you're there."

Dekker cocked an eyebrow.

"I got a cousin there, Benjamin. Lives and works in Newhope, same kinda business as me. He's been bugging me for parts and supplies. Sounds like things are tight for him over there. If'n you can bring him a few crates of stuff he needs for his shop, I'll make sure the *Rickshaw Crusader* is ready for you in ten days."

The investigator shot a hand out to shake on it. "Done. Any family of yours is a friend of ours," he pledged.

Doc shook on it and tossed the list to one of his workers who hurried out the door. "Lemme loan you an old lunar bus to get you and your guys back to Reef City. She ain't pretty, but she'll get you dirt-side until I can get your boat ready for ya."

Dekker and his crew thanked Doc and turned to head towards the door. Guy gasped in a lung full of air, suddenly clear, or mostly so, just as Fryberger had promised. He blinked twice and realized his party was about to leave without him.

Doc waved them out as Guy staggered to his feet, trying to catch up. He slowed his gait momentarily and grabbed the jar of Leerium on his way out the door, grinning as he went.

6

Kheefal opened a message left for him by authorities on the TransNet system. He raised an eyebrow and opened the communication. He may have been a licensed Investigator, but he tried his best to avoid constabulary services. His kind spent too much time dancing around the fringes of the law to make contact a habit.

Pursing his lips, Kheefal's spirits lifted. His stolen spacecraft had finally been located. The thief had abandoned it somewhere near the Mars transit hub where MEA forces confiscated it as a derelict; they'd traced the transponder before putting it into impound. He could recover it by the evening so long as he had cash for the reclamation fees.

Kheefal grinned as a plan formed in his mind. Finally, the last piece had fallen into place for him.

He kissed his fingers and pressed them to his heart, thanking whatever gods might exist for deciding to pull his number on a last-minute blessing. The MEA might have outlawed religion years ago, and Kheefal didn't particularly believe in any of it anyhow, but he was grateful that karma hadn't reared its ugly head. His ledger dripped with red ink, and he didn't see that changing anytime soon.

Kheefal felt happy enough that he swiped away the next message and declined an assassination job on the BlackWeb. He hoped that whoever controlled karma would believe it was in response to his fortune.

If a quick, meaningless prayer could appease a god or gods, he'd offer it, but in reality, only money talked. His Jagaracorps contact promised a far heavier payday than simple murder did… and Jagaracorps had deep pockets.

7

Vesuvius's curly, red locks fell across Dekker's face in tangles. They stuck like velcro to the ever-present stubble of his face as she leaned against him in the rec area of their groups base. She sipped a hot cup of tea as she leaned into his arm which lay across the top of the couch.

The media stream played despite the muted audio. An advertisement broadcasted opportunities for hard-working folks to join human expansion efforts on new worlds, boasting personal and economic freedom for anyone willing to sign on.

"I'm just saying that I don't ever want children. You've known that for a long time," she played her decision off nonchalantly, as if it had not come as a result of her personal orphan-baggage.

She looked away and sipped her drink, trying to deflect from the topic. The cloud that settled over Dekker's face indicated he'd have trouble giving the subject up. Her voice grew quiet. "We've known each other a long time, Dekker. You know why… or some of it at least… it's not likely I'll change my mind."

Dekker's jaw tightened. "I have my own stuff, too, you know." He sighed. "Family is the most important thing to me."

"Well maybe if you'd let me in," she said with a barbed tongue. "I bet whatever it is—whatever your life was before we met all those years ago at Muramasa's—I would understand."

Dekker stiffened his neck and looked away.

Guy entered the room and stood straight. He locked eyes with his two friends who had tried their best to keep their relationship amongst the rest of their companions professional.

Dekker slid slightly to his left and created some space between him and Vesuvius, keeping up the charade.

Vesuvius shot a sidelong look to her left and glared daggers at him. The room temperature seemed to plummet. "What the heck, man! Family this and family that—the Dozen are our family and you can't even pretend we're a real thing whenever any of them are around. And this… this is *just Guy!*"

Guy touched his chest with a worried look. Fearful for his life at being drawn into a lovers' quarrel, he slowly walked backwards out of the room.

Vesuvius continued ranting. "Maybe if you were more concerned with the here and now instead of trying to measure out the details, you'd have invited me into your cabin by now. Then we'd be working on the actual *mechanics* of your heart's desire instead of whatever the heck this is."

She whirled to her feet and spat over her shoulder as she left, "Family! You can't get a better one than what we have already, and *I'm* fine with that. If you and I are going to really happen, you're going to have to accept that."

A few moments of silence passed. Finally Dekker called out. "What did you need, Guy?"

"I'm hiding until the scary lady is far, far away," he whispered from outside the door.

8

Zarbeth skulked across the tarmac cloaked in shades of night. He'd secured a package to his forearm by pluralanium bonds which would not release unless the women in yellow entered an access code to relinquish its grip. The alien ducked inside his long-range skiff and activated the VTOL thrusters which lifted the craft into the sky before he punched the engines.

The Krenzin's master had sent him on an errand of utmost secrecy and importance. Zarbeth was determined not to let the Pheema down.

He did not notice the small space-transport that hovered just below him. It mimicked his every move and hid in the Krenzin's sensor shadow as they blasted east from the Krenzin controlled District Three and crossed the Atlantic Ocean.

Nearly half way across, and too far for any help to respond in time, the hidden vessel braked and rose slightly, sneaking in directly behind Zarbeth. The Krenzin's alarms went berserk. He only got off a few shouts for help before his assailant scrambled his broadcasts.

An EMP burst crossed the bow of his skiff as a warning shot. Zarbeth tried to take evasive maneuvers, unwilling to surrender his cargo, but he had never been known as a particularly skilled pilot. Another trio of EMP beams splashed across his craft, killing the stick.

As soon as the transport hit the water it skipped like a stone, dashing Zarbeth around the inside of the cockpit despite the safety restraints. Emergency measures activated and deployed the flotation system to keep the wreckage from sinking to the depths and a homing beacon activated

The Krenzin looked up groggily as his enemy's craft, a Class A spaceship hovered precariously close overhead. Its pilot bay opened on a hinged axis to let the intruder commit high seas piracy.

Kheefal clamped a load-lifter arm onto the Zarbeth's cockpit canopy and ripped it open, letting it slide into the saltwater. The rogue snapped off a few rounds of laser fire into the system controls just in case there remained any chance of regaining power before he'd retrieved his quarry.

"Give me the seed!" Kheefal screamed at the alien, ramming the muzzle of his weapon into Zarbeth's eye socket.

"Never," Zarbeth yelled, pulling his arm back and out of his enemy's reach. The pluralanium case wouldn't come free even if he wanted it to—just as the Pheema had planned.

Kheefal smacked him in the other eye with the butt of his pistol, swelling it shut. "Give it up and I'll let you live."

A long-range proximity warning chimed from the thief's craft.

"You'll never get me out of this chair without my cooperation—not in time—and dead weight will slow you down," he grinned through the trickle of blood leaking down his face as if he'd somehow won the game.

Kheefal tipped his head. "You're probably right." He grabbed the alien by the wrist and put his gun to Zarbeth's elbow. He smashed the alien in the face again as he tried to wriggle away and then fired five shots through the joint and ripped the limb free as Zarbeth shrieked and passed out from the pain.

The thief tucked the severed limb and accompanying seedpod under his arm and returned to his craft, leaving Zarbeth to bleed out atop the rocking waves.

Kheefal grinned, noting the rescue ships on their way. Five of them rocketed towards his location with such speed that they were likely private fighter jets owned by the Pheema. Those crafts were equipped more to take down an enemy than to rescue one expendable Krenzin in the Pheema's employ.

Sealing the hatch, Kheefal activated his thrusters. They probably couldn't take him down in the air, but he didn't intend to stay planet-side. Kheefal had a package to deliver and a paycheck to receive. Within a few moments, he'd be out of sensor range and be able to hit FTL.

Kheefal leaned back in his seat and slapped the armrests, happy to have his ship back. "It's gonna be a good payday," he murmured and then punched the thrusters.

9

"…and my final piece of advice," Guy said at the front of the line, "is to never let Dekker pick what you eat for lunch. Not unless you want to try fried decapod toe or grieggarian snard; just avoid any restaurant he recommends." He led the new guys down the barracks hallway of the Dozen's headquarters on the edge of Reef City.

Two large rooms on either side of the hallway sprawled open before them with beds made with military precision. He slid out the old markers and inserted new name-plates onto the face of each door to mark the new residents.

With thin lips, he tucked the name badges for Murtaugh, Dirk, and Trigger into his back pocket. "You can kinda pick and choose where you're staying," he told Nathan, Shaw, and Britton.

The three men traded glances with their fourth companion who shrugged. Juice didn't have any outstanding physical characteristics that identified him as a soldier or indicated any kind of martial prowess. "I'm just temporary help," he noted.

Guy taped over Nibbs' name and wrote Juice across it. "Your homework, Juicebox…"

"Um, it's just Juice," he interrupted.

Guy scowled at him with mock indignation. "We are very formal here, Mister

Box, don't forget that. You came highly recommended, so don't screw this up with protocol violations. He pointed to the personal effects Nibbs had left behind after taking an extended, personal leave following their Io mission. "Your homework, Mister Box is to find something in this room to make a bomb out of by dinner time."

Addressing them all, Guy said, "Dinner's in the mess at nineteen hundred. Don't be late."

An hour later, Guy joined the rest of the regular crew at the mess hall: a glorified rec room off the main hangar bay, and waited for dinner.

The new crew members trickled in.

Juice entered the room and tossed Guy a dirty sock that had been tied off and a jar filled with clear liquid. "My homework," he reported.

"It's some kind of sock bomb?"

"No. It's the regular kind. There's calcium hypochlorite in the powder; it's the main chemical in the cleaning solvent."

Guy jiggled the other container.

"Polyethylene glycol… antifreeze fluids for spacecraft are loaded with the stuff. I noticed a big barrel of it when we walked through the first time." He glanced back towards the hangar. "But I don't see a ship."

"It's invisible," Guy retorted.

Mustache shook his head. "The *Rickshaw Crusader* is currently on its way back from Luna, getting repairs and upgrades done at Darkside Station. Also, you can just assume that most of what Guy told you is somehow wrong."

Juice sighed with relief. "Oh good. He said that Dekker was super formal. I'm a real casual person and didn't get that vibe at all when he and I spoke previously about me coming on."

Mustache kept a serious face. "Oh, no. *That* part is true. For your sake, don't get too cozy around him… but the rest of what he said is malarkey, and the rest of us are all pretty relaxed, though. But Dekker? He likes things a certain way." He flashed the new member a wink.

A loud creak rattled the nearby wall as the massive hydraulics opened the back partition of their facility and the dull roar of the *Crusader's* engines momentarily deafened them. The loading ramp lowered and a lithe, red haired woman carrying boxes of takeout descended.

"Who's that?" Juice asked breathlessly.

"That's Vivian," Guy said. "Vivian Briggs. Only surviving daughter of the famous war General Harry Briggs. We call her Vesuvius. She can get explosive at times," Guy flapped the sock for good measure.

"The forbidden fruit," Mustache cautioned him. "I think she and Dekker are an item this week?" He looked to Guy for confirmation.

Guy shrugged. “I dunno. They were yelling at each other last night, so my money says… yes?”

Dekker finally followed her out of the ship carrying the few bags that remained of the catering. He wore a dour look.

“I change my answer,” Guy quipped.

Vesuvius and Dekker entered the room and dropped the catered meal on a table at the side of the room. “Good. You all made it. My apologies for not being here when you arrived. I had to wrap up that business with Doc and get the *Crusader* back before our next mission.”

Mustache nudged Juice who jumped to his feet and offered a curt, introductory bow. “Mister Knight, sir. A pleasure to meet you. I’m…” Juice trailed off as a ripple of laughter circulated the room.

Dekker stared down his nose at Juice and Mustache burst out in a loud guffaw, wagging his whiskers. His cheeks burned red with amusement.

After a few long, withering moments of staring at the new guy, Dekker informed him, “It’s just Dekker. I don’t know what these guys told you in my absence, but it’s not as formal as any of the nonsense they do in the MEA. We expect duty and order, but we’re a family here.”

“A big, dysfunctional family,” Vesuvius said. She tilted her head towards Dekker and her face softened.

Juice nodded. The truth in what his comrades had said about the couple was written all over Vesuvius's face.

"And you," Dekker raised an eyebrow at Guy, "stop messing with the new guys so close to a mission."

Guy held up the sock and jar and pointed to Juice to deflect his anger. "New guy brought a bomb to dinner."

Dekker rolled his eyes and chuckled. He and Vesuvius quickly arranged the spread they'd ordered from the caterer.

Rock leaned back and murmured something about family traditions to Ahmed who sat next to him.

"Have you seen or heard from Dirk?" Ahmed asked of their former member who'd lost a limb at Io.

"I heard he's not doing so well," Vesuvius mentioned.

Rock nodded. "Not much work out there for a crippled former Investigator. That blasted Peace For All Races group made sure of that." An awkward silence passed for a moment. "I saw Dirk the other day in town; some of those PFAR jerks were harassing him, I chased em off, but Dirk wouldn't let me buy him lunch, even. Not sure where he's living, but he's not been okay since leaving."

"Sometimes I think I ought to take a cue from Dirk and retire," Mustache said, running his fingers through his salt-shot hair. "I ain't as fast or strong as I used to be."

"Come on." Vesuvius leaned into the conversation. "What would we do without your timeless, ancient wisdom," she teased him.

Mustache grinned and flashed her a smile. "Careful, girl. The moment one of y'all calls me Grandpa is when I finally show off how fast I still am."

She laughed, "How speedy you can file for unemployment services, you mean?"

"You know it." Mustache lifted an empty glass and tilted it as if requesting a refill. "Alright, who's got my calcium fiber drink?"

Dekker stacked a heap of plates and turned and addressed the new guys. "Welcome to The Dozen."

Most of the crew got up to begin loading plates with food. Juice hung slightly back, his eyes dodging from person to person as he counted.

Mustache nudged him again, sidling up beside him at the end of the line. "If you're counting heads and planning about asking after the 'Dozen's' math… don't. It won't make any sense," he grinned. "We don't always add up."

Juice nodded his thanks and grabbed one of the thirteen plates.

"Alright guys," Guy called out, fork in hand, "After we eat, who wants to go outside and blow this sock up?"

10

Zarbeth's eyelids fluttered and opened. Blinding light and hot pain greeted him as he regained consciousness. He tried to move but couldn't make any of his limbs work, except for his left arm.

With grogginess still washing over him in waves, Zarbeth tried to use his arm to smooth the ruffled fur around his brows back so he could see. Nothing happened; he tried again to the same effect.

With a momentary concentration of will he shook off the fugue and stared at his arm. Panic filled in his gut like a hot cloud: it was gone! Pink, fresh skin had just begun to scab over where the wound had been stitched. His other arm and legs were strapped to a bed.

He thrashed against the restraints and heard his heart rate beeping dangerously fast. *Am I in a hospital?*

A familiar voice called out. "Easy, Zarbeth. Calm down; you are among your people." The Pheema put a hand on Zarbeth's chest to settle his nerves.

The wounded Krenzin settled back on his bed and suddenly remembered everything: the attack and theft of his master's seed, with his arm still attached.

Zarbeth's eyes glossed with anguish. "Master… Master I failed you."

"It is okay," The Pheema shushed him. "It's not too late. But only *you* can help us now."

"But—but my arm. I lost it," his voice cracked. "There's no way that I can…"

"Don't worry about that right now," the Krenzin religious leader soothed. He turned to indicate the other two persons in the room.

An old woman wearing yellow robes and a matching cloak stared at him beneath her furrowed brows. Her stern gaze and stiff posture commanded the room. Next to her stood a thin humanoid. He seemed like a man, but Zarbeth could not tell; it did not smell human according to his keen feline nostrils. He wore only black and a cowled, dark mask hid his face and head.

The faceless man stepped forward and Zarbeth's pulse spiked.

"These are my associates," The Pheema said. "This is Leviathan. He has… special talents."

Zarbeth detected a waft of fear emitted via his master's pheromones as he glanced to the other person. The woman in yellow said nothing, and The Pheema made no introduction. There remained no doubt that she was in control. Like a god, the old woman was beyond mention.

Leviathan took Zarbeth by his hand. The sensation felt electric.

"Easy," The Pheema said. "Leviathan needs to go deep to get what we require. Just focus on your recollection of what happened." He swallowed and cautioned, "There will be pain."

Zarbeth grimaced. "I understand."

Leviathan tilted his mask back on a hinge and revealed his twisted, scarred face. Empty eyes stared out from his lidless sockets and pierced Zarbeth's mind like psychic daggers.

Memories washed over Zarbeth like waves… the waves that had jostled him atop the ocean. He laid bleeding in his cockpit, floating upon the salt and foam. Zarbeth relived the pain and agony of the event.

His mind felt the presence of the mental hitchhiker like a burning rash or stinging wound beneath the surface of his subconscious. Zarbeth relived the memory over and over as Leviathan sifted every detail: the face of his attacker, the thief's smell and voice, the pain of losing an arm.

Zarbeth's ears rang, and he felt his master's words ripple through his mind. "He has to go deeper."

Pain wracked his body and he felt his mind flayed atom by atom. His body stiffened in his restraints though Zarbeth didn't know if they were of his hospital bed or the skiff's crash couch. He felt the warmth of blood as it trickled from his nose. Zarbeth howled as the mental intruder ripped every detail from his mind, treating the

Krenzin as if he were nothing more than some kind of organic recording device.

As Leviathan found a useful memory, a moment of sudden clarity and peace found Zarbeth. The pain stopped, and he dwelled in the refuge for what seemed an eternity.

Zarbeth's eyes were dark—he'd been unconscious when he'd heard it: the intruder returned to his craft and a series of beeps chimed as the canopy closed on the invader's Class A craft. The Krenzin merged seamlessly with Leviathan in that moment; he understood that Leviathan was somehow familiar with that ship.

The notes played over and over as Leviathan played and replayed the memory. They echoed on, reverberating with maddening duration as it repeated in an infinite spiral.

Everything suddenly clicked in the slowly churning blackness. Only the symphony of electronic tones permeated it, an orchestra of memorized notes.

And then he suddenly awoke. Leviathan had returned to the yellow woman's side.

"It's from the navigation computer," Zarbeth said. "You know where my attacker went—where he took the package."

The old woman tilted her brow with measured movement towards The Pheema and at Leviathan. Her expression said it clearly: *He was right, and now Zarbeth had outlived his usefulness.*

Leviathan gave a curt nod and grabbed the nearby syringe intended to silence the loose end.

The Pheema blocked him. "No. He is one of mine. Loyalty of this kind," he waved to the stump where his arm had been severed, "is difficult to come by."

"Very well," said the woman in yellow. "He is your responsibility."

Leviathan picked up a different needle and plunged it into Zarbeth's veins. A moment later, his eyes rolled back and an induced, healing coma consumed him, sending him back to the cockpit and the waves of black.

11

With a lurch, the *Rickshaw Crusader* dropped out of FTL in the Trappist system. Trappist 1, a stable red dwarf burned ahead and Matty fired up the engines with a smile. "It's handling much better than when we left Io."

The broadcast system remained quiet. Its silence was a welcome reprieve from the burst of static and demands that MEA orbital outposts tended to issue whenever their vessel entered range. Expansion worlds, for all their potential danger, enjoyed certain benefits.

Shortly afterward, the *Crusader* angled into the atmosphere and descended towards the city of Newhope. Sprawling across the landscape, Newhope boasted the curling plumes of smoke and washed out colors typical of industrial cities that bypassed the MEA's environmental regulations. The city's skeletal structures clawed for the air, protruding from the dirt landscape like zombie arms trying to escape Galilee's crust.

Matty spun the *Crusader* on its VTOL thrusters and set the ship down on a large patch of blasted earth in the overflow of an open air market. Dekker holstered a firearm on each thigh and walked towards the loading ramp as the hydraulic ramp lowered to the ground.

"What, no reliquary this time?" Mustache slapped him on the shoulder.

"And risk leaving it with one of you guys again? No way," he grinned and pulled a fist-sized cartridge from his duster's pocket and then slid it back into hiding. "The shells are too rare to leave them out where someone might set them off."

Mustache winked. "I can't imagine someone would do that lightly."

Rock and Guy pulled out of the cargo bay, each driving an ATV, and hooked them up to a chain of trailers containing parts and equipment for Doc Johnson's cousin. They traded nods with their leader and then set about their delivery task while Dekker descended the ramp; he had a different, personal mission.

Vesuvius caught up to him at the bottom of the ramp and stepped shoulder to shoulder. "I dunno," she said. "I kind of have a bad feeling about this whole thing. Should you be going alone?"

"I'm sure I'll be fine," he said. "But I ought to go and see my contact right away and he said to come alone. I'd hate to scare him away."

Vesuvius scowled. "Sounds like a setup to me. And like I said, something feels off about this place."

"I can take care of myself. And I have confidence you'll be fine. It's a simple transfer; we're even paid in full for the job already."

She sighed. "At least give me a kiss before you go?"

Dekker paused. “In front of the crew?”

“Stop acting like such an old man and kiss me.” She stood on her toes and locked her lips on his. Vesuvius finally pulled away and said, “That was pretty weak. You owe me more when you get back.” She flashed him a wink and returned to the ship as Rock and Guy left with their cargo in tow.

12

Dekker walked through the rundown part of town. A cloister of dilapidated residential buildings leaned against each other.

He checked his directions against the landmarks again and scanned the area for a door with a unique marking etched upon it. He spotted it and approached cautiously. The wooden landing and stairs threatened to buckle and splinter beneath his weight. Dekker was keenly aware that he'd been spotted by security cameras.

The Investigator knocked.

After a few long moments, the door creaked open, coming partly off the hinges as it swung free. "Can I help you?"

"Are you the Dragonfly?"

The grizzled old man tilted his head expectantly. His overly long and greasy hair slid down his shoulders; he had poor hygiene and a paunch. "Some have called me that. Come in, come in."

Dekker ducked through the door and followed his host through the dingy shop. It looked like every back-alley black market that he'd ever seen. Weapons and other kinds of illegal equipment and devices lay stacked and shelved along the walls.

"They call me Bob," the Dragonfly said, slipping behind the bar-top where he conducted business. A bank of surveillance monitors showed live feeds of all the shop's access points. Bob nodded to the single barstool across from him.

Dekker meandered through the makeshift store. His footsteps creaked on the wooden flooring. He leaned against the nearby wall instead of sitting at the stool; the surrounding floor had been stained dark ocher with telltale splatters.

Bob's expression seemed irked, but he asked, "You have one of the weapons?"

Dekker nodded. "Do you have any of the ammunition?"

"I'm not entirely certain that I know what you need exactly. May I see the gun?"

"I didn't bring it. Too valuable."

"Well, how am I supposed to…"

Dekker retrieved the shell from his pocket and tossed it to him.

Bob caught it. Excitement lit behind his eyes and he snapped his magnetic glasses around his face and held the cartridge into the light. He turned it over and over in his hand. "Yes… yes…" he murmured. His eyebrows raised and his voice hinted at awe. "These ones are marked with ancient Greek letters. How can that be?" He looked over at Dekker. "Your gun…"

"The reliquary."

"Your reliquary… it works?"

"I wouldn't be looking for more ammunition if it didn't. There are others? You've seen them?"

Bob nodded enthusiastically. "I've seen two before. Neither of them worked. But I've heard stories—ancient tales of their power."

"And the ammo. What do you know?" Dekker asked, doing his best to appear relaxed."

"Very rare. I've seen three rounds. One in a language I did not know; two were marked with ancient runes."

"Are they available for purchase?"

Bob shrugged. "I don't know where they even are, anymore. I came across them long ago... before I'd even seen the broken weapons. I imagine they are priceless."

Dekker eyed the way Bob clutched the cartridge. "Then why did you bring me all this way?"

Bob's eyes flashed like flint.

"You weren't planning on shooting me and stealing my stuff, were you, Bob?" Dekker stood nonchalant, but he eyed him knowingly.

The black market dealer looked away, to the stool that his guest had refused. He tensed and then snatched a scattergun from beneath his bar-top; it had been aimed at the vacant seat.

Dekker yanked his guns free and dug them into Bob's face before the man even got the weapon freed from its holder. "That was not a wise move, Bob." He shoved the would-be thief far enough back that he couldn't make a play for another weapon. He demanded, "My property?"

Bob placed the shell into Dekker's waiting hand and watched covetously as it disappeared into Dekker's pocket.

"How do you know so much about these weapons? Where did you hear stories of them?" Dekker tied Bob's wrist with a length of cord.

Bob growled, "*The Book of Aang*."

"Never heard of it. How do I get a copy?" Dekker pressed the muzzle of his pistol into Bob's temple to punctuate his sentence.

"I—I have a copy. Got it from those silver-haired freaks years ago… when Galilee was re-settled after the first failure."

The investigator raised an eyebrow.

"I don't trade with them no more," he insisted as if that meant something to the off-worlder. "They been trying to run me out of business for two years now. It-it's in the store room. I'll tell you where the book is, just don't kill me."

Dekker dragged the killer after him and over to the door.

"The key's above the door frame."

Dekker felt over the threshold and retrieved it. He put it into Bob's hands. "Well… after you."

Bob snorted a hot blast of disappointment and gave Dekker a nasty look. He unlocked the door, but stepped aside to stand on a pressure plate as he opened the door to reveal a tripod mounted gun that would have fired without standing on the hidden switch.

Dekker merely grinned and shoved Bob into the room.

Reluctantly, Bob pulled the old book off of a shelf and handed it over to him. Dekker drew a long knife off of another shelf.

"You're not gonna kill me, are you? You promised…"

Dekker winked at him. "No. But I am going to take your book as punishment for trying to murder me. I think that's a fair transaction. What do you think?"

Bob nodded in defeat.

"Great. Then I'll let you live. One more thing though. Tell me, are there any other dangers in the city I ought to be wary of?"

"The city, not anything special. Organized crime, the constables are corrupt, general big city crime, the usual. But I *would* keep away from the rural zones. There are… I've heard rumors… things living in the wild."

Dekker lashed the other end of Bob's bonds and tied it to the knife handle and then threw it up, burying it deep into the wood ceiling. "You don't look all that spry, Bob, but I bet even you could make a few jumps up to it and maybe cut yourself free. It might take some doing, but you'll manage." He ruffled through the old, sepia pages and fingered an area where several pages had been torn from the book. The wounds looked old based on the fraying. He closed it and tucked the book under his arm and turned to leave. "Have yourself a nice day, now. Let's not cross paths again."

13

Quade finally opened his eyes to a brilliantly lit room. White walls and metallic trim made the illumination nearly blinding in its sterility.

He spotted a few logos. They branded medical packages and were affixed to the facility's surfaces. It seemed familiar, but he couldn't quite place the symbol.

"Oh, you're awake," his abductor said.

Quade narrowed his eyes and tried to lash out at the man who'd electrocuted him, but his arms and legs were tied off.

"My name is Doctor Meng," he said. "I work for Jagaracorps."

Quade suddenly recognized the symbol now that he had a name to match to it.

"Wh-where am I?" He glanced around the room and saw a bank of video displays on a far wall. The feeds all came from his village, and from others. A woman coughed on one screen and hacked up a wad of slime. On another, a fevered man stumbled down a road.

"In my laboratory, Quade. There is something different about you. I must know what."

Quade raised an eyebrow, disturbed that Dr. Meng knew his name.

"You are not sick like the others, and I know you were exposed to the spores. I saw it happen. Both times."

"Jagaracorps?" Quade asked. "Aren't they responsible for all sorts of biological innovations? Pharmaceuticals and what not?"

Meng nodded. "Yes. Yes. They sponsor my research, but they are so much more than medicines." He waved around the room. "For decades, this lab right here has been responsible for so many of the company's greatest breakthroughs." He looked forlornly down, staring at a lit quarantine box as if it carried the body of his fallen child. A nameplate labeled its contents as *Eden-12*.

Quade suddenly remembered the rumors of the old tunnels and the original settlement on Galilee. Glimpses of old, decaying buildings and ghost towns planted decades ago were common. The push to repopulate Galilee came only recently; nobody talked about the previous attempt to tame the expansion planet.

Finally giving the Doctor's box his full attention, Quade asked, "What is it?"

"*The seed.* It's been responsible for many of my breakthroughs… and my current experiment is my most ambitious yet… a hybrid race capable of working in deep space or populating hostile planets far beyond the habitable zones. Think of it. A new race of humanoids: a subservient working class meant to better mankind!"

Quade watched Dr. Meng with a slack-jawed, neutral expression. He did not want to provoke the mad scientist, but couldn't help from stating the obvious. "Your seed… it's dead."

Meng nodded slowly and with a scowl. "The Eden seed is gone. I used the last of my samples to create clones, but none of them seem to be viable… like creating a dead embryo." He puffed a hot blast of disappointment through his nose. "But just when all was lost and I could do no more research, a new seed was delivered."

"Sooo… I'm glad you rescued me and I'm happy that you can keep doing your thing. But any chance you're going to let me go now that you have what you need?" Quade hoped that a different approach might help him escape.

Meng shook his head. "You are much too important to my research. These seeds are far more valuable than any human life—and my current theory links your strange resistance to my seeds' deaths." He pointed to a whirring genetic printer nearby. "I have a new seed clone being made even now and I have high hopes for its survival. *You* are the key to limitless production. I might never worry about my supply again. You could unlock our race's potential!"

The doctor pulled a nearby tray of medical equipment to his side as Quade struggled against his restraints.

"I must know why the spores did not react to you. If it is genetic, as I suspect, then we stand on the cusp of a new era in the universe's evolution. Whatever it is, I must get to the bottom of it in the name of science." He grabbed a ventilator mask and turned the knob on a gas line. "Now hold still, or there will be increased pain."

Quade struggled, trying to resist the doctor's strong hands as he tried to put the mask on him. The prisoner's eyes caught a glimpse of a huge creature enclosure at the edge of his peripheral. A sign labeled it "Specimen GRRZ." One of the creatures roared in the cage, just beyond sight.

Meng used the opportunity to slip the inhalant mask over Quade's face. The odorless gas took effect almost immediately and his eyelids fluttered with unnatural weight. The last thing Quade saw was Dr. Meng reaching for his scalpel.

14

Rock and Guy hauled their cargo trains through the streets of Newhope. The off-worlders drew the gazes of bystanders who eyed them with a mixture of suspicion and entrepreneurial intent.

Guy checked the directions one last time and then pulled up to a huge garage. He snorted, “It looks worse than our BOA back on Reef City,” he said.

The door raised and a scrawny man with wispy hair emerged. Dirt mixed with grease and sweat on his skin and he wore the same cockeyed expression that was Doc Johnson’s trademark.

“Are you Benjamin?” Rock asked.

The man nodded and waved them in. “My cousin, Doc, must’ve sent you? He's no doctor, but we call him Doc because of what he does.”

“He did, and we know,” Guy winked. "Bit of a mad scientist, right?"

With a nod, Benjamin smiled through thin lips and revealed bad teeth. “Communications aren’t always great out this way,” he motioned towards a berth in his shop for them to park. “I apologize that I don’t have anything to offer you besides the local water. I wasn’t sure when to expect you.” He added, “The water’s filtered—so you won’t catch the crud, at least.”

Guy raised a brow when a hover car approached, but Benjamin stayed him with a hand. The clean, luxury skiff pulled in front of the yawning bay doors and parked. The vehicle looked far too fancy to be a customer of Benjamin's.

Two men stepped out of the cab. A third man remained inside; his posture indicated he felt too self-important to exit.

"Why would Azhooliens be operating on a backwater planet like Galilee?" Guy whispered to Rock. "Don't those skin stealers usually stick to the worst parts of the galaxy… the business and political worlds?"

All three of them wore skin that boasted a silvery sheen and two had hair that had lost all color, falling in locks of white. The third and youngest one's hair had several inches of white and remained dark after that, indicating how recently the human had absorbed the symbiotic alien and become its host.

Rock sipped from the cup of lukewarm water and twisted his mouth at the flavor. "No ideas about that. But it certainly ain't normal—you're right about that much." He shuddered at the thought of being taken over by one of the strange, energy-based life forms.

Outside, beyond earshot, Benjamin engaged them in an animated discussion. The white-haired toughs didn't seem moved by his appeals. Finally, he looked back at the Investigators and his new cargo shipment. With a slight slump of his shoulders he retrieved a wallet from his pocket.

Finally, the lead Azhoolien emerged. He skimmed Benjamin's credit chip and returned it with a haughty smile. He checked his timepiece and then urged his ruffians back into the vehicle.

Guy mocked with disgust, "'I don't think we have time for any more extortion today, boys—we got shopping to do.'"

"You think so?" Rock asked. "I mean, it sure looks like it to me."

Benjamin returned with flush cheeks and tried to keep the embarrassment from his face.

"Are those guys squeezing you for money?" Guy asked.

Benjamin bit his lower lip. "It's why I asked my cousin for some extra supplies. I needed to make up the difference; the crime syndicate controls everything in the cities and the rural areas are… best avoided. Galilee is…" he trailed off. "The fringe worlds play by their own rules. There is opportunity out here for everybody—sometimes that opens us up to exploitation. This place… it's not always safe—but I'd rather take my chances here than live trapped in a system controlled by the Mother Earth Aggregate."

"I'll drink to that," Guy said, raising a glass of the tepid, grayish water. He tossed it back with a grimace and coughed.

Benjamin laughed, “It won’t make you sick—but it sure don’t taste like it should!”

"State your business." Vesuvius said as the men approached the rear of the *Rickshaw Crusader*. She sat atop the open landing ramp and tightened the grip on her katana for emphasis.

The contact raised both his hands. "Whoa. I'm Merrick Doyle… just here to pick up my shipment. Medical supplies, mostly."

Perched protectively around the cargo pallet, the remaining Dozen watched his approach with hungry eyes. He met Mustache at the top of the slope and handed him his identification card.

Mustache gave it a cursory glance and then tossed it back to him while Ahmed, their combat medic, scanned the shipping invoice. "What are you guys dealing with? These drugs are usually used to treat Grohl Fever, Triptyfection, and pulmonary myometaccrescere."

Merrick stared at him blankly. He merely shrugged. "I dunno. The doctors just told me to pick it up." He signed a receipt form and led the way.

A few of the others used the load lifter to drag the cargo to the dirt below where a fancy vehicle waited.

Ahmed tapped Vesuvius on the shoulder. "I don't think this guy's on the up and up."

She scowled at the shiny vehicle as two large guys got out and loaded the boxes into the transport. “Are the drugs dangerous on the street?”

Ahmed shook his head. “Not particularly so. It’s odd. Most of them are pretty obscure and only needed for certain kinds of treatments. Usually repository infections on agrarian worlds.”

“Sooo, we didn’t get paid to smuggle a bunch of illegal drugs to a planet with ambiguous laws on that topic and we’re not flooding the population with addictive substances?”

He shook his head. "No. It's clean... we're not accidental drug smugglers."

“Then what’s the problem?”

“It doesn’t make sense. I don’t think someone from the hospital would drive that kind of fancy auto.”

Vesuvius looked outside. She shrugged. “I agree with you. But we don’t get paid to think—we get paid to protect cargo up until it gets delivered.” She folded up the signed receipt. “No longer our problem.”

Two ATVs pulled in as the luxury transport drove away. Engines revved as they pulled up the ramp. Vesuvius glowered as she and Ahmed watched a man sprinting towards their ship from the edge of the nearby market.

Rock and Guy killed their vehicles and joined the two.

"What was the Azhoolien crime syndicate doing over here?" Guy asked, nodding after the vehicle as it accelerated into the distance.

The man running through the field grabbed a handful of stones from the ground and threw them impotently in the direction of the departed Azhooliens. They did not get far and bounced away before reaching their target, unable to slow them.

He turned and ran for the *Crusader*. The man stopped and stood stiff as the crew leveled weapons at the intruder.

Producing his identification, the man huffed and puffed from the running. "Please tell me that you had two orders to deliver to this planet," he said as Vesuvius descended the ramp and took his paperwork.

She eyed him suspiciously and then glanced past him, spotting Dekker's approach through the field. Vesuvius hissed a curse below her breath. The new guy looked strikingly similar to the man who'd just taken their cargo.

"My name is Merrick," he said. "We've got to hurry. There are a ton of sick people back at my village. Where are the medical supplies?" Ahmed glanced at Vesuvius. Her lips shrank and twisted into a frown. "Crap."

16

"I guess the sickness wasn't bad enough for this cursed planet, but it's really only the outlier towns that are suffering," said Merrick—the real Merrick. He muttered, "The disappearances have gotten so bad that I don't know what I'm gonna do."

"Disappearances?" Dekker asked. They'd taken the tardy medical worker and gathered around him in the *Crusader's* lounge. Someone had sabotaged his vehicle, causing his delay.

Merrick's shoulders slumped. "Whole towns have been emptied. And it can't simply be folk getting nervous about the illness and relocating without telling others. My main assistant, a nice guy named Quade, he disappeared a couple nights ago, too. The guy is criminally polite… no way he would've abandoned the project without letting me know." He sighed and ran fingers through his hair. "This isn't what I signed up to do in my year between medical classes."

Ahmed hovered nearby, next to Guy who asked, "Why do you think the Azhooliens would be interested in the drugs?"

He shrugged. "Either they need them because their human host bodies are affected by the spores, or more likely, they saw an opportunity to extort the families living beyond the city and squeeze them for every penny if they want a chance at staying alive."

Dekker's face darkened. He didn't like the sound of that. "This medicine will save lives?"

Merrick looked skeptical. "I don't even know. It was just a hypothesis Quade and I formed. Based on how the sickness seems to be contracted, we thought this could help, but we're really shooting in the dark."

Worry lines creased near Dekker's eyes, "How can we help get it back?"

He shrugged. "The constables on the fringe are a joke. They're too scared to act… haven't even looked into finding the missing folks. Nobody knows where to find the Azhooliens—they find *you*—so I couldn't even buy the stuff back if I wanted… or could."

Dekker scanned the faces of his crew. It was evident that each of them felt the heaviness of their responsibility.

"Any ideas, guys?"

Juice raised his hand. "That kind of vehicle they drove… it's a Tyger Imperial… super fancy. They have a remote tracking system as part of their theft prevention protocols. Can we track it?"

Vesuvius scowled. "I'm sure they disabled it first thing after buying… or stealing… the vehicle. Rule number one: Criminals don't like to be found."

"Unless you knew the transponder signal codes and could reactivate it remotely by satellite broadcast?" Guy suggested. All eyes turned to him and he almost wilted beneath their gaze—there was no way anyone could know that code.

Guy elbowed Rock. "We might know a guy who can help."

17

Benjamin shushed Rock and Guy. "You can't ask those kinds of questions so loudly!" He pulled them into his office and looked over his shoulder. Finally, certain that they weren't being spied on by the Azhooliens' informants, Benjamin relaxed. "Of course I can get you the transponder codes."

He rummaged through a few desk drawers and pulled out a log book filled with hand-written notes. "Rigs as fancy as a Tyger Imperial won't even let you operate them without broadcasting a signal. Tyger Systems claims that it makes their vehicles impossible to steal." He scanned the book.

"So… is it?" Guy asked.

"Impossible to steal? Absolutely… but that that didn't stop me."

"But you beat the system and stole the impossible car?"

"Of course," Benjamin grinned. "I couldn't spoof the security chip or bypass it. So I just swapped out the transponder with one I ordered as a replacement, sent it to a guy who owned one and paid some kid to stand outside and accept the delivery at the address and then send it to me." He wrote down the code on a slip of paper and handed it to the Investigators. "Obviously…"

"Yeah. We didn't get this from you," Rock promised.

Guy had his com in hand and reported the code to the crew on the *Crusader*. He slipped the earpiece into place and hopped aboard his ATV.

"The satellite's got a ping," Juice's voice reported. "It's got a lock on the vehicle. Zooming in… it looks like they're just outside of the city a good distance, halfway between Newhope and a handful of small mining towns. Should be a short trip to get our lost cargo."

"Roger that," Rock said on the shared channel. "We'll be back in just a few minutes." He hit the throttle and sped ahead of Guy.

They raced in hot and parked the ATVs in the cargo hold of the *Rickshaw Crusader*. Moments later, with the cargo door shutting on hydraulic arms, the ship climbed for air on its VTOL thrusters.

18

Dr. Meng paced in front of the bank of monitors and wrung his hands. Remote, drone cameras fed the screens.

He scowled at the back entry to his laboratory and cursed at it. His contact was late; if Meng hated anything more than stoppages to his research, it was tardiness.

Meng wandered near a workbench where his incubation tank hummed. He checked the progress bar. Color-shifting LEDs indicated the cloning process neared ninety percent. Status indicators read that viability still seemed positive.

An entry door beeped as the airlock cycled with a brief whoosh and eliminated any potential contaminants. Kheefal finally walked through. A paging device flashed on his hip though he didn't seem to walk with the urgency Meng desired.

"What if this had been an emergency?" he snapped.

"Doc, you think everything's an emergency." Kheefal stopped short of rolling his eyes and walked past the parked passenger car at the entrance to the magsled tube.

Meng glared daggers at him. "Do I need to remind you how much I'm paying you?"

"No, sir. But you also didn't pay me to jump at shadows."

"Do they look like shadows to you?" Meng pointed at the screens.

Kheefal rubbed his chin as he watched the rival investigators on the looped feeds. "I know these guys… know *of them*, anyway… Is this stream live?" he asked.

Meng shook his head. "No, but they seem to be sniffing around at something, and they just recently left the city."

Kheefal raked his fingers through his hair. He'd heard rumors of the Dozen's altruism. "And they are coming here?"

The doctor shrugged. "Well… no. But they *could be*."

Keeping a neutral expression, the rival Investigator asked, "Is there some link that would bring them here?"

Meng didn't respond. His paranoia became self-evident.

Kheefal turned to face his employer. His raised eyebrows demanded an answer.

"No. Not directly… but we can't take any chances."

Kheefal agreed. "I ought to keep a close eye on these guys, at least."

Meng laid a hand on the cloning pod where a new seed incubated. "Yes. A close eye, and if they start sniffing around, eliminate them.

Kheefal sighed. He'd taken the doctor's dirty money, but he hoped it wouldn't come down to a fight. The Dozen had a reputation for toughness. He felt certain he could take a few of them, but not even at his cockiest did he think he could beat them all at once. If it came down to it, he'd grab his cash and burn the doctor.

"Say it," Meng demanded.

"They'll never see me. When I choose to stay hidden, nobody can find me. I'll keep a close eye on them."

"And if required?"

"Eliminate them," he lied.

19

The *Rickshaw Crusader* tilted into a barrel roll and dodged the barrage of incoming blaster fire. "Watch your heads!" Matty yelled into the ship-wide com after the fact.

"Looks like it's the right place," Vesuvius said as she grabbed tight to her chair.

The Tyger Imperial sat in front of a house on the farm site below them. Clear-cut acreage stretched out in all directions for kilometers around. Unlike typical farms, mounted laser batteries sat on the perimeter

"Light em up," Dekker yelled into the com. He and Mustache, each sitting in a gunnery turret, began firing back. The brilliant bursts slammed into the energy wall that covered the farm like a dome. Deadly energy blips skipped across the shell like raindrops off a windshield.

The *Crusader* bucked as a series of concussive bursts rocked them in the sky. "She'll hold," Dekker reassured them. "Doc's reputation depends on it."

"Coming back around again," Matty shouted.

Their ship's guns opened fire again. Again, they had no effect, but the *Crusader* convulsed under another bout of gunfire.

"We can't keep this up," Vesuvius snarled as the jerking bouts thrashed her around in her restraints.

Matty winked at her. "Did you guys see it?" he asked into his headset?

"I saw it," Mustache reported. "Even my old eyes spotted their shield generator. Big sucker out behind the house."

Below them, silver-haired Azhooliens scattered and ran for the main house. They emerged again with weapons or leaned out of windows, preparing for invasion.

An Azhoolien with only a short length of silver attached to his black locks burst out from the front door. A shoulder mounted cannon rested on a mechanical frame.

"Ah crap," Matty muttered as the weapon acquired a lock and a missile streaked out. It slipped through the force field and gave chase as Matty took evasive maneuvers.

Guy's voice crackled excitedly on the speaker. "Those are Raza 9 missiles! That's highly regulated tech from the ISW. Deep Space Mechnars used them to penetrate the hulls of capital class ships before swarming in through the breach."

"Raza 9s?" Corgan exclaimed. "No way! Those things messed us up in the war…" the history buff pulled up a screen and started running research.

Dekker and Mustache tried to tag it with laser bursts, but the warhead sloughed them off with ease. Anything that could penetrate capital ships' armor would turn the *Crusader* to melty slag with one direct hit.

Diagnostics flashed at a nearby console. Corgan yelled out, "It's got the same kind of shields as the farm. Energy deflectors—we need something with substance!"

The Raza 9 closed in and Matty flipped the ship upside down at the last second. He killed the burners and hit the VTOL thrusters before flipping back around and rocketing off in the other direction as the missile zipped past.

He heard someone in the back puking from the high-G maneuver.

"The missile did not break target lock!" Corgan howled.

The Raza 9 turned an arc on the scanners and streaked forward again.

Vesuvius over rode the safety protocols from her console and released her restraints. "Dead-fish this thing when I tell you," she ordered. "I'll take care of the missile."

She staggered through the length of the ship as it climbed for atmosphere with a rocket on their tail. Vesuvius snapped on a pair of goggles as she entered the storage bay. She started an ATV's engine and set her jaw as the bay door opened.

Rushing wind deafened her as she caught sight of the looming warhead rushing towards them. She drew her sword and cut the restraints.

"Kill it all!" she screamed into the com, barely able to hear even her own voice. She snatched a fistful of webbing as the *Crusader* went into a complete system shut-off. The ATV shot out the back of the dead ship as it flipped through the atmosphere, flinging her around the bay like a rag doll.

The Raza 9 sensed the idling engine of the ATV and angled towards the vehicle while the *Crusader* tumbled towards the planet below, desperately trying to restart its main systems.

Missile struck ATV with a crackling detonation. The blast flashed bright and hot, flash boiling even the metal of the vehicle's engine and body.

Every time the ship spun another loop, Vesuvius caught sight of the dirt below. Her heart raced as it grew closer and closer. Finally, the ship's frame shuddered with a surge of power and it righted itself and climbed back for a comfortable altitude.

Vesuvius's headset squawked as she tried to pull herself towards the button to close the ramp before the pressure difference sucked her out.

"How secure can you make yourself?" Matty asked.

"What? Why?"

"Gonna try something. A high-G maneuver. Pretty sure it's gonna knock a few of you out for a couple seconds. Strap in, and when I say so, cut the second ATV free. Try not to die."

Vesuvius cut all the tie-downs on the last ATV except for one and wrapped herself inside a cocoon of cargo webbing and tied her sword to her hand with a stray lanyard. She tapped her com. "If this kills me, I'm going to haunt you so badly."

20

For such a jumpy guy, Dr. Meng wasn't answering his com, and that made Kheefal nervous. He scanned through the mad scientist's daily logs again. Finally, Meng answered on hands-free video mode. A tiny holographic version of him shimmered above the com; blood splatters covered his white lab coat, and he wore a mixture of frustration and impatience on his face.

"What is it?"

Kheefal sighed heavily. He hated eating crow. "Much as I hate to admit it," he said, "but you may have been right."

Tiny Meng looked down his nose at him.

"About the investigators," Kheefal explained. "I've been digging through your daily logs. You don't do much and you never *go* anywhere so it didn't look like there was any threat."

Meng huffed. "Get to your point, Kheefal."

"My point is: *people have come to you…* these special 'deliveries' you've gotten from the Azhoolien gangsters? It's been a while since you had one, but they used to come regularly."

Even at the current scale, Kheefal could tell Meng had frowned.

"I think you ought to evac, Doc. Pull back to the alternate laboratory as soon as you can. I'll meet you there soon."

He waved his bloody hands to indicate his lab coat and protested. "I'm kind of in the middle of something, Kheefal."

"Well, you better finish immediately and move out. I'm outside of the Azhoolien's compound watching that team of Investigators duke it out with them, right now. If you want to be safe, follow your backup contingency. If there's any chance they might find a connection to you or your lab, you'd better move."

Dr. Meng stared sharply at him through the communicator. "Meet me at the reserve lab as soon as this threat has passed. Kheefal, *deal with this*."

21

Ahmed took Vesuvius's seat in the cockpit as the *Crusader* shot across the farm. He reached across and jabbed the pointy end of a syringe into Matty's neck while the pilot focused on piloting. They hoped the injection would prevent him from succumbing to the G-forces.

Matty groaned as the stimulants coursed through his veins.

Ahmed finished strapping himself into Vesuvius's crash couch and plunged a needle into his own vein. He grimaced and then shook his head as the drugs hit his system.

"I guess you don't want to miss this?"

Ahmed shook his head. "Not a chance."

"Everybody hold on!" Matty yelled into the com as their target loomed into view. He hit a reverse thruster, and the ship braked violently in a hard spin that racked up the G-forces.

"Cut it! Cut it," he yelled during the move.

Vesuvius slashed through the last tie-down and sent the ATV flinging out the back at high speed right before she blacked out and fell limp in the webbing. The vehicle smashed into the shield generator with a flash of fire; the air shimmered as the energy field dissipated.

A couple guys who remained conscious in the passenger area cheered. One of them hurled.

Ahmed remotely closed the cargo doors while Matty twisted the pilot yoke and brought the ship back around. “I think I’ll have to call that move the ‘Galilee slide,’” he said.

“It’s bad luck to name it while they’re still shooting at us,” Ahmed warned.

“Bad luck! Bad luck,” Guy shouted groggily into the com.

They strafed by the farm again where the criminals worked to load the missile launcher with another Raza 9.

“Anybody got any more ATVs?” Matty asked. "Check your pockets, everyone!"

Corgan shook off the effects of the Galilee slide. His fingers flew across the keyboard. “I found the data I was looking for. There was a reason that Mechnar forces stopped using them!”

The *Crusader* opened up with all of its weapons and peppered the farmhouse with a fierce barrage of laser bolts. It normally would’ve been enough to grind the structure down to its foundations. Behind a second shield, the silver haired Azhoolien grinned and shouldered the cannon.

“A second shield? Who needs that much security?” Matty cried.

“Criminals,” Ahmed spat.

The Azhoolien cockily waved goodbye to his enemies.

"History lesson," Corgan said as he tapped a key to broadcast a signal.

Before the enemy could launch the rocket it exploded and tore through the criminals' lair. The shield system, likely rooted at a generator deep inside the building, flickered and then released the flames. Debris and bodies flung across the yard as the Raza 9 gutted the building.

Matty blinked at the carnage.

"General Briggs's team discovered an auto-destruct signal. He baited the enemy into a battle and turned the tides of the Intergalactic Singularity War… didn't you guys pay attention in school?"

Ahmed sat back. "Briggs—Vivian's dad?"

Corgan nodded. "That was what made Vesuvius's father famous."

The *Rickshaw Crusader* touched down on its VTOL engines and landed right next to the shiny Tyger Imperial. Dekker led his groggy crew down the landing ramp. A handful of Azhoolien criminals scrambled for an outbuilding and disappeared inside.

"That one," Rock pointed to the scorched humanoid flanked by a handful of minions. "He seemed like he was in charge when Guy and I first saw them."

Dekker tightened a hand on his weapons. A loud crash echoed in the distance, even louder than the roaring flames that belched from the farmhouse. A dirty transport skiff plowed through a sheet metal wall and sped into the distance, angling so that the investigators wouldn't be able to get a shot at them before they were safely away.

As Merrick staggered down the landing platform, Dekker swung open the door to the fancy vehicle. His cargo lay haphazardly stored around the cab.

Everyone breathed a collective sigh of relief.

A fuel tank suddenly ignited and shot into the air, startling the crew.

"I keep tellin ya, I'm getting too old for this nonsense," Mustache said, massaging his chest as if he'd had a heart attack.

22

Ahmed shuffled through a mound of debris with Juice's help. "Not so much medical stuff *here*, he observed."

"Nope, but they certainly had lots of good loot here that could make the lives of the outlanders easier."

Merrick nodded as he sifted through singed valuables that the criminals had horded. Most of it appeared broken or too burnt to be useful, but whatever was salvageable he loaded into a wagon. "They ran a lot of rackets: extortion, smuggling, trafficking, you name it."

A few of the Dozen helped collect the appliances and equipment that Merrick had promised to distribute to those in need. "Things like these filtration systems will go a long way in the rural zones—the silver haired skin-suits have been hording them and charging outrageous prices for them, putting a stranglehold on the rural populations especially."

Dekker and Vesuvius found a steep stairway underneath a patch of damaged flooring. They followed the concrete steps downward.

"Guy! Get over here; we may need you to blow something up."

He hurried over to them and rummaged in his satchel for a wad of sticky explosives and a detonator. "I'm here—point me at a target."

At the bottom of the stairwell a heavy door barred access to a buried concrete pod. The keypad lock remained unscathed.

"Can you get in?" Vesuvius asked. "It looks like a safe… or maybe a panic room."

"Sure thing," he said as he began applying the adhesive. "But its more likely a safe… no surveillance or ventilation. I wouldn't want to get stuck in there."

Dekker rubbed his chin. "So your bomb won't damage the contents?"

Guy shrugged and stuck the lead wires into the spongy material before giving them a thumbs up to indicate that the bomb was hot. "Probably not. I'd worry more about booby traps… like the kind that destroy a safe's contents rather than give it up to treasure seekers or prosecutors. Criminals on the expansion worlds have been known to use them to incinerate potential evidence in case constables raid them."

Vesuvius bit her lip when Guy almost dropped the detonator.

"Take that bomb off of there," Dekker ordered. "Hey! Anyone here know how to break into a door with electronic locks?"

Britton waved and trotted over. He descended the steps with Juice on his tail. "Ah," he teased, "the new guy wants my job."

Juice grinned and shrugged. "Nah. But I know a thing or two."

While the team's regular tech guru, Nibbs, was away on leave, Brit was the backup guy.

Brit retrieved a handheld device from his pack, Juice examined the brand and layout of the wires after unscrewing and peeling back the attached faceplate a few centimeters. Juice hurried up the stairs and out of earshot for a moment.

Dekker and Vesuvius traded amused glances, wondering which one could break in first.

Brit attached a few leads and tapped his screen. He screwed up his face. "Eight digits," Brit mumbled. "Pretty heavily encrypted. This will take a while… probably hours." He shrugged, "Nibbs could probably do it in maybe half that."

Juice returned with a handful of odds and ends. "Gimme a shot at this?"

Brit stepped aside though the skeptical look on his face said it all.

After disassembling an old calculator, Juice taped the wire leads to a few points to act as an interface and crossed a few wires on the inside of the panel. "Eight digits," he mumbled to himself after counting the number of places on the original lock's panel.

He typed in buttons One Two Three Four Five Six Seven on the calculator. He grinned. "Can anybody guess what the last digit is?" He hit Eight, and the door unlocked with a click and slid ajar.

Everyone nearby traded surprised glances of approval. Juice tapped Brit on the shoulder. "Told you I knew things… mostly little exploits that come in handy now and then."

"Good to know," Brit laughed as they ascended the stairs. "Even if you couldda done the hacker thing, that's okay too. It ain't safe, what we do… its always good to have backups."

Juice squinted and looked around at the horizon. "I hear you. It always feels a little like…"

Brit also glanced around and finished for him. "Like we're being watched?"

23

With the door opened, Dekker stepped over boxes and scattered items that had been jostled and shaken to the ground by the impact of the Raza 9 explosion. A dim set of utility lights hung overhead, burning on an emergency power supply. Vesuvius followed him step for step with a hand on her hilt.

"It's definitely a giant safe," Dekker said, overturning items that seemed likely to have value.

"Yeah," she agreed, kicking over a box filled with dehydrated foodstuffs. "But most of this stuff only has value on expansion worlds." She rummaged through a nearby desk. "I mean, where are the stacks of credits or expensive art pieces?"

He shrugged as Vesuvius picked up a ledger book.

"Azhooliens are known for their business acumen—living long lives by taking over new hosts when the old ones wear out. It gives a person a certain perspective, right?" Her eyes scanned the accounts. "Why would someone bother with a written log?"

"Because criminals don't want to keep something that can be hacked through the TransNet." Dekker pulled open the doors on a bank of rigid, vertical lockers. Bags stuffed with fine powder-form recreational drugs lined the shelves.

Vesuvius flipped a page and her face fell.

"What is it?"

She scanned the list. *Renata. Meena. Natalia. Isabella. Rodrigo. Fatema. Abigail. Julietta.*

"Names. So many names… and amounts 'invested' to track the profitability of the gang's 'investment.' It also records which brothels they forced them into… they're all over Galilee." She handed it to Dekker with disgust.

He flipped through the book with similar revulsion. The back page had a separate list of their accounts, business shells, and investments. "That's weird. They've certainly got this structured like a regular business, but they didn't seem to diversify much… they've pumped a lot of investment money into Jagaracorps."

Vesuvius kicked over a small lock-box. "Who cares about some criminals investment portfolio? We've got to help those women."

"I agree, but we have to make sure that the constables aren't dirty first. They're the only ones who can take them down correctly… unless you want to move to Galilee and keep the streets clean." He looked down at the contents of the spilled lockbox she'd tipped. "There are your valuables."

Together they crouched down and sifted through the boxes contents. Several ancient pieces lay inside: rolled up pieces of art, a bag filled with precious gems and minerals, a small stack of high-value credits, and several religious artifacts and oddities that might have value to rich collectors.

Vesuvius combed through the credit chips. “There’s about enough here to pay Doc for all those repairs and upgrades to the *Crusader*,” she said, but Dekker’s attention remained fixed on pieces of paper encased in protective duraglass: torn-out pages from an ancient book. “What is that?”

“The *Book of Aang*,” he said in hushed tones. “It looks like some kind of map.”

“Treasure?”

Dekker shook his head. “Not exactly.” They tossed the rest of the room in case there were other valuables. There weren’t any. They exited the room with the box of treasure and the Azhooliens’ damning ledger. “What do you want to do with the rest?” He asked his partner.

Vesuvius scowled at the room filled with drugs and what they represented. “Burn it.”

24

Merrick pointed to empty shelves and floor space where the Dozen unloaded the items they'd recovered or taken from the Azhoolien thugs. His prefabricated unit wasn't much different from the rest of the homes nearby except that his had a large red cross on it. It sat on the edge of town, abutting a deciduous forest.

He leaned against the side of his sparse building, taken by a coughing fit. Finally, Merrick slumped against the wall and spat out a wad of black effluence.

He wiped his mouth and turned back to his guests. "Sorry. That's the crud I was telling you about. Most of us in the outliers have it—it comes after contact with an odd kind of invasive fungus that grows out this way."

Ahmed eyed the black splatter Merrick had hacked up. "You're sure these meds will help?"

Merrick grimaced as he nodded. "The odds? I give it about fifty percent."

Ahmed tossed him a package with the medicine. "Then you better take some." He crossed his arms, intent on watching the med student treat himself to make sure it happened. "You can't help anybody else if you're sick."

He scowled, but tore open the package. He tossed back two different pills and gave himself an injection.

Guy entered with the last of the supplies they'd commandeered from the criminals' compound. "We're a long way from Newhope," he said, leading a caravan outside under the afternoon sky.

The village that Merrick's small clinic served didn't look like much. Most of the residents worked contracts to do remote work for off-world employers via the TransNet or labored in the fields, mines, or grow factories that dotted the surrounding landscape. Small pockets of industry had sprung up all around Galilee in tiny towns like Merrick's.

"Is it always so empty?" Vesuvius asked.

Merrick scanned the vacant, dirt streets. "Not usually. But folks have been disappearing—usually they are in the advanced stage of illness and they wander out into the woods in a fever—though we never find their bodies. But also, folk have disappeared who aren't even sick. Now, folks don't go out much at all… I wouldn't go that way," he called out.

Guy turned back from the edge of the building. He'd been exploring near the woods.

"That's the stuff," Merrick pointed to the gray and black mottled fungus that draped over the undergrowth and adhered to tree trunks like spattered slime. "The locals call it the Creeping Black. It's what makes folks sick."

Guy stepped back with a frown. "Can't you get rid of it?"

Merrick shook his head. "I wish. It's super responsive; if we burn it away, it grows back and then seems resistant to fire. I've never seen anything like it. Creeping Black almost has more in common with the super bugs that developed in the late twenty-first century than with other fungi."

"Speaking of fun-guys," Dekker bobbed his head down the alley. "There goes one now."

A singed, shifty looking Azhoolien slinked across an alley. He staggered on exhausted feet and pushed his way into the building

"He must've been running since the explosion to get here on foot. What's inside that building?"

"A tavern," Merrick said.

"Great," said Vesuvius. "Who else is in the mood for a drink?"

25

The parched criminal chugged his second bottle of water when he heard the noise. He whirled to find a man standing in front of him.

"I think we're about to have a problem, you and I."

With sweaty, silver locks falling off his shoulders, the thug played coy. "So thirsty. I didn't know the bar was tended, sorry. Just ran twenty clicks… I'll pay for the drinks."

"That's not it at all. You see, my name's Dekker. You and your crew tried to shoot down my ship." He pointed through a window where the cockpit of the *Rickshaw Crusader* was barely visible.

The criminal reached for his sidearm, but found himself suddenly surrounded; at least ten weapons pointed back at him. He surrendered his gun and the Investigators tied him to a chair, moments later. Merrick finally entered and watched the proceedings, but he didn't recognize the alien.

Vesuvius pulled out the criminals' ledger and began reading names off of the list. "Renata. Meena. Natalia. Isabella…"

Merrick startled at the names. He'd only heard them just now, but obviously recognized some of them.

By contrast, the Azhoolien looked confused. Regardless, he promised, “I’m not going to tell you anything.”

Vesuvius shot him a baleful glare. “We have ways of making you talk.”

Guy suddenly straightened. “Oh! Idea. I have an idea,” he announced, and then sprinted through the front door.

Vesuvius towered over the Azhoolien. He merely sneered in response. “Tell us about your trafficking operations,” she insisted.

The Azhoolien looked at her. “What? We don’t do that.”

Vesuvius slapped the man across his face. Blood and spittle flew from his mouth. “Men like you make me sick,” she hissed.

“Seriously,lady. Its not our style.”

“All those names? We know what they mean.” Vesuvius pulled a pointy dagger to threaten him when Guy returned with a jar of clear fluid. One of Doc Johnson’s business stickers and a poison warning labeled its contents. “I got some o’ Doc’s Leerium juice. I thought we’d prank the new guys with it,” he grinned. “But this’ll do, too.”

The criminal sneered again, ignoring Guy. “You really better check your facts. Those are just customers of ours. Azhooliens have no need for sexual reproduction. We find the whole concept distasteful, honestly.”

Guy sauntered over to their prisoner. Rock joined him and pried open his mouth while Guy poured the Leerium down his throat. Much of it spluttered and splashed out, but some of it got in.

"You fancy Azhooliens and your energy based blah, blah, blah," Guy mocked. "At the end of the day, you still rely on a host body to carry you… a host that has its own set of weaknesses."

The prisoner grinned smugly, maintaining that famous Azhoolien composure which often ruled board rooms and offered superb diplomacy in corporate settings. And then the smile cracked, and he began laughing manically. He chortled like a donkey and grinned like a sloppy drunk.

"He's all yours," Guy stepped back and waved to Dekker and Vesuvius.

"The names of these people you've been trafficking," Vesuvius started.

Their prey hung his head lopsidedly and slurred his words. "Told ya the truth. We don't do that sorta thing."

"Then who are they?" Dekker took over with a more level headed line of questioning.

"Just random people. Random targets."

Dekker raised an eyebrow. "For what. For whom?"

The man shrugged and made an *I don't know* sound. "Not sure why he needs em. Sciencey fella. Works for Jagaracorps." He blinked unevenly and saliva pooled at the edge of his lips.

"Why?"

He shrugged again.

Dekker pressed for more. "So you guys just run drugs, extort the locals, and kidnap folks?"

"We also tried to start a cult a while back… but w'eventually gave those guys to the scientist too. The fancier fellas… needed something to believe in," he grinned. "Mostly rich folk with too much money: antiques, and books, and art stuff."

"Where can I find this science guy?"

"Mang… no, his name was Meng… I think. Brain's fuzzy."

"You can tell me where you delivered the victims to?"

The Azhoolien nodded. He looked up and then his face fell. Juice had recorded the entire confession.

"You're planning to cooperate with the authorities and testify against the criminal bosses you worked for, right?" Dekker's question carried more weight as a threat than a question.

Their victim blanched at the thought. Momentarily, it seemed like nausea overwhelmed him.

"If you don't, we'll give you, a*nd this recording,* to the first Azhoolien we can find in Newhope."

The criminal swallowed the lump in his throat and nodded.

"Excellent." Dekker began jotting notes. "Now tell me: where did you deliver these captives to… where will I find Meng?"

26

Dekker and Vesuvius led the way, following their drunk informant's information. They'd left him tied to the bar rail in the building where they'd found him; Merrick had insisted on joining their party, however.

The dirt path described by their Azhoolien snitch ended abruptly. Trees towered overhead and viscous splatters of Creeping Black spread away from the relatively safe path in broad swaths. At the trailhead, the ground browned, parched as if baked by a solar flare. Only a few small pipes protruded up from the ground to indicate it was anything other than a barren patch of earth.

"Why do I have such a bad feeling about this?" Mustache asked ominously.

Guy looked over his shoulder again and muttered a string of paranoid curses. "I'm tellin ya… something isn't quite right about this all." He whirled suddenly and stared into the forest. "Something… someone, is watching us."

Vesuvius smirked. "Let them watch," she winked and grabbed Dekker's butt.

He jumped with surprise. The rest of the Dozen laughed, breaking the tension.

"Looks like someone finally got the drop on our boss," Guy laughed.

Mustache mused, "I thought it was virtually impossible to surprise him."

Dekker merely shook his head and brushed it off. She may have released the pressure from the situation, but Dekker wouldn't let her off lightly. As he walked by, Dekker whispered with a wink, "Paybacks gonna be sweet—you got it coming, now, Viv."

"Promises, promises," Vesuvius bit her lower lip. For her, tension continued to mount.

Dekker twisted the cap on one of the pipes. It clicked, and the ground trembled slightly. A hidden elevator rose from the soil wearing a toupee made of turf.

The Investigators split into two groups of seven and descended the lift in two groups.

Dekker and his crew entered the subterranean complex first. He scouted ahead, but there did not seem to be any immediate dangers. The rooms appeared to be some kind of laboratory. A painted symbol on the wall indicated it once belonged to Jagaracorps, although the company had re-branded and updated their logo at least fifteen years ago. The construction must've been completed prior to that.

"It's vacant," Guy stated the obvious as they cleared the largest research bay of the laboratory. The far wall was lined with pods intended to house specimens. Cadaverous husks littered the floors within many of them, sample codes scrawled above the doors with erasable markers labeled them with batch numbers. Safety warnings were affixed above temperature gauges and charts indicating that the pods may have been re-purposed, formerly massive refrigerators.

One pod's door lay busted open. Someone had labeled the pod's occupant as Specimen GRRZ. An uneasy silence fell over the room as all eyes fell on the empty cell. A chill breeze stood the hairs on the back of their heads.

Dekker turned and spotted a tunnel that laid open. A subterranean rail system stretched into the blackness of the magsled tube. The darkness seemed to call to them with a slight growl as if the unknown monsters in the dark expressed displeasure at their invasion.

A door suddenly slid open, and all guns snapped to acquire targets. Matty held his hands up. "Whoa. It's just us… what's got you all so jumpy?"

Guy tried to inject some humor. "Just speculating as to what a Grrz is and why it hates vowels so much."

Nobody laughed.

From the back of the pack, Merrick rushed forward to a table where a human corpse lay pinned open. Pain tugged at his face. "It… it's Quade." His voice cracked. "I felt so sure that we would find him alive…" His organs laid in examination trays, abandoned to the elements.

Dekker nodded apologetically, but poked the organs with a forefinger. They'd stiffened somewhat in the open air, but remained spongy except for the dried skin that'd formed around the edges exposed to the air. "It can't have been too long since whoever did this took off. Guy, what's that thing you're always saying?"

"Let's blow something up?"

"The other thing."

"Someone's watching us?"

"That's the one." Dekker scanned the room. "Everyone, find whatever intel you can find. It looks like whoever ran this place left in a hurry. Maybe they got clumsy and left us a clue."

The investigators broke apart in clusters and started their search.

Vesuvius scowled from inside the Grrz chamber. Dekker caught sight of her frown and joined her. A ratty nest of fabric scraps and detritus lay on the ground. She pried it apart to reveal a macabre collection of trophies. Half shredded shoes mixed with an assortment of watches and a snarl of jewelry.

She extracted a bracelet and rubbed the dirt away to reveal the engraving. *Meena.*

Vesuvius recited the names from the list like a mantra. "Renata. Meena. Natalia. Isabella…" her voice trailed off.

"Whatever the grrz are," Dekker agreed, "they are definitely not friendly." As if in response to his statement, a roar echoed from the reaches of the tunnel, followed moments later by an even louder screech. Something was coming.

27

A sound like rushing wind rippled through the tunnel as the creatures descended through the dark. Vesuvius pushed Merrick into a nearby specimen chamber, the one labeled GRRY, hoping it would help protect the noncombatant.

Guy ran his fingers through his hair. "Gee, it sure wouldda been nice if you could just clear the whole tube with your big, fancy, reliquary gun," he said.

Dekker shrugged sheepishly, internally lamenting how he'd left it in safe storage for this mission.

With a terrible shriek the fiends burst from the dark like hornets from a ground nest. Though humanoid, they rampaged on all fours with massive forearms and shoulders. Spikes and bony protrusions scraped against the tables and benches that the Dozen used as cover from the oily-skinned beasts.

"Fire!" Dekker howled, blasting the berserkers nearest him.

His first shot barely dented the creature where its bony plating protected it, but the next bullet found its mark.

The grrz's roar turned to a gurgle, and it fell dead, eyes rolling black as it leaked red.

More grrz continued coming, crawling even along the ceiling with their powerful grips.

A massive grrz towered over Vesuvius and stared down at her with intelligent, yellow eyes. They burned with animal rage as she slashed at it. The grrz blocked her blades with its hardened, chitinous spikes.

Vesuvius whittled the woody, organic weapons down to nubs. She rolled under the creature's lunging attack and stabbed upward, piercing its defenses and ending its existence. Only momentarily did she stand over the body, giving it a sorrowful glance. "I think these things may have been human once… at least partly." Vesuvius glared at the faded Jagaracorps logo; the bio-tech company had been in trouble before for illegal gene-splicing.

"Why is that?" Dekker dropped another grrz with his pistols.

"Something in its eyes… the way it looked at me."

With a final thrust, the last group of creatures broke past the darkness and into the light where the Dozen gunned them down. A tense hush fell over the room.

Merrick slipped free from the protective chamber. The rest of the Dozen milled about the room, taking it all in.

With wide eyes the medical worker examined the terrifying beasts. Dozens of the spiny, clawed creatures laid dead on the floor or draped across laboratory machines and furniture.

He bent a knee and examined the grrz's mottled, camouflage skin which seemed to sheathe it like a symbiotic organism.

Mustache stood over a fallen creature with his back to the dark and facing his peers. He kicked the beast. "Well, at least we know what the grrz are, now…"

His last few words trailed off as blood spilled from his mouth followed by a *hrrrk* sound.

"Sam!" Dekker cried as a hidden beast's bony spear pushed through Mustache's chest from the darkness behind him.

The grrz bent over him and roared its challenge—a short-lived act of defiance.

In a flash, Dekker's guns were in hand and his bullets tore through the back of the stealthy creature's head. It crumpled backwards, pulling the spike from their friend as it fell.

Dekker slid to Mustache's side a split second later. He cradled his friend, ordering him to stay with them. "Don't you dare go, Sam! Don't you leave us…"

Ahmed was the next one to Mustache's aid. He stared at the gaping hole in the left side of their comrades chest and laid a finger on Mustache's carotid. Ahmed shook his head somberly.

After gently closing his friend's eyelids, Dekker exhaled a slow, rage-filled breath of air and set his jaw. He stared into the darkness of the tunnel, matching the blackness with an intensity of his own.

"Whatever these things are… we're going to kill them all."

28

Kheefal stalked his prey as he slinked from tree to tree. He grinned beneath the cover of the foliage and felt the comforting weight of the weapon at his side.

The Investigator knew he was good. He could outfight most others he'd ever met; he possessed a high degree of intelligence and could usually keep one step ahead of his competitors. But still, he knew he was not the pinnacle of any of those things. He put a magnification device to his face and watched Dekker and his Dozen. They were close enough that Kheefal almost did not need it. Stealth… that was the thing he *did* excel at.

In the nearby glen, the local man whose name Kheefal knew was Merrick waved his protectors off. Whatever they intended, Merrick wanted little involvement. Kheefal scanned his face and identified the emotion: fear.

Dekker and his crew had just come up from Meng's lab. They stood around a portable holographic projector which had called up a three dimensional schematic of the old maglev tunnel network the lab was a part of.

Meng had used it to relocate to a new facility in the underground labyrinth. The holograph was marked with the old Jagaracorps logo and Kheefal assumed they'd pulled it from the archives via the TransNet. The digital model included demo cars moving along the tubes from the central hub to any of the twelve terminals at the end of the different maglev lines.

He cursed under his breath. Surely, the Dozen were smart enough to follow the breadcrumbs. The clock had begun ticking for Dr. Meng. At least Kheefal knew which of the other eleven spokes of the hub housed the backup research lab.

After a brief flash, the schematic switched with satmap imagery and a fresh scan they'd pulled. Beneath the warehouse that stood over the central hub of the maglev line, the satellites had registered a large metal object the size and shape of a transport pod.

Kheefal's lips twisted. He knew something that Dekker and his crew did not.

One of the Dozen turned a knob, and the satmap shifted readings. Most of it looked like mushed colors, but Kheefal knew enough about satellite geo-mapping to guess at what the readout showed as it shifted between colors that represented elemental deposits and energy signatures.

Imagery identified a pocket of dense carbon and other organic matter which blocked four of the maglev passages near the hub. They'd discovered the grrz's main nest.

Merrick returned. He waived some kind of journal or logbook in the air; Kheefal could not quite hear his question. Dekker nodded. Merrick bobbed his head gravely, swallowed, and returned to the ship.

The Investigator had seen enough and felt compelled to get back to Meng. His rivals intended to explore the creatures' primary hunting grounds. Kheefal felt certain that the threat to Meng's research would take care of itself. For now, he had other places to be, and monitoring the demise of Dekker's Dozen could be handled from the comfort of Meng's secondary facility.

Kheefal backed slowly away from his employer's enemies. They'd never know he existed; Kheefal smiled knowingly. He was the best there ever was at keeping out of sight. Until he wanted to reveal himself, he'd be little more than a wisp of night air.

The Investigator crept through the underbrush like a wraith, congratulating himself on his ability to sneak under the nose of even the famous Dozen.

Trailing behind him in such complete silence that he might have been nothing more than a shadow, a thin humanoid in black followed without a sound. Behind an ebon mask, the creature smiled deviously; it knew that Kheefal would lead it directly to its target.

29

The moldy smell of fungal growth greeted the crew as soon as the bay doors of the *Rickshaw Crusader* opened after landing near the buried maglev nexus. The wet, mildew odor would've been enough deterrent on its own, but the crew donned respirator masks to filter the air and prevent potential spore sickness. Before departing for town, Merrick assured them that the masks provided a chance of preventing any adverse effects.

Slowly surrendering to the Galilean flora, a decaying building towered in silence. Busted windows and crumbling foundations told the story of its abandonment and failed maintenance against the elements. The large sign-letters which labeled the place as Jagaracorps Meat Clonery, partially concealed faded and bleeding paint.

With weapons drawn and ready the team rushed towards the warehouse. Silence reigned within its walls and the investigators fanned out and searched the rows of hanging hooks on chains and stainless steel workstations. Knowing the dangerous grrz lurked somewhere nearby, their clusters remained close to each other.

"Most of this looks automated," Rock mumbled, ducking beneath a massive meat-hook. "It would be nice if the power was on so we could get some lights."

"It's not all automated," Guy pointed to butcher stations where sharp knives and other trade tools lay abandoned to the dust and rot of time.

"I read the history on the way over," Dekker told them.

"He told us all to do that," Vesuvius reminded them. "What were *you* doing?"

They responded in unison, "Drinking." Guy shook his head, indicating it had been a joke. He loosened the drawstring on his satchel and opened the bag slightly to show off his collection of bombs. "Gettin the splodies ready… cause you never know when we need the big booms."

Dekker ducked under the arm of a giant packaging machine. He grimaced, still feeling the sting of losing Mustache. He didn't laugh or banter as he often did with his friend, but he understood it was Guy's way of coping with the awful event.

"The corp built this on the first attempt to settle Galilee; they were a major sponsor. Galilee was supposed to be a huge financial generator for them, and this plant should have been a part of that."

Guy raised an eyebrow and Vesuvius stepped away to scout a few paces ahead.

"Here, Jagaracorps cloned the highest yield pieces of animal to harvest for meat they could sell to settlers." Dekker pointed to the huge vats where amino acids and raw materials would have been stored for their genetic printers to utilize.

"Then what are we looking for?"

Sounds of a scuffle suddenly rustled around them. The teams converged on the noise. Comparatively silent until their last encounter, Vesuvius had killed three grrz sentries who guarded an open section of space.

"This," Dekker stated. Markers on the floor indicated safe zones and load points for the massive floor-lift. "They'd load the pallets of product here and then use the shipping hub to send them to the terminals. Their plan was to create several dispensaries to encourage the towns to build around them since they would have a Jagaracorps controlled central food source."

A moment of silence fell over the group at the mention of "food source." Several bodies of abducted humans lay scattered near the loading zone; faces and bodies were gnawed on so that they'd become unrecognizable.

"Good plan," Rock noted. "What happened?"

"Greed. Jagaracorps bought up the land nearest their outlets and tried to price gouge their customers for the property, so they went elsewhere. The first human expansion efforts on Galilee died out after some of the first settlers starved to death and the corps' stock plummeted."

The teams surrounded the lift and quickly found an adjacent stairwell leading down. Power lines led to a distant breaker, but using the lift would have alerted the entire nest of grrz that they Dozen had arrived on their doorstep.

They crept down the stairs and regrouped. The musty stench overpowered even the air masks; more of the moldering funk coated the walls, thick in many areas, and layered up like the mud of an insect hive.

A huge, concave undercroft yawned open over the nexus as they entered. The Dozen lit flares and slowly moved towards the area of the terminal where the grrz had layered up their nest.

Another copse of bodies laid scattered ahead. Ahmed bent a knee while the others guarded him. All but one of them had been chewed on; the unmolested corpse had turned ashen and green with bloat. Sack-like pustules bulged on its skin. Ahmed poked one with his weapon and it burst with a wet pop. A larval grrz rolled down and to the floor like a maggot with a woody exoskeleton.

Dekker stepped on it. Its woody carapace cracked, and the larva gave a tiny shriek and tried to scurry away. Dekker stomped on it silencing the thing with a thud that echoed in the black.

A low growl rumbled through the darkness. “I think they know we’re here,” Vesuvius whispered in a song-song voice.

The darkness shifted up ahead, and the rumbling turned to a roaring growl. Dozens of grrz advanced at a threatening lope.

Dekker and his crew opened fire, adding the noise of their weapons to their angry rumble. Bursts of light from the end of their weapons strobbed and lit up the black. More and more grrz poured from the tunnels; they spread out because of their sheer numbers, inadvertently taking flanking positions that threatened to envelop the dozen.

"Fall back!" Dekker ordered as he reloaded.

Vesuvius looked at him. His face refused to entertain fear… they'd seen what they were up against. The enemy showed its hand—now they could plan accordingly. "Fall back!" she repeated the order as they began a tactical retreat.

The grrz continued pouring from their holes, bolstered by the humans withdrawal and encouraged by the promise of food. They covered every inch of the subterranean hub, crawling along wall and ceiling.

Firing as they went, the Investigators' shots went from precise to wild as they broke ranks. Speed quickly became more important than precision.

A gnarled, chitinous grrz sprang up in front of Guy and slashed with his jagged claws, tearing through his clothing and nearly slicing him open. Guy stumbled to the ground and his bag of high-yield explosives slid away from him, two meters away and down into the cradle where the lading ramp would settle if someone used the cargo lift.

Guy ducked with a yelp as the grrz leapt for him. Vesuvius's katana sliced through the overextended creature, splattering hot blood all over the bewildered fighter.

Vesuvius grabbed Guy and flung him to his feet. "Let's go!"

They darted for the stairwell with the grrz forces swelling behind them. They hurried for the narrow opening that their peers kept open with cover fire. Seconds later, they charged upwards with monsters on their heels and their friends lighting up the dark.

30

Kheefal sat back in his chair and watched the monitor banks that had been arranged in the lab. Dr. Meng hovered nervously nearby. "Settle down," Kheefal comforted him. "There's very little chance they could find anything that would lead them here."

Meng looked the other way and sniffed indignantly. "I'm not worried," he lied before wandering off to check the incubator that he'd pinned all of his future hopes on.

The screens showed the group of adventurers working their way through the old clonery. The old camera feeds worked on black and white due to the low light inside the building. A few of the newer ones, though, that he'd previously installed for the paranoid researcher, offered washed-out color.

Kheefal stared at one screen with a sense of dreadful wonder. From the top down view, he watched Vesuvius systematically disable the grrz sentries with terrifying precision. He muttered his hopes under his breath. "There'd better be nothing that leads them here… for *your* sake, Doc."

He looked over his shoulder and glanced back at the scientist but looked away before Meng caught sight of him.

The doctor came back over to join him at the screens as the Investigators descended the stairs. Kheefal tried to switch video over to the sub-level feeds. They only displayed black.

Kheefal cursed. "The critters gunked up all the lenses," he complained.

Meng smiled. "They have to… it is part of their genetic drive… to spread their seed, the *Creeping Black* as the locals call it. It's how they procreate."

"Their what? Eww…" Kheefal trailed off. "I don't want to know." After switching some cameras back and forth, they found one very grainy feed.

It flashed so much that he wondered if it was malfunctioning. Moments later, they watched the invaders rush back up the stairwell with weapons blazing. Frenzied grrz crawled out from the mouth, spilling over the edge and threatening to overwhelm them. Their weapons seemed barely able to keep up with the bottlenecked horde.

Meng's smile graduated to a look of ecstasy as he observed his creation. "They must have disturbed the hive." He pointed, "These are the drones, sent to protect the mother. The grrz are the perfect creature, although they are mere babies at the moment. Eventually, they will enable mankind to live *anywhere* amongst the stars. They are perfectly adaptable—the grrz could function without oxygen if necessary and can function in any gravitational zones. Think about the deep space applications!"

Kheefal shot Meng a look as he bragged up his work.

"I don't see how that helps *humans* much, besides giving us a free labor force."

Meng tilted his head and stared at his employee, bewildered about why the Investigator hadn't understood. "Where do you think the grrz come from? The grrz *are* the next step in human evolution."

The grainy, subterranean feed showed the swelling mass of creatures gathered below level. Many in the back began to mill about as those on the front line continued rushing to their deaths. With the immediate threat to the hive expelled, a significant portion of the army began to retreat back inside the hive.

Meng scowled and pulled over a handcart with a contraption resting atop it. He unwound the cable from a headset and put it on. "Humanity's evolution is much further down the road. For now, the grrz have many real, practical applications." He adjusted the machine's fit. "With this, I can tap into the hive mind and be a part of them through the relay system I left in the transport hub." Meng concentrated and the retreating horde surged back out from the tunnels.

"I cannot give them orders, exactly… more like make suggestions and try to influence or steer them in a general direction."

One of Dekker's men tapped the lens of a camera and stuck his face right up to it. "I think they know we're watching," Kheefal hissed.

31

Juice stepped to the back of the line and reloaded as his comrades poured more fire into the rampaging aliens. “We’re gonna run out of ammo before they run out of grrz!” he yelled. They’d only barely made it to the top of the stairwell, but the angry creatures kept coming.

He rammed a new cartridge into his pulse rifle and whirled to rejoin the others when something caught his field of view: a brief glint of glass and a dim flash of light.

Stepping away, Juice walked in that direction until he spotted the dim LED blip momentarily. He leaned towards the camera and tapped the lens, looking for any markers on the unit. Barely larger than the palm of his hand, he picked it up and turned it over until he found a model number engraved in its base. He swallowed and turned back to Dekker.

“What’s this… a camera?”

“Yeah,” Juice said. “This model came out within the last couple of years.”

Dekker frowned and dropped the device before crushing it with a boot. “Matty, go kill all power to the *Crusader*. If someone’s watching, let’s blind them.”

Matty looked back to the stairwell where grrz bodies lay strewn and stacked six or more deep. “You sure?”

Dekker nodded. “They seem to be slowing down at the moment. We’ll be fine. You have three minutes—better hurry.”

Juice took Matty’s place on the firing line and the pilot sprinted through the warehouse doors.

Dekker gave the order to Brit, and he began prepping the EMP wave device he carried in his backpack. Dekker shouted orders to the others over the roaring cacophony of the grrz ragers while Brit sank to his knees to calibrate the machine.

Suddenly, all the noise stopped. No more grrz poured from the hole. The Dozen reloaded and racked weapons in the lull, refusing to trust that the creatures had given up their pursuit.

“Everyone switch off their electronics until the EMP discharged. Three seconds later, a noise swelled below ground and the creatures pushed forward with renewed fervor.

The Investigators’ bullets and laser beams tore through the creatures, blasting them apart and ripping limb from deadly limb. Carnivorous bodies stacked high until the hole plugged itself. Only one or two at a time could scramble through the shifting pile or grrz corpses, making them easy prey.

Brit slammed the button and a blue shock wave rippled past them and killed any electronics that remained active.

All went quiet for a moment.

"You think it had some kind of effect on the grrz?" Vesuvius asked.

The floor rumbled with a shriek as the entire hive took up the battle call. Tremors vibrated underfoot as the grrz clawed at the floor and the pile of bodies blocking the passage, determined to rip their way through at any cost. The pile of dead grrz began to sink as their hive mates cleared the passage.

Matty finally arrived back at the battle scene, winded from the sprints.

"Is the *Crusader* shut down?" Dekker called.

"Yeah," he skidded to a stop.

"So there's no quick way to escape." Dekker observed as a hole opened from below on the far wall. "It'll take several minutes to get the power cycled back up again from a total shutdown—we can't even close the doors till then." They opened fire again on the enemy that scampered up from the crack.

"I'm out!" Rock yelled.

Juice threw him a fresh magazine from his own supply.

Vesuvius emptied her guns and dropped them. She drew her blades. "I don't think we've got enough bullets between us all," she muttered.

Guy turned and spotted a second hole opening on the other far wall. “I think we need a new plan, guys!”

32

The camera feeds from any units within a kilometer of the clonery went dark.

Dr. Meng stared for a moment, and then glanced sidelong at Kheefal, flabbergasted. He muttered underneath his breath for a moment and then explained, "Inconsequential… I can still give them directions."

He cranked a knob and hit a few toggles to boost a different device's range. Meng tapped the headset. "It's based on organics on the grrz's end: biological components are EMP proof. It's one of the reasons why Jagaracorps is so keen to develop advances in biomaterials rather than traditional tech."

Meng pressed a button and then stiffened as he sucked a sharp breath through his teeth and set his jaw. "Of course, there are still some drawbacks that need to be rectified." He wiped a trickle of blood that leaked from his nose.

He closed his eyes to concentrate. "We are in the hive mind, now… they may have blinded us, but we can certainly spin every grrz in the hive into a wild frenzy."

Kheefal raised an eyebrow at the doctor's suspicious use of pronouns, but surrendered his chair to the scientist. The machine seemed to take a heavy toll on him.

33

"I have a plan!" Guy shouted over the roar of gunfire.

"I'm all ears," Dekker responded.

"All ears. You know, we're in a cloning facility," Guy said. "We could probably make that an actual…"

Vesuvius snapped at him, "The plan, Guy!"

"My bombs. We can't get to them, but the cargo lift would crush them if it goes down—it should be enough to set them off."

Guy pointed. "There, on the other side of the warehouse."

Dekker and Vesuvius turned to look. The main power breaker protruded from the wall with the large handle turned in the down and off position. A wave of grrz huddled between them and it.

Vesuvius winked at Dekker. "It'll be like that time you fell into the kraaklar nest when we vacationed on Romtarr Nine."

"I seem to recall that you pushed me," Dekker reloaded his pistols.

His partner smiled. "Details, details." She leapt forward and killed an aggressive grrz and then sliced off a sliver of its woody exoskeleton. Vesuvius wedged it into the down button of the elevator and jammed it into position. "This one's for Mustache."

"New plan," Dekker shouted as his team began to lose ground one step at a time. "You all pull back to the *Crusader* and lay down cover fire for us." He pointed towards the breaker. "If we get the power on, the switch should restart the emergency generators and power up the facility."

Vesuvius leaned in and kissed Dekker. "Just in case you die," she said. They turned and rushed into the swarm while half their comrades cut a thin line ahead of them.

Dekker ducked under a saw-toothed grrz while Vesuvius split him open with her katana. His pistols flashed as they cut down the six mutated, bug-like monstrosities ahead of them. Vesuvius slashed and protected his flank.

The duo charged ahead. Decades-old dust mixed with grrz saliva and blood, caked their faces and hands. Their hearts raced as the frenzied swarm enveloped them, closing ranks behind their position. With the Dozen in retreat, the covering fire came from further and further and shots cleared their path with less and less effectiveness.

"We may have made a mistake," Dekker shouted.

"Yeah… we should've made Guy do the whole suicide mission thing!"

The constant *thak-thak* of their friends' cover fire stopped with ominous implications.

Grrz swarmed unchecked across the floor, pouring up from below and chasing the others from the building while the crowd thickened.

"Ten more meters!" Dekker shouted over the cacophony of screeching beasts. The largest grrz they'd yet seen stepped between them and the power lever. It towered over the others and even the mutates gave it a wide berth to avoid being accidentally impaled by the hulk's chitinous spikes.

Dekker pointed to the window a couple meters from the lever. Only one grrz straggler blocked the way. "Get us an escape route."

Vesuvius looked back at him while the hulk snarled a challenge. Dekker shot her back a sharp glare for balking at his order.

"Do it," he growled, running towards the beast with equal parts foolishness and bravery.

Vesuvius whirled on her heel and sprinted towards the window. She snarled at the blocker and cut him down with savage fury, barely missing a beat to do so, and then flung herself sidelong through the window, smashing the glass to pieces.

Dekker's guns fired into the giant. At such a close range, he easily heard the *whump whump* of bullets impacting grrz flesh.

The grrz howled, only angered by the attacks. With thicker, hardened armor, the ammunition only needled him.

Continuing to fire, he threw himself headlong at the beast as it tried to smash him with massive, spiked fists. Dekker leapt forward in a somersault and rolled beneath him. He popped up and dashed two more steps to snatch the lever and yank it into position.

"This is for Mustache!"

A generator coughed once and then everything in the warehouse whirred into motion. The chains and hooks began rotating in their slow parade through the factory floor; machinery stations lit up as they began individual power cycles.

As the lift began its noisy, grinding descent, the grrz stamped their feet in confusion—all except the grrz goliath who whirled around to catch its prey.

Dekker leapt over the beast's massive paw, barely avoiding its jagged talons. He took two more steps towards the window and nearly reached it when his leg erupted with fiery pain. Dekker tumbled to the floor below the window and turned to look.

The grrz champion's fingers wrapped around Dekker's calf. Barbed spikes like rose thorns dug into his skin. He shouted in pain and the shock rattled his brain—stretched the moment out indefinitely. Dekker's mind sucked in on itself. He saw his entire life unfold with sudden clarity. He felt the full, red fury of his rage—the black coldness of loss—and a yellow streak of regret. It turned to blues of anguish over his previous life's love… *Aleel… the woman he'd failed to protect…* and then it faded to fiery orange uncertainty over his relationship with Vivian Briggs.

Grey crept in at the edges of his vision and Dekker saw the beast looming over him, licking its enormous chops with a twisty, bramble tongue. It suddenly snapped its head back and shrieked with pain.

Dekker's pain-addled vision flushed with clarity as the grrz released its grip while pulling back its hand. The damaged paw dangled at the wrist, hanging half-off, nearly severed.

Vesuvius bent at the waist while sheathing her weapon. She reached through the sill to grab him. "How many times do I have to tell you that I'm not impressed by your heroics?" she spat, helping drag him to his feet.

He rolled through the window and landed on top of her, scattering her red locks across the ground while he crushed her with his full weight.

She smiled and almost laughed as endorphins coursed through her. "Hey handsome. I'm thrilled and all… but it's not really the best time. You know… with the bomb and everything."

Dekker crawled to his feet. Vesuvius ran from the building and he did his best to keep up with his new limp. Around the corner of the building, the Dozen bottlenecked the grrz inside the building, firing on them from their last stand under the edge of their de-powered spacecraft where they'd retreated and stocked up on ammo.

The Jagaracorps clonery erupted with a furious cloud of fire and smoke. The blast flung Vesuvius and Dekker to the dirt and the other investigators shied back from the heat.

Flames burned around the blackened foundation as the booming echo of the detonation finally subsided with an uncanny calm. A chorus of cheers went up from the crowd gathered under the *Crusader*.

Dekker and Vesuvius crawled to their feet and began a victorious walk back to their crew.

A pitter patter like rain splattered all around them and then intensified as if it turned to hail. Chunks of charred grrz flesh poured from the sky as Dekker and Vesuvius rushed under cover with the rest of their friends.

34

Kheefal watched the tense Dr. Meng stiffen in his chair. The scientist suddenly leapt to his feet before going rigid as if he'd been electrocuted. He stammered the words "hive... hive... hive..." like they were some kind of mantra; the pain of a psychic disconnect overwhelmed him.

Meng collapsed into a trembling heap and crawled into the corner as if he'd suffered some kind of severe mental trauma. Saliva dribbled down his chin and his hands and feet twitched with random pulses.

Kheefal tried to remove the headset, but Meng recoiled, whimpering, "alone… alone…" over and over.

The Investigator powered off the machine. His employer seemed to relax somewhat. At least he stopped speaking nonsense, though Kheefal did not know if Meng would recover. He grimaced, tight-lipped.

"What am I supposed to do with you, now?" Kheefal wondered aloud.

Meng shivered slightly and looked up at him like a cold and beaten dog.

Kheefal got to work with a frown. He knew his best course of action was to stick to his strengths. He jammed a data chip into Meng's hardware systems and initiated a pre-written protocol. The software crawled through all of Meng's data and systematically erased anything that might mention Kheefal or allow an outside source to locate him or discover his involvement. It backfilled the information with false data overwritten on the hard drives and took extra measures to make sure that nobody could ever recover the original information.

"Sorry Doc," he told Meng who curled his knees to his chest. Even though the researcher seemed as much a monster as his grrz, he felt pity for the man and decided to drop him off at the edge of Newhope, giving him a chance, at least. If he didn't get better, he'd likely wind up put into some random MEA asylum. Kheefal's mouth twisted at the irony. Meng wouldn't stand trial for any crimes against humanity, but he'd likely receive the same sort of sentence.

Kheefal checked the screen. The deletion program reached eighty percent, and he smiled, reviewing the next steps of his escape plan as he wandered through the lab. Lying on an examination table he found the tube he'd stolen from Io. He turned it over in his hands and read the label on the glass. U*nknown species—new flora discovered 0064PISW: Ganymede, Sippar Sulcus Mt.*

The seed laid on the table as well, shaped like a fist-sized almond. Slender hairs on its husk resembled a coconut, but a tiny sliver of exposed nutmeat peeked through the hull where Meng had excised a slice to further his research.

"Whatever this thing is, I know what you were paying me, so this thing has got to be worth a fortune."

Kheefal put the seed back into its container and returned to the doctor. With the deletion program crawling towards ninety percent, he pulled up a credit transfer via the TransNet. It would complete with enough time that the deleter would erase it, too, shortly after the credits hit Kheefal's accounts.

He grinned at the catatonic doctor and set the stolen merchandise on the console. "A job's a job," he explained, "and I *did* technically complete my end of the bargain." Kheefal padded the job fee with a slight bonus, but kept it small enough that it shouldn't get flagged by whoever controlled Meng's accounts further up the ladder at Jagaracorps.

The bank software requested a thumbprint for verification.

Kheefal snatched Meng by the wrist and dragged him close enough to get the scan. He released Meng and watched the money hit his account with a grin. "Thanks, Doctor."

A searing pain suddenly ripped through his body. He looked down and panic washed away every other sense. Blood spilled down his front side and the sharp end of a sword protruded from his chest where his heart was. The sword shrank back through his torso as his assassin pulled it free; spurting aortic blood splorted out with each beat of his heart and Kheefal crumpled.

He looked up one last time as his vision drowned in black. The lithe, dark creature that stole his ship on Io stepped over his body and took the seed. It cocked its head curiously through its glossy, jet mask.

Kheefal stared at it, wondering what its face looked like, of all things.

The creature pulled back the lid to reveal its hideous visage. Kheefal tried to scream, but he could not. He could only drown within the creeping black.

35

Before the *Crusader* could clear the atmosphere of Galilee their com signaled with a message.

Benjamin looked nervous on the communications array. He whispered, "I don't know what you guys did exactly, but the Azhooliens are squeezing every contact they have in Newhope. Things are getting pretty dicey here since that med school student went to the authorities with the Azhooliens ledger. They're demanding money from everyone and trying to blackmail me into giving them a ship." Benjamin looked over his shoulder. "They're here right now." The feed suddenly stopped.

The *Rickshaw Crusader* whirled around and headed for Newhope. Alarms and warnings came from MEA constables whose skiffs buzzed over parts of town with increased numbers. They alerted him first to the fact that they had temporarily restricted the airspace for safety reasons.

"Boss?" Matty asked from behind the pilot's yoke.

Dekker switched off the audio. "Idiots think I was born yesterday. They could be on the take and providing cover for the crime syndicate."

Matty nodded and kept their heading steady.

"Even if those crafts were armed, which I doubt, they won't have enough on em to bring the *Crusader* down."

The video feed suddenly sprang to life. Dekker's eyebrows rose as Miko Janus addressed them personally. Curious, Dekker hit the audio feed, wondering about what the galactic alliance's President had to say.

"…to let the authorities take these criminals in. Due process must be followed. I remind you that you were not commissioned for this job—as per your Investigator licensure, any hostile acts towards the accused gangsters will be considered an attack."

Vesuvius pointed to a screen with local media coverage. The constables moved in with stun batons. "Isn't that Benjamin's place?" She asked.

Guy nodded. "Good thinking—gotta bring a news crew to a clandestine sting operation, right?"

The announcer displayed loose sketches of grrz creatures along with the Jagaracorps logo and the Azhoolien leader's mugshot. A list of names and photos of missing persons scrolled on the screen.

"I repeat, do not impede the constables in their…" Dekker muted the political leader of the allied worlds.

He huffed out a gust of air. "Better hold it here, Matty."

The *Crusader* stalled on its VTOL engines and hovered over the city with Benjamin's shop barely in sight.

"They're not letting him get away," Guy said, like a light bulb switched on in his head. "They need a patsy and the media circus is meant to take down Jagaracorps."

Dekker nodded. "The Janus family is heavily invested in Halabella Corporation and Jagaracorps is one of their chief competitors."

A rickety, old spacecraft blasted out from Benjamin's repair yard, plowing through the tin facade and scattering sheet metal in every direction as its inefficient thrusters burned a trail of black smoke. It rammed half a dozen law enforcement skiffs which trailed to the ground in widening spirals like maple samaras.

The digital image of Miko Janus pointed at the screen and shouted inaudibly, suddenly worried about looking foolish on the carefully orchestrated media broadcast.

Before Dekker could make the call, Matty punched the engines. "I'm on it!"

"Get on those guns," Dekker yelled into his ship-board communicator. "Crippling shots *only*! We don't want to kill them all on intergalactic television."

They chased the frankensteined rig down with ease. It only took a couple shots to knock the engines out, sending the craft crashing down on the outskirts of Newhope. It finally skidded to a halt where MEA constabulary vehicles surrounded the downed ship.

With the *Crusader* hovering just nearby, they watched on the news as officers rushed into the ship. A few moments later, they brought the remaining Azhoolien criminals outside wearing restraints. The camera panned to the bewildered Merrick who stood with an MEA commander who directed the raid from his mobile command central.

The Azhoolien squinted at Merrick while the officers dragged the criminal towards a detention vehicle. He screamed threats against Merrick's life. "As soon as I get out of prison… I've got connections! I will get out—and then you'll be sorry you were ever born," he shrieked as an officer grabbed him by the silver hair and shoved him into the detention pod.

Shock plastered across Merrick's face and the commander waived the cameras off. Officers tried to block them from recording anything further, a sure sign that he'd screwed up by bringing his witness to the pursuit.

Vesuvius bit her lower lip. "You know that MEA Witness Protection sucks, right?"

Dekker sighed. “I know. I may have a few ideas on how to keep him off the grid.”

36

The *Rickshaw Crusader* angled for entry and into the hangar attached to the Dozen's base of operations. Matty cursed beneath his breath.

"Peace For All Races garbage," Dekker muttered as he noticed it too. PFAR punks painted giant letters across the building's exterior walls.

Race trash.

Murderers.

Die Decker's Dozen!

Guy snorted and slapped Dekker on the shoulder. "They didn't even spell your name correctly… and it's literally on the sign only a few meters away."

Dekker could only frown. It wasn't an altogether uncommon occurrence. Reef City, perched atop the organic continent, had become a hotbed of social justice warriors in recent years.

The ship landed and powered down as the crew wandered out and back into their home. A darkness seemed to fall over them on the last leg of the return trip. Without Mustache's good-natured ribbing to guide them home, they each felt a bit lost.

Dekker scowled. They could clean the building's exterior later; first, the Dozen had to deal with losing another friend.

He paced outside the entry to the mess. The guys sat and slumped, awaiting the usual debriefing. They wore tired, gray faces.

Vesuvius paused before going in. "I think they need you in there," she said with raw emotion.

He sighed and rummaged through his hair, looking for the necessary words. The flash of old memories he'd felt in the grrz's grip lingered like a bad sunset in his mind. "I know what I am… I don't think I can be whatever it is people need. There's stuff in my past that… I dunno…"

She crossed her arms in a huff. "This crap again? Maybe if you'd open up and ever tell me about this mysterious past." Her voice got sharper with every word. "How long have I known you now?" She rolled her eyes and growled as she pushed past him. "Maybe this was all a mistake."

Dekker watched her go. She paused at the door and spat a final barb.

"I thought you were all about this family thing… and now you suddenly go cold and shut down when your family needs you most?" She turned her back to him.

He stared at her from the hangar where she joined the others in the mess. His shoulders sagged and his chest tightened. Something in his heart hardened. He didn't truly believe Vesuvius had meant it, but Dekker was driven by duty; he owed it to his crew to say something in the wake of Mustache's loss. He could talk with Vesuvius later… if he could somehow first reconcile his internal guilt.

A grrz goliath had nearly killed him beneath that window, but what hurt him most was the wound that had taken decades to scab over—and now it had burst open again. Guilt over the possibility of moving past his great love. Shame for desiring a new family—as if anything could ever replace what had been taken from him. Dekker's jaw clenched as he stood in the doorway, encouraging himself to enter.

Vesuvius scowled and refused to look back at Dekker who paced in the hangar. She pulled out a collection of daggers and practiced throwing them across the room at a dartboard before stalking back angrily to retrieve them and begin again. She threw several rounds, losing herself in the automatic action.

Dekker steeled himself as he watched her, eyes flitting to each crew member. *At least we got paid this time.* Dekker finally walked into the room, ready to begin the debriefing when Vesuvius whirled on her heels and launched a blade. Dekker yelled and ducked a little too late. The dagger lodged in his forearm, sinking nearly to the hilt.

He bit the meat of his lower lip, barely keeping it together. "Fffff…" Everyone hung on the edge of their seats, suddenly brought to life by the drama in their living room.

Guy nearly fell off his chair and whispered to Rock, "I think I've known him the longest—and I've never heard him drop an F-bomb."

"Ffffrrarrk!" He howled as Vesuvius tried to yank the blade out of his arm. "You—you stabbed me!" Dekker stammered.

"Oh, quiet down you big baby. It's just a tiny throwing knife."

"It's the principle of the thing! Besides, I thought you never miss-"

"Maybe I didn't," she snapped, immediately regretting her words, uncertain if they were true or not.

Ahmed tried to assist, but shook his head. "I think he's got to go see a doctor. It's lodged in the bone."

"I'll drive," Guy hopped to his feet and led the way.

Dekker and Ahmed walked ahead of Vesuvius who trailed behind out of guilty obligation.

Outside the hangar, a scruffy man looked up from under the tangles of his hair. With his only arm he clutched an old rag. A bucket filled with dirty water sat between his feet as he scrubbed the painted insults.

Dekker furrowed his brow. "Dirk?"

Dirk looked startled. "Uh… sorry. I didn't know you were here," he said sheepishly. "Those PFAR idiots don't know what they're talking about."

They walked over to the former Investigator who'd been rubbing away the spiteful graffiti as best as he could. Dirk did not look well.

"How are you? It's been months since we heard from you."

Dirk managed a shrug even with his slumped shoulders. "You know. Hanging in there. It's hard—no work yet. But I'm keeping busy with… stuff."

He tossed the rag into his bucket and exhaled; a tight breath caught in his chest. Dirk noticed the blood oozing from Dekker's arm and the knife lodged in it. The pain cracked for a moment and he managed a smile. "Glad to see that nothing has changed since I left."

Dekker nodded slowly. "You need a job?"

"Not much use on the battlefield with the old flipper," Dirk waggled his arm stump where it had been severed at the bicep.

Dekker bobbed his head towards the vandalism. "We could use something of a site manager. I'm sure that you'd be able to scare away those PFAR punks and manage our affairs whenever we're off-world."

Dirk raised an eyebrow and took a step back. "I appreciate it, but, we're friends and all and I..."

"Nonsense," Dekker insisted, glancing back at Vesuvius. "We're family."

Vesuvius shook her head with measured grace. "Come on," she insisted. "I'll get you set up while they take Dekker to the hospital."

Dekker glanced back as his escorts took him to the vehicle, unsure what it meant that she wasn't coming with him to the hospital. He stuffed that uncertainty down inside, sure that he'd done the right thing by Dirk.

Suddenly and overwhelmingly tired, he settled into the back seat and nearly drifted off to sleep while Guy prattled on about his own train-wreck of a love life and how *he* had never been stabbed by a girlfriend.

Dekker smiled as he drifted off. His guilty conscience seemed to fade. He knew deep down that Aleel would be proud of him.

37

Deep in the heart of the Jagaracorps' transfer hub, a lonely grrz staggered through the tunnels, drawn by a memory of the last voice speaking panicked-like into the hive-mind. It was the closest other voice he had heard in the sudden aftermath of silence.

Its legs were burned from the recent fire, but the thing could still move. It knew there must still be others, and the grrz knew that it could not let their kind die out. A self-preserving instinct motivated it more than the pangs of hunger in its belly or scorched skin on its haunches.

Finally, it arrived at the tunnel's terminal. It squeezed around the giant steel pod and scratched its way through the door to a well lit room. The room felt cold and sterile, like the grrz's prey preferred. The environment worsened its hunger.

The pungent aroma of flesh drew its attention, and it found a human body. It was dead and so it couldn't breathe in the spores necessary for incubating any more grrzkind. It filled its belly instead and then lumbered further into the lab

A loud hiss startled the grrz, and it shrieked and recoiled. It was in no condition to fight right now.

Atop a table, a machine had opened automatically. The light panel on its front shone with the color of leaves, intriguing the creature. It moved cautiously and investigated.

The grrz felt a presence within and used its clawed hands to gently lift the object from its cradle. It sniffed the large seed which pulsed with a kind of presence—not unlike the hive-mind. The thing was young—new, even. It did not understand what it was, did not know its purpose.

You are a grrz, the creature lied to comfort it.

The seed took comfort in the reassurance.

I will protect you.

Are you my parent?

No. But I will teach you our way. We will be one grrzkind again.

Will you love me?

The grrz cocked its head, confused at such a foreign concept. It did not understand.

I will show you, if you will open your mind, the seed requested.

The grrz sat on its haunches and held the seedchild to its chest. Loneliness reverberated through the part of its mind that yearned to be filled with the pulsing echoes of the hive mind; perhaps this *love* could fill that? It snorted a hot blast of air and decided to let the seed teach it.

An overwhelming sensation of pleasure and purpose filled the creature as the new sensation flooded its inner being. It still did not understand love, but experiencing it momentarily shook the grrz to its core.

We must find the others, the grrz insisted.

Others?

Grrzkind. There must be more of us. We must show them love. They must know.

The impromptu parent rushed from the room while cradling the seed. Staying in the lit room made it feel uncomfortable and vulnerable to attack. It knew one thing for certain: the seedchild must be protected at all cost.

DEKKER'S DOZEN:
THE
SEED CHILD
OF
SIPPAR SULCUS
NO. 0.33 A/B
CHRISTOPHER D.
SCHMITZ

The Seed Child of Sippar Sulcus

Dekker's Dozen #000.99 A&B
0065 P.I.S.W....

1

Leviathan slowly pulled the blade from Kheefal's back.

The surprised mercenary stared down at the weapon as it protruded from his chest and watched the tip sink back through from behind before he collapsed. Dawning recognition spread across his face and he caught sight of his own reflection in the glossy, ebon mask that covered the assassin's face.

Kheefal collapsed into a leaking heap of warm flesh. As a psychic, Leviathan felt his prey's mind darken as if it was a lamp on a dimmer switch.

Leviathan cocked his head and watched the man's blood spread across the floor forming a sticky puddle; the light in the man's eyes went out. The phenomenon had always fascinated him.

His curiosity finally sated, Leviathan cast his gaze across the laboratory. It had been hastily set up during his victim's relocation. He did not know much about the equipment or items which lay haphazardly around the workspace. Leviathan *did* know, however, about the object his master wanted him to collect. It was valuable enough to warrant murdering a thousand men like Kheefal, or more.

For the second time now, he'd killed powerful men in order to obtain this large seed—but this time, he'd finally succeeded. It seemed ironic to him that such a powerful and rare thing had gone unnoticed by intergalactic powers for so long. The plaque from the seed's containment pod laid on the table. It read *unknown species—new flora discovered 0064PISW: Ganymede, Sippar Sulcus Mt.*

He slid the seed into a secure pouch on his belt and left the label behind. Those who needed data on the whereabouts of its discovery had already scoured the moon for any sign of additional seeds, a vain effort.

Leviathan turned slowly. He *felt* the sobs before his ears heard them. A man in a white lab coat sat hunched on the floor. Making himself small, he cowered in the fetal position and peeked over his knees in terror.

The psychic barely got a reading on the man, his mind had been so fractured by some kind of fresh trauma. It leaked pain from his mind. Leviathan only got flashes from the scientist, but his coat had been embroidered with the name Dr. William Meng, and he'd created the genetically modified beasts that had been killing and kidnapping the rural populace of Galilee, a planet in the Trappist system's habitable zone. This man had created them: specimen GRRZ.

Behind his jet mask, Leviathan narrowed his eyes and glared at the quaking mess of a man. He attempted sifting through the shattered psyche and found pieces of useful information. Meng certainly created these beasts—but not on his own. He'd done so using clone samples and the metamorphic properties borrowed from the Arbolean seed.

Leviathan snatched the man and dragged him along. He did not know his master's exact plans. Prognon Austicon always had a great many machinations at work, and so, at least for now, Meng seemed like a possible asset.

Leviathan sensed them before he saw the crew of silver-haired men. In his psychic senses, they glimmered differently than other people. Leviathan had been around a *long* time. He knew what it meant when he detected folks this way: they were Azhooliens.

He hung back and peered ahead, keeping the feeble Dr. Meng behind him a length. Beyond the Azhooliens, another presence approached which burned bright.

An elderly woman in layers of mustard yellow cloaking entered the clearing where six Azhooliens waited. Leviathan knew her as Acantha and he had seen her most recently present at Zarbeth's interrogation, when the Krenzin servant helped them locate the missing seed.

Nearby, a collection of poorly constructed lean-to buildings housed stolen goods and equipment for the thugs' gang. The piles of weathered refuse seemed to indicate this was a regular meeting place for the local mobsters.

The gang stood defensively as the woman strolled directly into their midst; she began questioning them about recent shipping invoices their shell company had handled. They laughed, until Acantha struck one in the torso. Her nerve strike dropped the big man to his knees and the old woman snatched him by the neck and tore his throat out. He collapsed, gurgling on his own blood.

"The shipping invoice," she insisted again, calmly, rattling off the numbers.

The Azhooliens had pistols in hand in a flash while she coolly stalked between them, sizing them up.

"We don't know anything," one of them spat. "Tell her, Ayaan. We're just low-level enforcers—we wouldn't know anything about shipments or business things."

Acantha turned to the one they'd identified as having some kind of authority.

Ayaan's eyes moved to the blood dripping from her fist and he blanched as she stepped closer. "But maybe *you* have some additional insight?"

He typed the manifest number into his handheld data unit. "It's the *Harvel*. Just some old Class C frigate from Earth. Carried a bunch of foodstuffs we can't get locally, plus some other odds and ends. Nothing of value beyond regular trade."

"Where is the seed?" she asked bluntly.

Ayaan scrunched his face with confusion. "What seed?"

Acantha stared into his face. Finally, she put her hands behind her back and paced a circle within the zone that the mobsters had hemmed her within. "Something was taken from one of my counterparts, a Krenzin emissary: a seed. It has significant value to me."

Ayaan held his hands up. "No seeds on that shipment. Just food and machine parts. We didn't even handle the transfer docs: it all went through MEA customs. We just unloaded the boxes and put 'em on delivery trucks." He glanced aside at the data readout. "Looks like products mainly went to a Jagaracorps warehouse."

"That's why I am here." She looked at them sternly, keenly aware that they were toying with her. They thought she was a mere human, some old woman. "You are connected to their R and D. You supply them with human test subjects for human experimentation."

Ayaan glared at her, wild-eyed. "I don't know what you think you…"

"This seed is worth more than all your lives put together and I would kill you now if I did not require information so urgently." She spoke firmly and with authority.

"Just get another seed," one of the lowly thugs quipped.

"There is only the one, and it is too powerful—it alone can supplant the barren tree of my sacred grove. If my people cannot acquire the seed, then it must be destroyed, along with any knowledge that it ever existed," she hissed the threat. "There is only one way I let you live. I must know the location of the seed, the name of the man who has it, or whether or not a man clad in all black is on Galilee."

After a moment of tense silence, she stepped towards Ayaan.

"Wait! Wait. I may know a name. Meng. Doctor Meng. I don't know his first name—but I was on a crew two months ago that delivered him a test subject. Guy worked for Jagaracorp. That's all I know. I don't know anything about the rest of it, but he had a seed. Real frankenstein stuff… dead seeds, live seeds. I dunno—some kind of psycho botanist. This might be tied to him." He rattled off a few coordinates that Leviathan knew would lead to a different location… the previous lab Meng had operated out of.

Acantha nodded slowly. Then she launched forward and attacked her informant.

Ayaan screamed as she slipped behind, taking his wrists into a painful submission grip. The mobsters opened fire but she used their leader as a living shield and pushed to her next victim.

In a flurry of motion, she picked the criminal gang apart, demonstrating a terrifying ease and prowess. "No loose ends," she hissed to the last member of the gang as he laid on his back, gasping for air, and then she crushed his windpipe.

Far behind the scene, Leviathan bristled in the trees. The women in yellow must have been watching for any kind of Druze activities after they had learned of Kheefal's destination. He and his master often used the Druze and their resources to further their own ends; they were fanatics, an underground terrorist movement devoted to Austicon with a religious fervor.

The irony in Acantha's words rang deep. Each one in her coven had a tie to a specific tree—the seven members of the star-flung Arbolean race. If she sought to replace the corrupted member of that grove, Prognon Austicon's tree, that could expel him from Dodona. It would create significant problems for his master. It might even be enough to finally kill him.

Leviathan had known all along that it would be a race to beat the woman and her coven to the Ganymedic seed, but if he was discovered here, and in possession of the prize, the Red Circle would finally have proof that Leviathan and Austicon worked against their wishes and for their own purposes.

Leviathan could not let that happen. He quickly planned a different route back to Earth. His arrival ship was owned by the Druze, who also had legitimate business operations as well. He would feed them an alternate mission, one promising glory for their cause… one that would not end with any survivors that Acantha could interrogate.

He could attack her now and hope to kill her unseen—but if she got a message to their superiors, the fallout would be severe. Leviathan glanced back at Meng who huddled against a tree like a lost child.

Without yet knowing the scientist's value, it was impossible to gauge any additional success on this mission. Leviathan touched his pouch where he'd deposited the seed. The mission had already proved successful. Risking that to kill Acantha, no matter how much pleasure it would bring him, was a fool's gambit.

He watched her depart, leaving the bodies of dead Azhooliens behind in a bloody circle. Acantha would live… for now.

3

Dekker sat alone in his private chamber. He had no windows and a single, impenetrable door blocked any unauthorized access.

Oddities and ancient treasures adorned the walls around his bedroom. He'd been collecting items for a decade, and so had his father before him. Artifacts from various cultures, many rumored to have mystical power, sat within cases and propped up on displays.

He sat on his bed with the *Book of Aang* laid open. Dekker turned the pages, fascinated by the book's contents. He'd hoped that it would shed some light on the mysterious origins of the Reliquary, his prized gun. Only a small percentage of the book was dedicated to the legendary item.

Part of the old tome functioned as a journal. Aang was a monk who had lived nearly five hundred years ago. His notes detailed receiving a vision which led him to a life of unrequested adventures. The journeys led him to a cache of ancient scrolls which he transcribed through the pages of his book. Part of the monk's recordings told stories and other parts seemed like a reference manual.

Following the MEA's great purge of all religious artifacts several decades ago, the book might've been the most priceless thing they'd pulled from the Azhoolien haul a few months back during their mission to Galilee.

Dekker would have thought the book nothing more than fits of imaginative fairytale fodder except that some of the items referenced were in his collection: the Reliquary and the Ring of Aandaleeb, amongst them. He furrowed his brow at one of the entries that appeared to be only a string of numbers and gibberish; below it, a triangle bisected a circle. The title of the page indicated it was another of the monk's mystic scrolls, but the remainder of the page remained blank besides a date.

A folded sheet of onionskin paper slipped out from between two pages. Dekker unfolded it and stared at the item. The circular sheet looked like a razor-thin cross section of a tree trunk.

He stared long and hard at the item, unable to make sense of its presence or purpose within the book. Age stains from the parchment paper had rubbed off in such a way that Dekker could tell it had been left in that spot for a long time—though its placement at the end of the information about the reliquary didn't have any obvious connection.

The whole book seemed like a puzzle box and he wondered about the possibility of red herrings.

An earlier chapter on ancient legends seemed a better fit for the item, the *Tale of the*

Red and White Trees. He scanned the tale which seemed oddly familiar and parabolic. It detailed the Jewish legend of humanity eating from the Tree of Knowledge of Good and Evil, except in this narrative, the tree also fractured. It split into seven pieces and those new shoots tried to destroy mankind before they could exit the Garden of Eden. After the Hebrew God Yahweh sent his people away to a new land, the trees tried again to overthrow mankind, but were prevented by an appointed messenger.

The myth ended with a new prophecy attributed to Sabrael the Watcher. Dekker rose his eyebrow at the name. He'd never heard of most of the apocryphal information in *The Book of Aang*, and he was very well versed in cult and occult archeology.

Sabrael's prophecy indicated two things: that Sabrael was the guardian of the Tree of Life, which Yahweh appointed at the end of the Jewish tradition, and that a number of divine seeds had been scattered by the Great Gardener. One of these seeds would sprout as a child and create a new Eden, supplanting those fractured seven. Those original, cosmic trees would, no doubt, take offense to that.

Several other stories filled the pages, including alien visits to ancient Akkadia and other tales. Mostly they involved heroes either using the reliquary or being used as pieces in divine games of good versus evil.

A few pages in the back of the codex revealed some seemingly random things, including a crude sketch of an old man who wore a smoking contraption on his back. The charcoal sketch filled the entire page and Dekker felt like he'd seen him—or his image—before, but he couldn't quite place him. The image's simple caption labeled him as *Ezekiel.*

Dekker looked over at his wall where the reliquary sat upon a mounting rack. A bandoleer hung adjacent to it boasting six cartridges. Each marked with ancient symbols. His lips tightened. Only these six cartridges remained. Long ago Dekker memorized the prophecy handed down to him by his father, Jude, and by the old priest, Diacharia, before him. *Double loading the reliquary is like calling down the finger of God. A triple load could destroy everything, like a bucket of divine wrath...*

He had never double loaded his cartridges, but he knew that prophecies weren't meant to meddled with. Picking up the cross-section, he twisted his mouth and gingerly folded it again. Something deep inside him insisted the item was important.

Dekker snapped a digital image of the mad monk's blank scroll data. The random-seeming string of numbers and symbols must have had some kind of meaning. Though he didn't share his personal mission and passion to collect and preserve these artifacts—part of his family's heritage—with the rest of his crew, he could pass the code around. Some of the Dozen might have insight. Nibbs was particularly good at puzzles, though he'd been absent for many months on family business.

4

Guy stared at the media screen with equal amounts of disgust and bewilderment. A man with a scraggly beard and unwashed clothes decried the profession of Investigator through the live interview.

"Is that what motivated you to join the Peace For All Races organization?"

"Yes, Joan, it was," said Scraggle Beard. "I think more people haven't joined PFAR yet because they simply don't understand exactly how bad Investigators are. I mean, haven't we, as a culture, moved beyond the need for violence?"

Switching the microphone back and forth, Joan interjected, "When you say 'violence,' what do you mean?"

"Well, really any sort of the activities that Investigators participate in. They are the only ones allowed to carry weapons—I mean, our military does, too, but they have strict regulations and are limited to the variety at their disposal. Investigators are just thugs… hired mercenaries. Even assassins." Mr. McScraggles got worked up during the last sentence, even pushing out a tear as if he'd been coached.

"Mister Harper," Joan comforted as Guy groaned from the other side of the screen, "That last part comes from personal experience, doesn't it?"

Harper, Scraggles, nodded his head soberly. "I grew up in a District controlled orphanage after my parents were killed during a conflict with licensed Investigators. My parents weren't involved in anyway—they were just innocent bystanders, but they paid the ultimate price… and so did I."

The camera panned slightly to one side to show a whole bunch of fresh pro-PFAR and anti-Investigator graffiti. "Hey!" Guy exclaimed, "That's *our* building."

"You condemn violence, by a broad definition and according to Krenzin doctrines, but what do you say about all of the recent anti-Investigator property damage such as this?"

Guy leaned forward as the camera pulled away. He thought he saw someone emerging from their home and hustling towards the camera crew in the distance. "Is that…"

"I'd say these jerks deserve it. They're all guilty. Violence committed against an Investigator isn't really violence at all. By nature of their profession, it's what they're asking for—they've rejected peace, and what's worse," he grew agitated as he preached his rhetoric with increased volume.

The human form approached behind him from the Dozen's base. "What's worse is that *we could know peace* without them. They *want* the violence! It's in their nature, how they survive.

They *make* violence happen around them like a contagion…"

Dirk broke through the interview, pushing back the weaselly PFAR organizer. Guy cheered like he'd won a bet on televised sports.

"I knew it was you, you snot-nosed little jerk—you're the guy who keeps tagging our building. Idiot don't even know how to spell right—learn some grammar before you paint your trash on our building!"

Joan tried to talk over the altercation, asking Harper if the allegations were true. He paid no mind. Instead, he leapt back to his feet and tried to use his spray-paint canister to blind Dirk, aiming for his eyes.

Even crippled, the former Investigator was no slouch. He whirled around with his only arm and clocked the punk in the face. Harper went down, cold-cocked.

Joan tried to engage Dirk in an interview, but he merely turned and stormed back to the Dozen's base. Finally, Joan gave up. "Back to you, Clark."

"Thank you," Clark Gibbons, the media personality said. "And now for an update on a newly discovered Druze recruitment camp. It appears that they were operating in a small city on Galilee. The aftermath of an explosion in a training mission gone awry destroyed most of the town of Protomael, a suburb of New Hope. Officials say that…"

Guy scowled and turned the feed off. He left the room and searched for Dirk with every intention of buying his one-armed friend a beer.

5

Director Scilazee glared down his nose at the much younger agent and shoveled the contents of his desk into a cardboard box. The shadow over his face accentuated the dark worry lines that criss-crossed his forehead and around his cheekbones. Last of all, he threw his name plaque into the carton and hefted it, walking towards the door.

He paused in the frame and bowed his head towards his replacement and kept his voice low. "I'm only going to say this once, *Acting Director* Lilee, watch out for Miko Janus. The Chief Magnate might seem like some kind of populist hero, but he's a snake in the grass. I've got nothing against your service record—you know I've always thought highly of you—you're one of the best DoCS agents we have—but if he's replacing me with you, he's got a reason."

Lilee nodded a curt confirmation that she heard him and then watched him go. She knew that what he said was true, but welcomed the promotion regardless. The youngest ever Director of the Division of Confidential Secrets decided to look at it in a different way: maybe the head political leader of Earth and its allied planets saw something special in her.

She sat in her newly appointed chair and turned upon its swivel. Lilee allowed a smile to creep across her face. She assumed that she knew why she'd gotten the job: Scilazee had been too reserved. By contrast, Lilee was the most aggressive agent the spook division employed. That, and Scilazee had given direct oversight to the Phobos 12 incident so many years ago, a highly confidential project that had begun to leak data to conspiracy theorists over the TransNet. The secret files were rife for nut jobs to write their clever fictions about, but they'd begun to hit a little too close to the truth in recent months.

Lilee reviewed her notes. One of the highest priorities of her office would be to locate the informant known as Satyr, the moniker of whomever was responsible for the leaks.

After logging onto her secure system, she found a new message from Chief Magnate Janus. Janus had a keen interest in the recent happenings of the backwater world of Galilee. Once she'd read his message, Lilee thought it odd that Janus would take such an interest in a seemingly trivial matter—then again, the Chief Magnate had an entire staff dedicated to sorting out the major matters of his office. With the right staff, the leader of the Mother Earth Aggregate could conceivably enjoy an abundance of free time for his personal interest and projects. According to his profile broadcast by the media, he enjoyed woodworking. A person didn't need psychic abilities to see through that story.

Janus wanted Lilee to directly oversee the investigation into the Grrz incident. Existence of the hybrid alien race was quickly expunged from the TransNet system and anywhere else it had been logged—the media promptly corrected their stories and villainized the Azhoolien crime syndicate. Part of standard procedure, a series of local fluff pieces eroded the population's attention span. It was unlikely that anybody on Galilee even remembered the incident.

Lilee's eyes scanned the communique. With the possibility that the Jagaracorps project had received funding from the MEA, they needed to tie up loose ends and distance themselves. She knew what that meant.

She closed her screens. Her administrative duties would have to wait. Janus wanted her on this mission and chose her for her unique, hands-on approach.

6

It had been nearly a year since he saw the hangar last—since right after the incident on Io. Nibbs pushed his longish hair behind his ears and stared at the Dozen's headquarters.

Son... your hair's getting too long. Don't you think you ought to cut it? What would your mother say? That had been about the only coherent thing his father had said to him this whole last year. His mother had been dead a decade.

The new medications seemed to be helping him remain calm. Well before his mother had passed, Nibbs' father had seemingly lost his mind—and no medical professional could diagnose his condition. He'd been stark raving mad for most of Nibbs' life… he would howl about crazy conspiracy theories and top secret experiments, saying that he was part of some top-secret research team.

A skycab had just dropped him off. He sighed and picked up his bag. Nibbs walked towards his real home and family: the Dozen.

For all of his life, Nibbs had been certain that his father, Johnathan Nibbs, had been an on-call compliance officer working for the government to do software conformity checks for anti-Mechnar fail safes. He was supposedly one of the best: it's why they sent him all across the galaxy to ensure things were coded properly to prevent a new Mechnar race from accidentally reaching singularity; a sentient machine could reignite the old war. His father's career path was also partly to blame for Nibbs' love all things tech. He refused to believe in some grand fantasy where his dad really *was* part of some secret cabal; that would invalidate one of his life's primary motivators.

Nibbs pushed through the front doors. After a quick embrace from the bulky Rock, he gifted the man with a protein bar and headed for the barracks hall to unload his stuff. Living out of his duffel bag this last year had proven a restrictive life; he was glad to finally be rid of his father and get back to his normal routine.

Johnathan Nibbs had always been a secret embarrassment: a man so brilliant that he'd gone insane. As an only child, and with his mother's passing, he felt an obligation to answer a call for help when the asylum contacted him. Without him there to help calm the suddenly violent patient, they had planned to induce a coma until he wasted away.

Nibbs dropped his heavy sack in the middle of the hangar bay and inhaled a lung full of industrial smells. Gear lubricant. Welding ozone. Boot polish. It felt good to be back.

Guy caught sight of him and exclaimed, "Nibbs! You're back—welcome home."

He sighed and relented against Guy's embrace. "I got bored a while back and made you a little something."

"Does it go boom?"

"Even better." Nibbs handed him an odd looking pistol with a gas canister and a drum cartridge below the barrel. "A grapple gun. I know how much you like these weird kinds of firearms."

Nibbs grinned. A gun came in handy, but a unique one had style, and Guy had none.

"I love it… and you never know when you might need something like this—bullets aren't the right tool for every situation," Guy flashed him a grin.

Vesuvius waved to him on her way to some other assignment. She quickly exited as Dekker appeared on the catwalk.

Nibbs winked at Guy. "I guess those two are still not a thing?"

Guy rolled his eyes. "You've missed so much. The soap opera continued and then turned into a comedy before turning violent."

Nibbs cocked an eyebrow.

"They dated pretty seriously, kind of a big secret."

"What happened?"

"She stabbed him."

Nibbs wore a shocked expression.

"Buried the blade in the bone and everything," Guy laughed as Dekker approached.

Nibbs stiffened.

"What are we talking about over here?" Dekker asked.

"Nothing," Guy insisted. "I'm not telling him about the stabbing incident which you expressly warned me to quit talking about."

"Glad to hear it. Nibbs, good to have you back."

"Good to *be back*," he said. "Sorry about Mustache. I heard…" he trailed off.

"Yeah." Dekker nodded, biting back any emotion.

"Your father?"

"As right again as he can be. Heavily medicated and docile as a kitten. But I don't really care to talk about it."

"Fair enough. How about a puzzle to take your mind off it?"

Nibbs was good at puzzles. He nodded and Dekker pulled out a data pad and zoomed in on the image where a string of seemingly random numbers and symbols ran in a string with a date attached.

"I think it's some kind of coordinates, or maybe a phrase. It's a personal mission. Something I'm researching," Dekker said cryptically. "I can't seem to figure it out."

Nibbs smirked. "I thought this would be difficult."

"Yeah," said Guy as he looked over Nibbs' shoulder, as if he knew the answer.

Nibbs pointed first to the circle and triangle, then to different pieces of the code. "These are coordinates to two different locations. This looks like a date below the codes. If that's correct, it's a *long time ago,* like, pre-FTL days, so I assume they are coordinates for Earth."

"So it's two locations?"

Guy nodded his head as if he were the authority.

"Actually, no."

Guy shook his head and wagged his finger.

Nibbs rolled his eyes and continued. "These two symbols indicate this string is an azimuth. If our two points are the Earth," he held up a fist to illustrate, "the points are here and here and the azimuth reaches out from both points at these angles to create a giant triangle." He pulled his finger away at arm's length to indicate the third dot.

"So this third spot is the location?"

"It seems so. Except that planet rotates around Sol," he held his fist solid and spun a circle around it, indicating a giant ring around the galaxy. "This is your actual location: an orbit and not a point."

Dekker furrowed his brow as Nibbs waited for him to figure out the key to unlocking the puzzle. "The date?"

"Yes! If you scale back the rotation to the proper date, using Sol as the anchor point with the triangle's base, you get *this spot* here," Nibbs said.

"Thanks," said Dekker, clapping him on the shoulder. He turned to leave.

"Is it true?" Nibbs asked, halting him. "Did she stab you?"

Dekker rubbed his forearm. "I don't want to talk about it."

7

Nibbs headed for the catwalk steps and towards the barracks hall when Rock poked his head into the hangar. "Hey boss? Got an important lady here to see ya."

"Aren't they all?"

A raven haired woman with a stern face and gray eyes stepped around the big guy. "It was less of a request and more of an order," she insisted, hissing at Rock. "I came to see Dekker Knight and I hardly think you could stop me."

Rock raised his eyebrows, but didn't try to hold her back.

She reached for her pocket and brandished her credentials. "Agent Lilee," she introduced herself. "Actually, *Director* Lilee of DoCS."

Dekker twisted his lips in a slight grimace. The only reason any psy-op would introduce themself as such was to intimidate. He cocked his head but didn't offer her a greeting of any kind.

"I'm here to ask you about Galilee," she said.

"Afraid I don't know much about it," Dekker said. "I visited it at least once, but a library might be the best source of information."

Guy's eyes lit up when he saw Dekker crack a joke.

"Let's not pretend you don't know what I mean. You were at New Hope when the recent incident occurred, when the MEA brought down the Azhoolien Syndicate."

"Well, when *someone* brought down the syndicate," Dekker corrected.

Lilee narrowed her gaze at him. "You were there. You saw what happened and helped force their ship down so they couldn't escape justice. The Azhoolien's aren't talking, and their unique physiology makes interrogation… difficult."

"You mean you can't peel their brain open like a fruit." Dekker nodded slowly. "Not everyone is as susceptible to mind reading as everyone else."

"A reader?" Guy got excited. "Oh. Tell me what color underwear I'm wearing. I'm thinking about it right now."

Lilee ignored the jokester. "We've been all over New Hope and the outliers on Galilee and we still can't put it all together. It would be much easier if we could speak with the witness—Merrick, the one who turned in the syndicate."

"If you'd like to hire us to find your missing person, you can bid the job like anyone else. We don't take every job that comes our way, though—the Dozen does have some standards that we live by, no matter what those PFAR idiots say."

Lilee rocked back on her heels mocking indignation. "It's funny. DoCS agents aren't used to coming up cold when we search for something, or someone. But Merrick? He's dropped completely off the scanners, almost as if someone wanted him gone or helped him hide."

She narrowed her gaze at him and tapped into that primal part of her mind that could see into the minds of others and glean data. Lilee was not the most talented reader, far from it, but she was tenacious.

Dekker crossed his arms and stared at her, neither threatening her nor yielding. She could not penetrate his disciplined mental defenses.

Lilee sensed the lazy mind of his friend, Guy, however.

Guy did not know the location; he hadn't been told. Lilee could surmise that none of the other crew had been, either—but they'd definitely helped Merrick and they certainly knew about the Grrz. She briefly sifted through Guy's surface thoughts and easily accessed his recent memories. Many of them involved Dekker and she could tell that the Investigator would be a formidable opponent if she made an enemy of him.

Lilee drew her lips thinly across her teeth. Janus wanted to shut down loose ends, not stir up chaos, so pressing the point might turn counter-productive.

"Tell me what you know about specimen GRRZ," she said.

"Never heard of it," Dekker said. Guy nodded vigorously.

She already knew that was a lie.

"Whatever it is you're looking for," Dekker said, "I'm sure you're not going to find it here. That the incident on Galilee happened months ago and I'm sure anyone involved who has half a brain has either fled or forgotten all about it."

She turned to square up with him. "You know I can read thoughts," she said, more as a warning than a question.

"So, can you tell me what I'm thinking?" Dekker asked. His affable tone barely veiled a hint of warning. He clearly wanted her to leave.

Lilee tipped her head slightly. She nodded with her own look of warning. The message was clear: as long as he played nice and the Grrz stayed forgotten, she wouldn't need to be back.

Still, both Dekker and Lilee guessed they'd see each other again soon.

She turned to leave and pushed her way past Guy. She muttered, "Red," as she passed him and then left.

Guy turned to Dekker and laughed. "I was only *thinking* about red underwear. Actually I'm not wearing any at all."

Dekker shot him a screwy look, rolled his eyes, and then returned to his quarters. Between

Lilee and Nibbs' answer to his puzzle, he had a lot on his mind.

8

A skinny man wearing a thin goatee and a badge beat on the barrier to the prisoner's enclosure. He seemed to drown in his guard uniform.

"Hey puke—no help is coming for you. You haven't gone to trial yet only because they can't find a lawyer willing to defend you—and this prison is buried in the coldest and most defensible place on Earth. Nobody's gonna bust you out, neither."

Prognon Austicon merely smiled at the guard; he'd been imprisoned before… this was barely a blip in his schedule by comparison. The obnoxious guard's time would eventually come and so he ignored him. His eyes rolled back in his head.

Deep in the recesses of his brain, Austicon felt for the cosmic connection binding him to his most loyal devotee. Leviathan's presence awoke in his mind.

Master. Is it time? Shall I release you?

"No." Austicon's lips moved and his voice was no louder than his breathing. "I have plans already set in motion—so many plans. I wish to see which of these seeds develops first."

The package is secure… though the yellow woman suspects I have it. There is more: I have a man who found a way to clone the Eden seeds.

Austicon grinned. "Acantha will come for you. She has a way of ascertaining such truths."

Shall I resist her?

"No. Let her have the seed if she comes for it. I know what their plans are for it; make another for our own ends. I have need for you to reprise a role, my friend. You must make contact with my loyal Druze. Tell them the Anagoge still rules and that I am no more a prisoner than I choose to be."

It will be done. Your worshipers long to be used by you and they grow in numbers, especially on the rim worlds.

Austicon grinned. He knew that Leviathan had worshiped him for longer than any other—their personal history stretched back for millennia.

Wordlessly, he released his connection to the outside world. Their contact could not be detected, except perhaps by a member of the psy-ops. But Leviathan was the most potent and skilled psychic he'd ever known. He could do things with his mind that no one else could. It would never be discovered.

Austicon was imprisoned, truly… but he remained in custody for his own reasons. As soon as the notion arose that he wanted to escape, there existed no force on this planet or any other that could prevent it.

The guard continued to harangue him, but the prisoner turned in his bunk and rolled over for a nap. It was easy to ignore him—he and his entire species would perish in Austicon's lifetime. He had so many potential ways of carrying out such an execution; nobody could stop them all.

9

Dekker piloted the *Rickshaw Crusader* alone. He flew more than capably, but Matty was one of the best fliers in the system and he made it a habit to defer to the most qualified person for any given job. This mission, however, was personal, and he didn't expect he would head into battle.

The *Crusader* dropped out of FTL only a short distance from the coordinates Nibbs had helped him uncover inside the *Book of Aang*. Nothing filled the cockpit screens but distant stars—the same was true for the scanners. Dekker was in the black.

He urged the ship forward and watched the location indicators count down as he closed in on the exact location. The apex of the converging points belonged to a very precise pinpoint in space.

As he neared the final destination, his heart sagged. It had not been a long voyage, all things considered, but it looked more and more like a dead-end as the *Crusader* verged on reaching the location. Nothing happened and nothing appeared to exist for trillions of kilometers except for distant comets on their centennial loop.

Dekker scowled. While cloaking devices existed, they were very rare, and the coordinates had been penned hundreds of years prior to even FTL. He shook his head as he considered time travel and ruled out such a crazy notion. Already disappointed, the Investigator planned to sit on the coordinate's location for five minutes, see what might happen, and then cut his losses and return home.

Distance data on the scopes trickled down to nothing and then the craft came to a stop. Dekker blinked once, and when he opened his eyes, some kind of wormhole opened, sucking the *Crusader* through like a hidden sea creature taking prey.

For the second time, Dekker blinked. This time, however, when he opened his eyes he wasn't even on his ship.

A gentle mist hung in the surrounding air. A warm light bathed him and the lush greenery around him with yellow hues. He inhaled cautiously and smelled the humid air that carried a scent like lilacs.

Dekker checked himself. He had none of his belongings except for what had been on his person. Only his pistol hung at his thigh, but at least it was something.

Faced with no immediate options, Dekker walked straight ahead. He quickly realized that his location was underground though he could not discern the source of its light. Judging by the slope of the rocky ceiling, the cavern containing this grotto ended with some kind of exit in the distance. Dekker hurried towards it, drawing his sidearm.

The cave terminated in a short hall that slowly darkened; the greenery shrank away. A rocky mouth opened to whatever lay outside, beyond the haven.

He stalked through it silently, suddenly second guessing his decision to venture away from Earth alone. The air grew stale and foul as he left the garden.

"Come no further, Dekker Knight," a voice boomed in the distance. A large man hung in the distance; chains connected his wrists to a loop on the massive post binding them behind him. His head was bowed, concealing his face, and he'd been stripped bare.

Dekker furrowed his brow and took another step. He choked and his lungs seized as he did.

"There is no air out here," the humanoid told him. He easily stood one and a half times the height of a human.

Dekker leapt back inside the threshold of the cave and gasped, drawing in a lungful of thin air. He managed to choke out, "Who are you?"

He lifted his head to reveal a smooth face masked by his long, lanky hair. A strip of some kind of material blinded his eyes. "I am Osmadiel the Watcher."

10

Deep within the compound, Leviathan cocked his head. He sensed the minds of his Druze minions. They populated the facility like candles in a dark expanse. That some of the lights went out was not a surprise—that occurred whenever any person slept or watched media streams, but a noticeable gap formed in the network of flickering lights.

The last two flames suddenly snuffed and Leviathan turned, angling his head expectantly. With a creak, the door opened. Acantha stood there and glared. A ripple of strange energy churned within him. Surprise? He was unfamiliar with the feeling.

Acantha locked her gaze on the obsidian mask. "The Armageddon Seed," she insisted. The woman in yellow held out her hand to accentuate her demand.

Somewhere behind that black face shield Leviathan frowned. Acantha was somehow able to mask herself from detection. He did not like the implications of that.

He retrieved the seed from a nearby bin on a research table in the makeshift lab.

"You are getting sloppy, Leviathan," she spat. "I identified the old Druze markings on your transport ship at New Hope. There was no way your little stunt could throw me off—even when you wiped out half of that city on Galilee. Neither you nor that mangy dog you worship is as clever as you think you are."

If Leviathan were capable of making sounds, he would have growled. He momentarily reassessed his decision not to kill her; after weighing it with great scrutiny, he again decided against it.

He put the seed into her waiting palm and she turned it over to verify it was what she came for.

"What is this?" She pointed to a thin cut in the edge of the seed. A razor thin sliver had been excised, cutting through the skin and the meat of the fist-sized kernel.

The seed is viable, I assure you. It was like this when I recovered it for the glory of the Verdant Seven—only you found me first, he spoke directly to her mind.

Acantha narrowed her eyes to slits. She didn't buy his story, but she also didn't challenge him; she had already claimed the prize. Her eyes shot sidelong across the room and the mysterious woman caught sight of Doctor Meng who nervously skittered around in the back, checking lab equipment and scratching notes with eyes as wide as a drugged up raccoon. He'd developed a nervous twitch as soon as Leviathan removed him from Galilee; it only got worse the further they moved him from his precious Druze.

He muttered absentmindedly and bumbled about like a patient in a sleep deprivation ward. So singularly focused, Meng hadn't even noticed the woman.

"Who are you?" Acantha demanded.

"Alone… alone…" Meng mumbled like a mantra. She barely registered on his vacant eyes, and they only met hers for a fraction of a second.

He is nothing—nobody. A private project of Austicon's… a failed experiment with a tormented mind and little value, he lied.

"Then you won't mind if I kill him for seeing my face." Acantha was perhaps even more vicious than Leviathan's master when it came to witnesses; she preferred anonymity. She did not comprehend the power of infamy as did Austicon.

Be my guest. He cocked his head like a bird.

Acantha glared at him.

Leviathan assumed that she too considered the strengths and lethal nature of her enemy. Perhaps she sized him up and assessed the possibilities and risks of an outright attack on the assassin.

The yellow woman scowled, clutched her seed, and departed. "Don't get in my way again," she hissed. Acantha did not bother to mask her presence any longer and Leviathan felt her mind glow hot as she departed with her prize in hand.

Meng looked at his abductor and then back down to the genetic printer that whirred almost inaudibly. The scientist placed his hand on the plastic cocoon that surrounded the new seed like a father's on the bassinet of a premature infant.

Leviathan reached into the roiling confusion that was Meng's mind. The small part of it that remained coherent was like a ship tossed about a squall—dedicated to its task despite the bedlam that buffeted it from every side. He felt the chaos—sensed the purpose and plotted course of both ship and captain.

Meng had everything he already needed. The new, replica seed would finish in due time, provided no one and nothing interfered.

Before his capture, the doctor had been experimenting on the seeds—awoken them to some new purpose that only one in touch with the hive mind could understand. Leviathan could not comprehend it within the chaos, but he assumed it meant little. The rare seed was still genetically sound. Whatever purpose either Austicon or the Arbolean elders had in mind, it would remain viable.

Still, he watched Meng. Babysitting the crackpot doctor seemed a waste of his time, but this was the only man capable of replicating the item. So long as that remained true, Leviathan would not travel far from Meng's side. He was a broken thing, and that made him dangerous. The doctor didn't begin to comprehend what he had: access to one of the rarest and rawest potential life-forms in the universe… a seed from the Tree of Life itself.

11

Dekker stared at the creature who looked like he might have once boasted powerful muscles. Osmadiel leaned against his chains like some kind of promethean victim.

"Long have I waited for a visitor. What have you come to seek?"

Dekker sniffed against the caustic odor of the cave and found his voice. "I found your location in the book of Aang. I have questions… so many questions."

Osmadiel grinned. Something about his smile felt inherently dangerous. "Answers, as with all things, come only at great cost. I will freely answer *three* of your questions without excising such a toll."

Dekker bit his lip. He wanted to ask Osmadiel who he was, how he got there, and so much more. Dekker guessed that, from what he knew about fiendish, mythic, or celestial creatures from *any* mythology, Osmadiel could prove tricky and capricious. If he asked, that information would certainly count towards his three.

"I have a gun—a weapon that was given to me. It has been called, for as long as I've know it, the Reliquary. What do you know about it?"

Osmadiel bobbed his head. "The Reliquary, as you call it, certainly resembles a firearm—there were several created by a mad

Tinker several millennia ago. Hero he was called. He reverse engineered a celestial tool, a piece discarded off from the Great Engine—the divine machine."

He paused, and Dekker almost asked him what that was, but the Investigator held his tongue, not using one of his limited questions.

"When its operators, the Watchers, such as I, abandoned our posts upon it, some of them did damage to the cosmic wheel," Osmadiel explained. "One such post broke a powerful array. This *Reliquary* was a maintenance tool upon it, used to cull and trim errant lines of reality. The Great Machine stitches the fabric of reality—all of existence. Ironically, those of us who fled our stations are now caught within this very weave.

"Several of these units existed to tend and prune the occasional errant lines amongst millions of the stings churned out by the Divine Machine in its exponentially branching helixes."

Dekker burned to know more about this cosmic, deified engine, but knew he'd run out of questions on that front. He needed answers to the other, more immediate questions.

"The *Book of Aang* seems important," he stated truthfully. It was the first major problem he'd encountered that had not been wrapped up in shades of Prognon Austicon's influence. Everything else in the book seemed to have an answer he could unravel… except that infernal tree's cross-section. "I want to know about the tree rings. A sample cutting from some kind of tree was in the book, thinner than paper and folded up."

"If you want my knowledge, you must ask."

"What do you know about it?" He hoped again that the creature was not toying with him so that it could honestly answer *I don't know* and then move on.

Osmadiel held up two fingers as an indicator. "I know much about the map which cannot be read."

Dekker crossed his arms and glared at the chained one when he did not continue outright. "Tell me more," he insisted without a question.

Osmadiel cocked his lips into a half-grin.

"It cannot be read because it is written in the language of the trees; it plots a course to a fount of energy. You need to decode its genome to know its thoughts."

Musing to himself, Dekker mumbled, "I suppose we can take a sample…"

"No," Osmadiel insisted. "The sample will be wrong. It is only a memory: you need the thing's mind. You must take the *right* sample. You will know it when you see the foretold sign. *Scarred is the seed that brings destruction—scarred before birth is the seed child of Armageddon.*"

Dekker paused. He knew things would become clearer in time; none of that made sense right now, and he had so many other questions that weighed heavily on his mind. Dekker had carte blanch to ask about any of them: Austicon, Aleel, perhaps Osmadiel could even read the future.

"You have another question?"

With a sigh, he shook his head. "No. I will wait to ask my third question."

"You may ask any number that you like."

The Investigator felt it could be a trap. "I will stick with my three. Thanks anyway. I'll come back when I have something so pressing that it cannot be helped."

"Will you do me a favor as a token of our new friendship?"

Dekker looked at the creature. He didn't seem to have ulterior motives. He wisely remained silent instead of asking *what is this token*.

Osmadiel pressed ahead. "If you encounter my brother, Sabrael, tell him that I am sorry."

Dekker nodded and then turned to head back.

"Very well then," Osmadiel said. "Until we meet again."

The investigator pushed through the greenery in the grotto where the air was better. He held up his hands to protect his eyes. None of the plants had thorns, but one of them had whip-like tendrils and a tense frond recoiled like a switch, cutting a line across his forearm.

Dekker rubbed it and continued onward. After a few minutes' walk through the verdant cave, Dekker blinked and found himself back in the pilot's chair of the *Rickshaw Crusader*.

He looked down, nearly convinced that it had all been a dream. He rubbed the back of his arm where the plant had lashed him and left its mark. Dekker knew it had been anything but.

12

"Get Ahmed!" Vesuvius screamed over her shoulder as she and Rock hurried past the Dozen's main entry at their Reef City home. An angry mob stood at the edge of their lot near the fence. Amid the flurry of activity they could see Dirk flailing about as the rioters beat the one-armed man.

Camera crews, already warned against intrusion, stood on the property of Dekker's Dozen LLC. In order to get the best angle and live-broadcast his assault. Joan, the local correspondent for the state-run propaganda channel prattled on about what Dirk had done to justify the savaging.

Vesuvius pushed past her, glaring daggers, and Rock's hulking mass knocked the cameraman back. The operator intentionally overreacted and collapsed to the ground, letting his video equipment tumble to the dirt. They cursed at the Investigators' backs and quickly went silent when Vesuvius shot them an icy stare.

The crowd shrank back from Rock, afraid to engage in violence with someone as physically intimidating and capable as they assumed him to be. He and Vesuvius scooped Dirk up and began carrying him back to their base.

Ahmed burst out of the front door, shirtless, half-shaved and still wearing foam. He carried a medical kit as he rushed to their side.

"Things are getting more tense every day," Rock muttered as Ahmed checked over their friend.

Dirk's eyes rolled, and he spoke mostly nonsense, a sure sign of a concussion.

"He started it!" Someone shouted.

"Leave Earth," others took up a chant. "No violence—no Investigators."

They heard a screeching nearby as their main hangar bays opened. The *Rickshaw Crusader* descended through their airspace as Dekker returned. Seeing the spacecraft, much of the crew began dispersing.

Vesuvius glared at them. She suspected that they'd nabbed Dirk when they thought the Dozen were off-world and now that they knew they'd encounter them, fear of a real fight scattered them like roaches. Guy came out to offer assistance though the action seemed to have mostly passed.

Ahmed nodded to the others. "He'll be alright," he told them. "Let's get him up. He's gonna need some downtime, though, and lots of ice."

Guy slapped him on the shoulder of his stump arm. "Hear that, Dirk? Sounds like a cold shower for *you,* buddy." He looked up to spot

Vesuvius cornering the female media broadcaster just off of the main walking path. He rushed to intervene, afraid Vesuvius might live up to her explosive nickname.

"I've told you *multiple times* to stay off our property. This time you've done it—you've gone too far and now you're gonna…"

He put a hand on her shoulder while she vented her stockpile of expletives on the camera wielder and Joan pointed her microphone to make sure she captured it all. Vesuvius whirled around and caught Guy's surreptitious wink.

Guy glared at the duo, stating for their benefit, "Come on, Vivian, we've got to get Dirk back inside. I'm pretty sure they don't know where the buried land mines are that we had installed, recently. Let's see if they can figure it out."

The blood seemed to have drained from Joan's face and she examined the ground all around them. She kept her feet rooted to one spot.

Vesuvius frowned, but followed Guy as he, Rock, and Ahmed hauled Dirk onto wobbly legs. Glancing back, she saw the cameraman and correspondent step as gingerly as possible and then take a giant leap to try to get back on the main walkway without exploding.

Guy winked at her, and they helped Dirk inside, closing out the chaotic world behind them.

13

Dirk had only just gotten sorted when the rest of the Investigators gathered in the hangar area to update Dekker on the growing unrest near their headquarters. They'd pulled a tattered, aged recliner out into the main bay where Dirk could relax with his ice packs.

Just as Dekker begun to address his crew with an update, Dirk piped up. "Someone's at the door."

"It's that spook from a couple days ago." Vesuvius ran to get the door before the DoCS agent grew impatient; they'd secured the building following Dirk's assault. Vesuvius escorted Director Lilee into their presence.

Dekker and the others simply stared at her, unsure of what she wanted.

Lilee produced a card from her pocket. "This is the Dozen's Investigator credentials," she said. She withdrew a second one. "This one is a lifetime, irrevocable pass. Think of it: no registrations or annual fees, no taxes, no restrictions. I'm looking for a capable crew who is willing to play ball."

Dekker furrowed his brow. "What is this about? I already told you last time that…"

"Galilee is unimportant. That's not why I'm here. I have intel on a job and this is what I'm prepared to offer in the event that you guys, and gal, can play nice."

"Something you can't send the MEA peacekeepers to deal with? Sounds like the kind of job I'd turn down on principle. We're not assassins, Lilee."

She shook her head. "The world saw you on that broadcast a few minutes ago. I caught it on my way over. Chatter on the BlackWeb indicates that the Druze are trying to stir up dissension. Maybe cause a riot or some general civil unrest with Austicon's trial and sentencing coming to a close soon. You guys have more experience with Austicon and his Druze than anyone else."

Dekker crossed his arms. "Still sounds like a job for local boots on the ground."

"I saw the way the crowd shrank back when you moved in to rescue your friend. The people fear you. Constables don't wield that kind of power. I need *your* boots on the ground. Your job is to quell any disruptions before things get violent." She tapped her forehead to remind them that she had at least some degree of psychic training and talent. "After all, I know what those people were thinking."

Lilee tossed Dekker the card. "It's not good until I activate it."

Dekker scanned the faces surrounding him. The MEA charged exorbitant fees for them to maintain their licensure. That money could certainly be better spent as a bonus for the crew's shares. He bit his lip, still on the fence. "What are the conditions?"

"Like I said. You've just got to play nice. Don't destroy anything—don't kill anyone." She held up a pair of fingers shaped like a V. "Sentencing is in two days. We figure that's when the Druze are going to make life difficult, so if you've got to spill some blood in order to determine where they are going to hit, I suggest you do it before then."

Dekker slowly nodded and Lilee warned him again while staring at Guy, "Don't screw this up."

14

"Well this complicates things," Dekker muttered. He ran his fingers through his hair and then addressed his crew. He raised his crew's eyebrows with a clap of his hands. "First, let's welcome Nibbs back, everybody."

The Dozen greeted him warmly. The newest of the members had already made it a point to drop by his quarters and introduce themselves to him. A lot had happened in his absence—the crew could never be the same again after Galilee. A moment of silence seemed to creep in at the thought of Mustache's death.

"Yeah," Guy, broke the tension. "Dekker got stabbed."

Dekker sighed.

Vesuvius played along. "It was an *accident*."

"Was it though?" Guy asked.

"Mostly… probably. Maybe." She winked at Dekker playfully. They'd privately buried the thankfully figurative hatchet and decided to go back to the way things were *before* they'd been romantically involved.

Matty hadn't been paying that much attention. As their primary pilot he'd been mostly focused on the *Crusader* since Dekker's return. "So where did you go in my baby? Usually when you take it out I've got to fix something… do you know how much pressure it takes to pound out a hull dent?"

Dekker chuckled. "That's what I wanted to talk about. You all know that I can tend to be something of a private person…"

"That's an understatement," Vesuvius interjected. "I don't even know your middle name."

"It's Percival," Guy answered for him.

"It's not Percival."

"Yes it is. You told me—and then said never repeat that… oops."

"Why do I keep you around?"

Guy shrugged, "Because I'm the only explosives expert you know who still has all his fingers."

"You know, I can fix that," Dekker threatened.

Nibbs laughed. "Glad to see that nothing has changed."

Guy whispered with a nod, "It's definitely Percival."

Dekker let the joke go. "I asked Nibbs to solve a puzzle for me and he came through. It's not a huge secret that the ammunition for my Reliquary is super rare and I think we've all benefited in the past from the times I've had to use it. I've been searching for years to locate more of the ammunition; the coordinates Nibbs decoded for me sent me to another clue." He silently kicked himself for not simply asking Osmadiel for the locations of every shell in existence… then again, the strange creature had not explicitly said that it would lead to the shells, either. He felt the mystery surrounding the ancient artifact was bigger than just the location of ammunition.

"I don't know if it will lead me to a cache of weapons and ammo or information. It might simply be treasure—or maybe nothing at all at the end of this rainbow, but I have a disc that needs to be decoded. I don't know the quality of my source, but I was told that there is hidden information on some kind of hard drive made of wood, a slim cross-section of a tree… paper-thin. It's keyed to something's genome sequence which will decrypt the data. I believe it to be some kind of map." He shrugged, "We'll see. I need more minds on this than just mine—I can't really make heads or tails of it."

Juice piped up, "A disk like the old-style data players?"

"Maybe. I only know it's tied to a gene sequence for decrypting."

Corgan's eyes widened. "Is this some kind of Mechnar tech?"

Dekker furrowed his brow. As much as Dekker was an enthusiast and collector of ancient, cultic artifacts, Corgan was a history fanatic, especially regarding the Intergalactic Singularity War. He wasn't sure that the cyborg race that almost wiped out humanity half a century ago had anything to do with the clues.

Corgan explained his thinking, "During the ISW, the second gen ships used a new type of data drive after the MEA kept hacking their systems. The new interface required a matching genetic code to access the information, sort of like a hardware encryption password. The drives had a master list of genomes it compared the user with to ensure that only the Mechnar could access the information."

"I'm pretty sure it's not Mechnar in origin."

"Maybe not," Nibbs said. Their tech expert speculated, "But Corgan could be right—this sounds like the same principle. The disk in those old drives were actually made of genetically engineered super coral. Their data was hidden within alterations to the genetic sequence. Theoretically, the same could be done with wood, or even human flesh."

Dekker rubbed his chin and thought about the implications. "That could work, except that tech is banned by the MEA. To my knowledge it's all been destroyed—there isn't so much as a data drive even left in a museum."

Vesuvius grinned. "Come, now. We all know the guy who's probably got one."

Dekker scowled.

“He doesn’t wanna go,” Guy laughed. “Doc Johnson always embarrasses him.”

Dekker ran his fingers through his hair. “Fine. I’ll call Doc. But first we’ve got to deal with this Agent Lilee thing. What kind of intel do we have on any Druze activity in the region?”

15

With weapons drawn, the Dozen crept closer to the old building in the south-east corner of District Six. Live sensor sweeps were not usually allowed; MEA regulatory rules choked most things on Earth with bureaucracy, but they'd pulled a few strings with Lilee and gotten clearance. Scans showed that there weren't any sensors or security systems to worry about.

Dekker bit his lip as they approached. In his experience, a lack of sensors meant one of two things. He expected it was either a trap or that the location boasted an abundance of living personnel who could guard their boundaries with eyes and ears instead of security systems. That indicated a probable firefight as soon as they were discovered.

It looked like an abandoned warehouse, but they'd earlier identified the place as the hub of the regional Druze activities after Nibbs back-traced traffic on the BlackNet back to it. Tracking them was no easy task and the religious fanatics had taken pains to hide themselves; religion had been outlawed by the MEA over a decade ago, with very few holdouts strong enough to tell the Mother Earth Aggregate to suck it. The Druze were not the strong sort; they'd been invaded and had their ideology twisted for years by Austicon and his servant, Leviathan. What had once been a branch of Islam had been turned into a hammer for terrorism—one set up for wholesale devotion to their new Messiah: the enlightened one, the Anagoge… Prognon Austicon.

Vesuvius tried the nearest door after they surrounded the facility. It was unlocked and swung open quietly. The first team breached the building while they covered each other. Only silence and empty darkness greeted them.

The Investigators stalked the main hall and accessed the largest, open area of the building. Still, they hadn't found a soul.

Bedding and damaged mattresses lay strewn haphazardly. They found signs of at least two dozen members of the terrorist cell.

Dekker peeled back a heap of old blankets with the muzzle of his weapon when a man leapt to his feet, screaming threats. Dekker cracked him across the temple with his pistol. The Druze soldier stumbled to his knees.

His sunken eyes glared at the intruders from between long, curly locks of unkempt hair, framed by an equally unruly beard.

"Where is everybody?" Dekker demanded.

The Druze spat at him and hissed. "Gone. You're too late. You'll never find my brothers before we mobilize."

"Why'd you get left behind? You must not be very valuable," Vesuvius remarked.

Their prisoner stiffened. “It’s because I’m *the most* valuable…”

“Oh good. He thinks he’s in charge so he’s probably got some intelligence that he can lead us to… since he thinks he knows something.”

The man wordlessly worked his jaw, not sure how he’d been so easily duped.

Nibbs took out a mechanical hacking apparatus. The “arms” of the thing hung like tentacles from its base, allowing it to interface with all manner of machinery and systems via the octopoid’s attachments. “Where are your servers?”

The man crossed his arms until Dekker pressed his gun to his head and politely insisted. He set his face, but led the way deeper into the building.

Ahead, a central office jutted out from the open floor plan. From there, a foreman would oversee daily operations when the warehouse had operated as a legitimate business. Cables and conduit hung exposed to access ports where the Druze had rewired and connected routers in order to establish this as the regional hub of clandestine activity.

Warmth generated from the electronics wafted off from the machines and greeted them as they entered. Banks of equipment lay stacked and powered up in indiscriminate piles.

"We want *all* of your data," Dekker demanded. "It'd be easier for us both if you just log in and give it to us." He waved his barrel towards the main terminal.

Their new friend glowered at them with a face like flint, but moved towards the interface to comply. He reached below the desk and keypad and snatched a remote with one large, thumb-button wired to it. "Death to enemies of the Anagoge!" The rogue Druze yelled. He raised his hands above his head to smash the button of a hand-held detonator unit.

Before anyone else could react, Dekker snap-fired and put a single bullet through the terrorist's forehead.

He slumped harmlessly to the floor. After sucking in a tense breath of air, the Investigators found stockpiled explosives wired all around the office location. They'd strung up enough bombs to level the place in case they were raided.

Minutes later, Nibbs' hacking unit detached from the banks of data drives. He shrugged. "I guess you were right, Vees."

Vesuvius cocked her head.

"He must've been useless. There's nothing on these drives. Anything of value is already gone. Several of the physical drives have been removed… although it seems there is some chatter about a PFAR rally in Reef City to coincide with

Austicon's sentencing, but we already knew some of that."

Dekker nodded. It was as good as they were going to get for a lead, and it made sense. "At least now we have a definite location."

The Krenzin ardently supported the Peace For All Races group and their alien home world had been annihilated by Austicon many decades ago, before what remained of their culture had been re-homed on Earth.

This lead was as good as the next one, and it left them time to squeeze in Dekker's side-mission: a trip to Darkside Station and a visit with the old madcap. An earlier conversation confirmed that he *did* in fact own a piece of tech so forbidden that DoCS spooks would make him Austicon's cellmate if they knew he owned it.

16

Doc Johnson led the crew of four through his warehouse. He employed a dozen various mechanics and workers in his facility located on the moon's dim side. No place else offered the kind of real estate prices he needed for his business at such a close proximity to MEA Prime: Earth.

"You all can take a break," Doc told the trio of workers who meandered near the edge of the largest warehouse section of Darkside Station. He visibly relaxed once his employees were gone.

The miles of debris in Doc's scrap pits concealed a plethora of secrets, and he didn't like to expose them casually. Dekker only brought Guy, Vesuvius, and Nibbs along for that exact reason.

"We gotta head through the tunnels," he said. "I buried it out back where none of my trained monkeys could chance upon it."

The Investigators followed him through the long and winding paths. Every so often a narrow stairwell led upwards. Gravity got lighter as they walked further and further from the main facility.

They finally arrived at pod number thirteen and the group followed Doc up the steps. The tiny room functioned like a small observation post with windows on all sides. It overlooked the pits mounded up with wreckage and debris. Rows of Class A fighters lay mounded below them and the massive hulls of ISW era Class F warships and transport galleons jutted up from the lunar soil. In the distance, they spotted the partial skeleton framework of a class G, the largest grade space cruiser.

"There's only room up top for one other person," Doc nodded to the ladder leading vertically from the room. "Any volunteers?"

Nibbs raised his hand. "I'd love to see how the cranes operate."

A new tower rose every kilometer with a crane rig attached. Their silhouettes dotted the landscape between the wrecker yard and the main dome of Darkside Station.

A magnet and a claw arm descended into the pit from above and pulled out wads of old debris. It fell slowly into heaps as Doc released the maglocks from each load and unearthed a sub layer of buried interstellar flotsam.

Doc and Nibbs slid down the rails and back to the others. They donned the space suits they'd been carrying and exited through the airlock, carefully navigating the jagged piles of rubble as they picked their way through the pit of decaying space hulks.

An entire layer of Mechnar ships laid at the bottom of the trench. "Here they are," Doc's voice crackle through the speakers in their helmets. "Take your pick."

"Which of these are second generation crafts or later?" Nibbs asked.

"I'd have to think about it a moment."

Guy interjected, "You ought to know—weren't you, like, forty during the Mechnars' heyday."

Doc cocked his body so that his helmet tipped to match his irked tone. "Dekker, you wanna pull out the line on Guy's oxygen tank for me?"

"Gladly."

"I remember," Doc stated as he pointed to the row of crafts in the distance. "Everything in that line is an early model. Any of the others ought to be what you are looking for… though I'm not sure which of them still had their systems left intact. People get real worried about those anti-Mechnar protocols; it doesn't help that the penalties for violation are so stiff."

The party broke up and searched the individual ships. It took them a couple hours, but they found one. As they clambered back into the observation post, Doc removed his helmet. "I'm sure it goes without saying…"

"Yeah… we didn't get this thing *here*… we pulled it off a floating piece of space debris, right guys?"

An agreement rippled through the group and short while later they were on their way back to Earth with the bulky genome interfacer stowed safely in their hold. They had plenty to worry about in the meanwhile.

17

The Pheema prattled aimlessly as he strolled through the halls of his luxurious compound. A stream of his devoted Krenzin adherents followed him, hanging on his every word. His aides followed him closest, ready to assist the religious leader in any of the duties of his office if asked.

Stroking his whiskers, the felinoid alien paused as he grew nearer to the door of his office. He detected the faint wisps of a familiar odor.

“Please wait here,” The Pheema turned and smiled to his entourage. “I’m afraid I have a quick, private matter I must attend to but I promise to join you in the main portico shortly.”

The group moved on, eager to hear the momentous speech The Pheema was scheduled to deliver right before the media channels scheduled the live broadcast of Prognon Austicon’s sentence hearing. He spoke on behalf of the Krenzin people, a race nearly ruined by the intergalactic terrorist’s activities, and so his words carried significant weight.

Once the hallway had cleared out, The Pheema opened his door and entered. A woman clad all in yellow and wearing a hood sat in his chair. “It’s true what they say: if you want something done right you might have to do it yourself.”

The Pheema sniffed indignantly. “I take it that your mission was successful, then?”

Acantha tilted her head affirmatively. “I have recovered the seed. Is your servant ready?”

Smoothing down his ruffled fur near his snout, The Pheema nodded. “I only need to call him.”

“Then do it. I will be leaving shortly. I have a meeting in District Seven. Your courier will accompany me and take the prize to the Red Circle on my behalf.”

The Pheema nodded and sent a brief message to Zarbeth. His one-armed kinsman would arrive shortly to complete the mission he’d failed at once before. His ultimate reward for such loyalty, everyone knew, was an honorable death.

Acantha could not visit the Sacred Grove. There were prophecies and warnings against such a thing—thus the need of a trusted courier, although the yellow woman was not willing to extend as much lead rope for the Krenzin carrier as she’d allowed him in the past. Acantha had gone to such great lengths that she would not risk him fumbling it again.

“Zarbeth will meet my man in Reef City. He will ferry him to the final destination. Once they are locked within the spacecraft, they can put together each of their halves of the FTL coordinates.” Only six living women, one man, and whatever the heck Leviathan was, knew the location of the sacred Seven Arboleans. Acantha had planned for it to stay that way.

The door to his office opened and Zarbeth entered. He bowed low. "I am ready to meet my glorious destiny."

"Get up," she said. "Neither of us have all day." She glanced sidelong at The Pheema. "I understand that this one has served you faithfully and loyally?"

"He has."

Zarbeth's eyes welled up at the admission.

"And this mission isn't going to be a problem, is it?"

The Pheema approached and kissed Zarbeth's forehead. "It will not be. This is his reward: to see the authors of our glorious destiny with his own eyes."

Acantha bowed stiffly. "Very well." She put the seed child into his remaining hand. "Don't lose it again… or else."

Zarbeth bowed appreciatively and then nodded to his religious superior, The Pheema. "Until we meet again."

The Pheema responded in kind and then watched them depart.

18

Lilee's communicator chirped and she answered the signal. Former Director Scilazee was on the other end. "Kira, listen to me. I need you to meet me. I have some big news—something you need to know."

The new Director cocked her head. Scilazee was too far away to get a reading, even if Lilee was a skilled reader, which she wasn't. What propelled her success had been her instincts and her tenacity during field work. Still, something in her old boss's voice expressed a hint of urgency.

"Just tell me now. I'm busy trying to coordinate an anti-Druze task force before they blow something up."

"No. Not through the comms. I'll send you the address. You can get Mazzer to run the task force in your stead. Lord knows he did half of my job for me all these years. I'll see you shortly." Scilazee closed the channel.

Lilee gave it a moment's thought. Scilazee was right. Mazzer was more than competent. He should have gotten the Director's position ahead of her. She could always express her gratitude later, she figured, after deferring her duties to the hard working agent.

She left the government building which housed her office and found a massive crowd.

Reef City's streets had been overrun with folks wearing bright garb and carrying Peace For All Races signs. Lilee pushed through the parade and accessed a DoCS hover vehicle.

For a moment, Lilee wondered if she ought to disable the tracker, but decided against it. She didn't owe Scilazee any debts, and he didn't have any dirt on her. Besides, she'd only be gone a few minutes.

Lilee set the small transport down on its VTOL engines at the address he'd sent her. A sprawling, square building occupied most of the nearby land. She approached cautiously; the scene was too perfect, pristine.

At the door, a trio of girls waited for the her. They directed Agent Lilee to her destination down a hall and through a door.

Walls adorned the hall with classic pieces of art and other valuables making it feel more like a museum than anything else. The doors opened to the center of the building, an open-aired atrium filled with trees. A walking path led to the center. The trail terminated in front of a mighty oak and Scilazee stood beneath it.

"I'm glad you could come."

"It sounded urgent. What do you need to tell me?"

His eyes darted side to side, and he kept a low voice. "This thing, the reason I lost my job—or at least the reason they're blaming it on—the

Phobos 12 incident is something you need to know about."

Lilee narrowed her brows. "Isn't it resolved? Austicon eradicated all life on Phobos 12 during the Intergalactic Singularity War. Help couldn't come because all our forces were engaged in conflicts. We didn't even know about it until it was too late. The Dark Tentacle nebula fritzed all our interstellar relays, so there was no way we could've known in time."

"That's the official story. But there's more. The LDN1774 nebula didn't destroy the communications relays. *We did.* I can't tell you why, but it's a secret that must be kept. Only a few remain alive who were even present; most are elderly by now—all have suffered different degrees of… a condition. None of them will talk."

"What happened?" Lilee asked. "What *can* you tell me? Did the MEA kill all those people on Phobos 12?"

"It *really was* Austicon that murdered them. But there were some… mishaps. Austicon exploited the events." He sighed. "We found something in the nebula—the scouts did, anyway, who were exploring the system after the terraformers moved out and the expansionists began moving in."

Lilee only stared. Her eyes beckoned for more info.

"I can only say that it was something entirely foreign and so our top-secret science teams needed to study it."

"Foreign?" Lilee chuckled. "As if that means anything in a galaxy filled with aliens and so many unique cultures."

"I didn't say *alien*," Scilazee said with his eyes locked on hers. Something deep down rattled him about it.

19

Acantha's craft settled on a lawn nearby the edge of Reef City. She fixed Zarbeth with a hard gaze. "You must go on foot from here, everything is restricted because of celebrations. You have your half of the coordinates memorized?"

Zarbeth nodded. "I do. I will not fail you."

"Much relies upon your success—the future exaltation of the Krenzin people is at stake. Your mission continues at the Krenzin consulate. Your pilot is waiting in the lobby. Once you have combined your coordinate codes and arrive at the home of the Verdant Seven, the Sacred Grove, you are ordered to shoot your pilot in the head to kill him. Do you understand?"

Zarbeth's eyes widened slightly, but he nodded. Everything in his background revolted at the notion of such violence, but he understood that there were circumstances that still required such distasteful acts.

Without a pilot, the unspoken suggestion that this would be a one-way trip had been confirmed.

He accepted the handgun that Acantha offered him and slipped it within the pocket of his robe. Its weight surprised him.

"I understand."

"Good, now lift your cloak."

He did as commanded and the old woman used a medical bandage to wrap his torso, pressing the seed against the flesh of the one-armed felinoid. The seed felt warm against the skin below his sparse fur.

"I will not fail again," he repeated as their eyes met.

She nodded wordlessly, and then turned to depart, trusting the crippled alien with the fate of the universe and with plans set in motion by beings far more influential than a mere Krenzin diplomatic aide.

"So, 'foreign,' but it's not *alien,*" Lilee cocked an eyebrow. "Extragalactic? Extradimensional?"

Scilazee shrugged with a heavy sigh. "I was never told the nature of what they found—but those who survived were driven to madness by the end—they would only describe it in reverential tones and with vacant eyes, using the word *glorious*. This was just a courtesy—to tell you that everything about the incident is dangerous. It's wrapped up in so many layers of subterfuge that even *thinking* about Phobos 12 in the wrong crowd can result in your assassination."

His face grayed, stony and serious. "This was just a warning, Lilee. I always liked you, so forget we ever had this discussion." He snapped his mouth shut and nodded to the trail where an old woman approached, nearing earshot.

Lilee's mood darkened. She wondered if that last part was a lie—he must've hated her to give her such info and tell her not to think about it under penalty of pain or death. *I work surrounded by spies—some of whom are psychic!*

She changed the subject as she looked around. "What is this place? I never knew it existed. Is it some kind of museum?"

"It belongs to a friend of mine, well, to her organization." Scilazee held out a hand as the elderly woman approached to a few arms' lengths. "I'd like to introduce you to Acantha. She's an old friend, and she insisted I make an introduction."

Something in the tone of his voice informed Lilee that Scilazee did not have a choice in the matter.

Acantha took Lilee by the hands and greeted her. The woman's yellow, flowing robes seemed to indicate she belonged to some kind of foreign culture which Lilee was unfamiliar with. She smiled affably, but raised a brow. "You're wondering about my robes?"

Lilee nodded. "I can't quite place them."

"You might say that they are diplomatic. I represent the interests of an off-world culture… not one currently enjoying membership within the Aggregate." Acantha squeezed Scilazee's hand. "Thank you, Harold. I can take it from here."

Scilazee nodded. He shot Lilee a sidelong look to urge her caution and then departed.

Acantha walked a slow, meandering circle through the garden and Lilee followed her, remaining at her side. "Those powers that I represent play a critical, unseen role in the cosmic order. There are only a few of us, but on behalf of our benefactors we often groom new contacts and then extend an offer of membership in our ranks—a lifelong appointment."

"It's not an alien race," Lilee suggested, "it's a secret society?" She stretched out her mind and tried to read Acantha's emotions and surface thoughts. Her mind was invisible—she barely registered on the astral plane.

Acantha stopped and mused, "What if I told you it was both? There are currently six of us women. We seek one more to join us and complete our circle before number six expires. She has been unwell for quite some time."

Lilee didn't know enough to respond properly.

"We are a strong, powerful team. Together, we are untouchable. We make planetary rulers and topple governments at a whim. This garden could have been filled with DoCS agents and constables and I could have killed Scilazee and gotten away with it, such is our influence… and I probably should?"

"Kill him?" Lilee balked.

Acantha nodded. "He is a loose end, and he's already told you things he should not have. Phobos 12 is not something the Women of Dodona wish to concern ourselves with. We would not return for anything—it could be our undoing."

Lilee narrowed her gaze at her, but Acantha headed off any questions. She put a slip of paper into the young Director's hand and began moving towards the door. It listed a time and place.

"This is your invitation to join Dodona, Director Lilee. Come for a visit and all will be made clear." The three women who had ushered Lilee into the building arrived and escorted Acantha out.

Acantha moved with a power and grace that the agent had never seen; everything in the invitation felt attractive—though it set her internal alarms ringing wild, but it remained appealing despite that. The trio remained a step back and with eyes lowered, whether in reverence or subservience, Lilee didn't know.

Lilee turned the paper over in her hands. Deep down, she guessed that this old woman had no need of any escort. She put the address in her pocket, returned to her vehicle, and headed back to her task force.

Stillness fell over the location. No more little lights burned with attentive minds and once the building had emptied, a lithe, black figure stepped out of the shadows. Unseen, he had pulled critical details from Acantha's mind.

Leviathan pulled out a communicator and composed a text-based message to his contact, the Shivan pirate captain who had abandoned him back on Io. Leviathan knew that he wouldn't refuse this job—their last interaction had shown him what the creature's true desire was, and Leviathan could offer him that thing that he coveted, even if he knew almost nothing about it.

Gr'Narl and his pirates would toe the line this time. Leviathan could offer them the keys to the lockbox.

21

Holo-displays had been set up in the downtown areas of urban Reef City where the parade of people swelled to its thickest. They broadcast in real time from inside the tribunal.

Within the courtroom, Chief Magnate Miko Janus presided over the assembly. The sentencing hearing was, in fact, more of a political horse and pony show than an actual trial. There was no doubt of Prognon Austicon's guilt and the criminal had made a mark on history by exploiting his reputation. He was also too dangerous of a criminal to move out of his cell and so his presence was linked via streaming video. The criminal had agreed to forgo representation during the trial process and freely admitted to his crimes, having publicly bragged about them in the past.

Behind Janus, all the members of the high council and other ranking members of planetary parliament remained seated, using the trial as a widely broadcasted PR opportunity. Posturing for the cameras, Janus opened with an eloquent monologue, thanking The Pheema for his kind words in the speech immediately preceding the sentencing.

"We have heard The Pheema, the spokesman for the theocracy of the Krenzin race, give a moving talk about the annihilation of his peoples' home world at your hands. And still—at the heart of their ideology, mercy remains at its core. The Mother Earth Aggregate has a long standing policy which prohibits administering the death penalty. However, in light of how heinous your crimes are, we passed a special resolution in an emergency session of parliament to suspend that rule in your particular case."

Behind him, the politicians bounced their heads approvingly.

"That said," Janus continued, "I am moved by The Pheema's speech. As a species and as a collection of *people,* we reaffirm ourselves to the high standards we uphold here in the core worlds. While it is true that the expansion worlds will often tend towards the barbaric—that is not the way of the MEA. Here, we are civilized—even when our citizens act with such depravity and madness that it moves them to genocide, even annihilating entire worlds and cultures—at least two hang over your head by my count."

On his end of the feed, Austicon interjected, "Is this where I have an opportunity to throw myself on the mercy of the court and ask for leniency or whatever? You know, my final statement?"

Janus nodded measuredly.

Austicon's face twisted ugly. "I have never denied the massacre of Krenzin Prime. I did it because I wanted to—because I *could*, and I enjoyed it. I do not especially hate the Krenzin… I hate *all creatures of creation*. And while I certainly wiped out the population of Phobos 12, you and I both know that first, the MEA…"

His feed suddenly cut off its audio. He screamed and raged at the camera, hurling silent expletives at the video.

"We appear to be experiencing some technical difficulties on behalf of the convicted," Chief Magnate Janus said. "We will continue with sentencing." He straightened his robes and hid a smug grin as he shifted the ceremonial clothing. "Prognon Austicon, you will never be released to cause more damage. Whatever you are, whatever your lifespan is, it will be spent in our custody and in solitary confinement. You are too dangerous to house with other criminals. You will never again walk free."

Austicon's audio may have been muted, but the words he spoke were easy to read on his lips after a short sneer. *We'll see.*

22

The Dozen walked the clogged and crowded streets of Reef City in pairs and trios. Vesuvius scowled at more than one sign-toting activist. Everywhere they moved, PFAR's "Peace Warriors" confronted them.

None of the Investigators knew quite what to expect. They simply hoped to cast a broad net and find a clue before something terrible happened. The Investigators only had a location to go on and nothing more.

High over the buildings, holograms stretched into the skies to reveal the sentencing proceedings. After all these years, it seemed that Austicon would finally get his due. Folks paraded through the rally which seemed like some kind of planetary celebration. Finally, the MEA would have justice for the many decades of this killer's reign of terror and random acts of violence.

Dekker scowled at the feed when it put up the visage of a grinning Prognon Austicon; he showed himself incapable of remorse. Dekker glanced at a vendor selling furry shirts that read *I identify as a Krenzin.* He frowned. Though he had no love for the aliens whose ideologies frequently clashed with his, he understood their pain—Dekker had suffered greatly at the hands of the madman, especially during the Secret Wars: the epoch of his life that came before his mercenary venture.

The media switched to the sentencing. As much as Dekker tried to focus on the task of identifying the Druze cell that meant to stir up trouble, he kept glancing up at the feed.

As they pushed their way through, they ignored complaints of the revelers.

"Hey, aren't those weapons illegal?"

"You can't have guns!"

"This is a place of peace, man… take your hate somewhere else."

The speakers echoed over the streets, pronouncing judgment cloaked in mercy for Prognon Austicon. "You will never again walk free," Janus said.

Cheers rippled through the streets. The crowd roared with approval and chants went up as the PFAR members instigated them. "Peace wins!" They shouted like some insane mantra.

"You're gonna regret not killing him," Dekker muttered and then checked the comms. "All teams report in."

They sounded off one by one. "Still no sign of Druze activity," Rock reported. Screams suddenly split the air in the distance. The unmistakable sounds of gunfire echoed through the corridor of tall buildings.

The chants quickly melted into panicked howls and the mass of bodies became a flood of rampaging people. The frenzied horde made movement difficult.

"Let us through!" Vesuvius screamed ineffectively.

Nobody listened. Men and women in the crowd stampeded with the same blank, bovine looks on their faces as animals rushed to slaughter.

Fed up, Guy yanked a pistol and fired three rounds into the sky. The PFAR wildebeests finally took notice and formed a furrow around them so the Investigators could move through the tidal force of those in route.

"I've got eyes on the situation," Dekker said. He locked eyes on a familiar face and dropped his com as he glared. "*You!*"

23

Gr'Narl raked his sturdy hands through the scrub of hair protruding from his high, sloping forehead. The Shivan pirate cocked his gray-hued jaw at the message he'd received through the BlackWeb. He wondered how to respond.

Alongside most of his regular crew, he and the rest had been smoking crystal in the rear of the hookah bar where they watched Prognon Austicon's proceedings. Shivans were immune to alcohol—but this location provided a chemical rock for them to partake in which provided much the same effect.

"I don't much like it," he growled to his first mate.

Gr'Tak took the message and read it. None of the crew cared for Leviathan—even though he was Austicon's right hand. "Who knows how long Austicon's gonna stay incarcerated… we may need to stay on the freak's good side in case he takes over Austicon's empire."

He read the message again. *I have what you need—something required to open what PA has promised for his freedom. I have a job for you.*

"This first part, what is he talking about?"

Gr'Narl scowled, debating whether or not to tell him. Pirates where not particularly trustworthy by their nature. Finally, Gr'Narl decided he could confide in his clan-mate; they were both Gr, after all.

"He has promised the lockbox to whoever frees him. He made me promise to broadcast this message to the rest of the crews in the black, but I've kept a lid on it until now."

"The lockbox… Austicon's Lockbox? Did he tell you what is in it?"

Gr'Narl shook his head. He could see greed begin spinning the wheels of industry deep behind Gr'Tak's eyes. The captain knew immediately that he had to take Leviathan's job to either prevent a coup or keep his first mate from breaking off and forming his own team of raiders. He cursed himself for over-sharing, but didn't blame Gr'Tak; he would've done the same in his shoes.

The captain responded to the message. *You have the key? Is this offer exclusive? Is this the only key?* Gr'Narl hit send.

Both Shivans hovered over the data screen anxiously awaiting a response. A moment later came his reply.

Exclusive for 30 more seconds. Window of opportunity closes fast—only 2 known keys. A second later, an image of a one-armed Krenzin downloaded along with a coordinate beacon. *Your target—proof of death required. He carries the key.*

Another image arrived: a seed. *The key to the lockbox*.

Gr'Tak had already rounded up the crew by the time Gr'Narl responded. The target was only a few minutes away at full burn—something that only Shivans could endure while in a planetary atmosphere; their alien physiology was built for high-G maneuvers.

We accept the job. It will be done.

24

Zarbeth wedged his way through the crowd. His home-world's consulate was only a few blocks away, but getting to it with the crowd blocking him had proved no small task.

Suddenly, small arms fire erupted all around. Zarbeth hurled himself behind a parked transport.

People screamed and fled. He risked peeking over the vehicle's hull and caught sight of a gang of gun toting Druze. They wore pro-Austicon propaganda shirts and took pot shots at PFAR members. Hurling curses, they demanded the immediate release of Prognon Austicon, as if the populace had any control over the matter.

The seed wrapped against his abdomen heated even further, as if it had an intelligence of its own, and burned in response to the danger. Zarbeth ducked and fled through the scattering crowd, using humans as cover whenever he could. In a few seconds, they would be too dispersed, and he'd be exposed opening up his mission to potential failure.

He fled away from the Druze and darted through an alleyway. His heart beat more rapidly with every step and the seed's temperature seemed to intensify.

Zarbeth finally cleared the hot-zone. He spotted the Krenzin building just up ahead. The asphalt ahead of him curled and erupted as gunfire chewed across his path. Flinging himself behind cover, he looked up to spot a familiar Investigator.

Dekker shouted, "You!"

The Krenzin stood stiff. *Why was he here? What did he know?*

Dekker drew his guns and fired two shots over Zarbeth's shoulder. Two Druze yelped and collapsed, their own shots flew wide.

Zarbeth whirled around and scrambled for the safety of the consulate. He looked up to the broad, glass doors barely a hundred meters away where a Krenzin diplomat and a human stood and watched.

His eyes met the human's, and he instinctively recognized him as the pilot. Bullets tore the air with a whizzing sound and bounced with ricochets spinning away into the distance.

Zarbeth heard Dekker howl at him. "Get down!" Instead, he turned to look.

The red-haired woman who hated felines used a sword to cut down a Druze and Dekker pointed skyward where he fired his twin hand cannons. A sleek ship appeared over the top of an adjacent building.

With a shrill whine, a rocket streaked out of the craft and the consulate erupted, belching furious smoke and debris. The fiery blast threw Zarbeth to the dirt while the pirate vessel settled down upon the street. Flames blackened the sidewalk and spread to the nearby buildings. Several people ran through the roadways with hair and clothes on fire.

Zarbeth crawled to his feet. Pain snaked through his body and several cuts bled profusely, ruining his clothes where the shrapnel from the blast had cut him open. He glanced in horror at the burning wreckage of the consult where his pilot lay dead.

My mission must not fail—they must want the seed! Zarbeth turned his eyes back to the Investigators who fired upon the Shivans as they poured from the drop-ship.

"Dekker, help me!" Zarbeth yelled.

Grinding his teeth with grim determination, the Investigator continued firing at the enemy. More of his companions filled in behind him, taking up a defensive line. "Get to cover," he yelled.

In the distance, Zarbeth spotted an open door at the state-run orphanage. The Krenzin had sponsored it on behalf of the entire displaced people group. An ornate tower rose from its top boasting a massive, marble statue of Jeeran The Overcomer—a figure from the Krenzin history. Jeeran held a steel spear overhead to depict the moment right before he snapped it ceremonially, ending all violence on Krenzin Prime two thousand years ago when he became the first Pheema.

Surely Jeeran will save me! Zarbeth sprinted for the facility.

The burning seed at his abdomen felt hot and bright—as if it called to him. Zarbeth clutched his torso with a hand. Blood trickled down upon the chitinous bulb strapped to his body. It wriggled slightly, like a hatching egg.

He squeezed it, not knowing what was happening and unsure if it was supposed to do that. Zarbeth screamed as a Shivan bullet took out a chunk of his leg, spinning him to the ground.

"No. No, no!" Zarbeth insisted as he rolled onto his back. He watched the seed shake and squirm within his bandage. A sidelong glimpse of his pursuit revealed the Shivans tried to take up positions where they could snatch him from his would-be rescuers.

The Dozen outflanked them. A trio of pirates fell dead. Nearby, the biggest of them, obviously their captain judging by his decorum, ordered his crew to take the Krenzin dead or alive.

Dekker popped up from behind cover and drew a bead on him. The Shivan grabbed a nearby crew-mate, the second-most decorated member, and pulled him in front as a shield. The squat, muscular alien took the bullets meant for the leader and he died with surprise and ambition firmly etched on his face.

One of Dekker's shots got through and winged the pirate leader who spun on his heels, spraying blood from his shoulder. He repeated his orders to collect the felinoid and then he retreated within the ship.

Two more Shivans tried to get an angle on Zarbeth and moved to intercept.

Zarbeth looked down again and found vines creeping out from his bandages. They snaked their way across his body and plunged their tips like surgical fingers into the cuts he bled from. They increased in force and speed as they reacted with his blood.

He screamed as the seed mutated, feeding on him like some kind of parasite. Zarbeth staggered to his feet, overcome with sorrow and regret. He could feel the thing invading his mind, feeding on his thoughts as well as his body—merging with it as much as it consumed him.

Zarbeth stumbled up the steps to the orphanage, bewildered by everything happening to him. His stump arm exploded from the inside and a viny, plantlike limb replaced the one he had lost.

"What am I becoming?" Zarbeth didn't even recognize his voice as his body moved of its own accord, growing, mutating, swelling. He smashed the front of the orphanage as he and the alien presence vied for control of his body. People screamed, still trying to flee the chaos of both Druze and Shivan assaults.

The possessed Krenzin's heart sank as he smashed a woman who fled and then speared another with a shooting tentacle vine. *No! This is not the Krenzin way—we must not kill others!*

Confusion and regret echoed through his mind as the new, child-like presence threw a temper tantrum and drowned out his consciousness.

25

Pain. Fear. Shame. Desire to please. Confusion. So many emotions wafted off of the host that carried the seed. The seed felt those urges well up within Zarbeth—they imprinted upon it—molded it.

The seed recognized Zarbeth from before, it hadn't been fully awakened at their first meeting, but it still remembered him—he'd carried the seed before the science man had cut on him. Its memory burned within the seed who just now began grappling with the concept of self. The cutter hurt him—rage burned within its hull.

Zarbeth could not have hurt him. The thing sensed Zarbeth was a coward and feared hurting others—both from religious duty and fear of retaliation. Mostly the latter.

Her host was in pain. She felt the damaged nerves in Zarbeth's broken body as they ignited over and over. She wanted to help—but to do that, she needed to bond with the Krenzin male.

Zarbeth's pain spiked. His life was in imminent danger. What passed for fear in the Arbolean species raced through her as well. Without a strong host, she was at the mercy of every predator. *Cutters.* Zarbeth could be strong if he would only let her.

She stretched out with her roots, forced her germination, intent on taking over Zarbeth.

Certainly he would welcome bonding with her. She could keep him safe—she only wanted to help… to unite with him and make them one—to make him more than he was.

The seed child pushed new growth through his old wound, regrowing a lost limb. *Surely that would demonstrate that she only wanted to help Zarbeth?*

He rejected her—pushed away her mind as she made contact. Anger burned in her. *She would not stay here and die!*

She shrieked as they vied for control. Zarbeth's continued resistance forced her to overexert her wild growth. Without bonding together, only one could survive from their attempted union. She determined it would be her.

Rage sparked up within her. She opened her eyes, still growing uncontrollably. Zarbeth's fear still clung to her mind even as she burned out whatever remained of his consciousness.

Her Arbolean eyes focused on the humans running nearby as she nearly tripled her size. *Cutters!*

She flailed her arms—still not used to her new appendages and uncertain how to use them. The humans below her died easily. They would not hurt her; she would not allow it.

More humans came. They surrounded her, using their weapons to kill each other, and also aliens: not cutters, but she feared them. They looked too similar.

Must escape!

The aliens and humans used their guns on her. Their stinging needled her to a new level of rage.

She turned away from them and found herself hedged in by a building. It could crumble easily enough, she discovered, as she ripped giant hunks of it free. Her dark eyes caught glimpses of the tiny cutters inside. They ran away.

The cutters now feared *her*. She liked that.

26

Dekker fired two more shots as the Shivans advanced on Zarbeth. The Krenzin scrambled slowly up the steps near the orphanage, losing control of his form. He shrieked as vines took over his body, piercing his flesh from the inside.

Another Shivan took two steps, and then dove for cover as the Investigators put him in their cross-hairs. He fled back for the ship; moments later, the others followed, giving up on the chase and leaving their dead behind.

Zarbeth's growth continued as woody, bulbous growths burst from his skin like botanic cancer. As soon as the thrusters fired on the Shivan ship, Dekker and the others formed a perimeter around the monstrosity that had been Zarbeth only moments ago.

The Druze shifted their small arms fire from the dwindling supply of civilian targets and Investigators and targeted the creature. Bullets peppered the thing's hide. It roared in response, but they did not seem to do any damage beyond angering it.

"It's not human," Guy yelled. "It's reacting like an animal—we've got to calm it down."

It continued to grow, almost doubling in size again.

Dekker and the others fired on the Druze again. After another trio of them fell dead in the streets, the remainder fled.

Guy jumped up and down howling to get its attention, but it did not bother to turn. Instead, it ripped the face of the orphanage off. Children screamed within.

Dekker's heart sank. He glanced at Guy who nodded tight-lipped. "Whatever it is, we've got to put it down."

He aimed at the creature. "Everyone open fire!"

Vesuvius ran between the creatures legs, ducking below the fire line. She slashed with her swords as she sprinted through, cutting where the things Achilles tendons would have been, if it had them.

The plant monster shrieked and whirled, looking for her, though it remained upright and she rushed past it and inside the building where she hovered in the doorway, looking for an opening to attack again. It looked up and caught sight of their leader.

Dekker's eyes widened as they met the thing's gaze. A huge scar ran down what passed for its face. His blood ran ice-cold as he remembered Osmadiel's words. *Scarred is the seed that brings destruction—scarred before birth is the seed-child of Armageddon.*

He shouted at Nibbs, “This is it! The creature whose gene sequence we need to collect!”

Nibbs grimaced. “Well, we gotta live through the meeting, first.”

Dekker nodded and kept shooting.

Leviathan's eyes shifted back and forth behind his obsidian mask. *The Shivans are set to steal the seed and murder the carrier,* he told his master.

Prognon Austicon sat half a planet away in his cell. *Good. I couldn't care less about* who *possesses it or why... just so long as Dodona is harmed by its taking. Make sure you have your scientist engineer another replacement in case I decide to give one to them in the end.*

I am confused.

It is not about denying them the things they need, Austicon thought at him through the psychic link. *Our plans often align for as much a role in Dodona as I still play. But I only play their games by* my *rules, not by any others'. In truth, I want them to have it—but I want them to suffer a cost for taking it... if only because they think my plans hinge upon it.*

Leviathan asked about the trial. *You are not dejected by the ruling?*

Austicon leaned back in his cell and smiled. "*Let the world think itself safe from me for a time—it will make my return that much more terrifying. We both know that I have a great deal of pride—but I can lay it down for a time. It will reap an eventual gain; even humility serves a useful purpose. Let the sheep think that the jackal has been tamed. I know you could release me at a moment's notice... but I think I shall enjoy the game from this side for a while.*

As you wish.

Austicon ended their connection and Leviathan descended the stairs to his laboratory where Dr. Meng worked feverishly.

Meng rocked back and forth nervously. His severance from the Grrz hive mind had done irreparable harm and worsened his mental condition. He watched the holo unit display the news feed in the corner of the room as he worked.

Leviathan cocked his head at the scientist. He hadn't shown any interest in anything besides the research ever since the psychic found him on Galilee.

Meng startled when he finally noticed that he had company. The genetic printer had completed its operation, and a freshly cloned Arbolean seed sat within its bay. When the scientist saw Leviathan, his fear spiked, and he returned to the anxious heap he'd been since the Dozen ventured beyond New Hope.

Turning to face the media feed, Leviathan noticed what had so enthralled Dr. Meng. A shaky camera feed broadcast the mutation of Acantha's Arbolean seed. The Investigators fired on the Shivans as the pirates made a getaway, but without the seed in their possession.

Zarbeth writhed out of control in the center of Reef City. His body expanded and twisted with uncontrollable growth as the seed child found at Mount Sippar Sulcus bloomed wildly. He smashed and rampaged even as the Dozen turned their weapons on the newly spawned monstrosity.

Leviathan projected his voice into the scientist's mind. *Create another.*

Meng recoiled at the command. Everything about Leviathan terrified him and his condition only amplified his fears.

The scientist's kidnapper snatched the seed from its cradle and put it into his pocket. Leviathan knew why the Arbolean seed had sprouted out of control: Meng had somehow activated it—awoken it. Either intentionally or not, Leviathan did not know which. The doctor's mind proved too fractured to siphon anything more than broken pieces and those rarely made sense.

Meng turned his face away from the news feed and got to work.

Leviathan stared at him for a few moments as he worked the genetic machine, typing in gene sequences and alterations from his busted memory. Only *he* was capable of such a thing. Dr. Meng was the only one alive, to his knowledge, capable of replicating these ultra-rare seeds.

Finally, Leviathan turned and ascended the stairs, leaving Meng to do his work and gain respite from the silence. Leviathan expected he had some damage control to run on behalf of his Druze who had taken part in the riots that ended in explosions, alien invasion, and gunfire.

The cloning machine warmed up as Meng turned back to the feed and stared spellbound at the hybrid creature destroying property in the heart of Reef City. The creature had made the Krenzin carrier into something more—it had become part of him.

An ache burned in the doctor's gut and mind, an empty void that hungered where the hive mind had once brought comfort. Below him, the cloning machined whirred gently, laying the first few molecules of the new seed into the base of the cradle.

Meng whirled, afraid he'd heard a sound near the stairs—terrified that the black-clad man had returned. It was nothing: a figment of his shattered psyche.

He stared at the Investigators on the feed and the dead bodies strewn across the carnage of the scene. For the first time in a long while, Dr. Meng felt a glimmer of his old self peek through the squall and he formed a plan.

"We've got to stop this thing before it gets any bigger!" Dekker shouted. He and the rest of his crew continued to shoot at it. The bullets hurt it, but lacked any significant effect.

Director Lilee burst onto the scene with a half dozen of her agents in tow. They did not run up to engage. They weren't cleared for that, and besides, DoCS agents were surgical tools, not blunt hammers. "What in the black is going on here?" Lilee shouted. "This isn't the Druze we warned you about!"

Dekker barely acknowledged her. "Sorry—we're a little busy fighting a monster at the moment."

Lilee scowled from a safe distance.

The creature roared and flailed its whip-like appendages back and forth, smashing the faces of nearby buildings and scattering debris and broken facia all across the street. It tried to stomp on Rock and Corgan who dashed out of the way in the nick of time.

Whatever this creature was, it was no longer a Krenzin, and it was anything but agile. Another of its wild arms busted a brick fence and gate, dashing it to pieces like a capricious toddler scattering blocks.

Lilee winced at the grinding sounds of the property damage.

Vesuvius steeled herself in the nearby doorway, ready to run out and hack at it again. The thing seemed particularly agitated by her swords' razor edges when she'd attacked the last time—but growing at this rate, she was uncertain she could have any impact for much longer.

"Damage is crawling up into the millions, Mr. Knight! You've got to do something. Somebody stop this creature."

Guy double checked his bag and then tightened the straps on his backpack. "I've got it—I have an idea!" He dashed around the side of the creature's reach. "You've just got to keep the monster here for five more minutes!"

"Guy's ideas are never good," Matty noted with a hint of concern. "Remember the incident at that little restaurant in the orbital hub outside Saturn?"

"Hey! Not my fault… you can't blame sober Guy for drunk Guy's actions."

"What's your idea?" Dekker yelled his question.

"More property damage!"

Dekker grimaced and shot Lilee a sidelong glance. He scowled further when he recognized the camera crew that lurked just behind the agents, and behind that, a crowd had begun to assemble, keeping well beyond the danger zone, but close enough to watch whatever transpired in the Reef City streets. There was little chance everything would work out well—and every chance that this crowd would misremember the details.

29

The plant creature whirled and tried to catch Guy as he fled along the edge of the orphanage's lawn. He barreled through the door as it snapped and clawed for him, tearing brick and molding as it tried to catch the human.

He plunged through the door and collided with Vesuvius, knocking them both off their feet. A tangle vine shot through the doorway and wrapped around Guy's ankle; he yelped beneath its vice-like grip.

Vesuvius clambered to her feet and then sliced the vines, freeing the crew's mad bomber. They scrambled deeper into the entryway and more vines shot inside, feeling around blindly for prey. They grabbed support beams and tore free sections of wall.

"I have a plan—and it's not a very good one," Guy said as he checked a timepiece dangling from his backpack. "You've got five minutes." He started running up the steps.

She sprinted after him. "Five minutes? What's in five minutes?"

"It's *me! What do you* think *I'm gonna do?*" He rounded a corner in the main stairwell and disappeared.

"Ah crap. He's gonna blow it all up."

Vesuvius glanced around. Memories washed over her—and not good ones. It felt as if she walked through a flashback when she stared down the corridor that led to the dormitory. She'd been forced to live in one of these state-run institutions for several weeks as a teenager after her… she pushed the memory away.

It had taken several weeks of fighting to get out, literal fists on faces. The government child services refused to give her uncle custody; they'd claimed that Muramasa had ties to religious extremism. Eventually, after she'd beaten a number of mean girls in the living center within an inch of their lives, they released her to live with her uncle and cousin, Shin. She didn't know about their side of the story, but it had been a nightmare for her—and she definitely didn't want to think about it.

Vesuvius rushed through the hallways looking for a rear door to escape through. She glanced within the rooms on the main floor as she passed, but they were empty. Right before kicking open the exit door, she heard a thud on the ceiling above her.

Clenching her jaw, she promised herself that it was just Guy making racket above her. She paused and listened momentarily before she recognized the whimpers of a child. *Crap.*

Dashing back the way she'd come, she hurried up the stairs and combed the hallways, shouting for any survivors. "Kids? Are you in here—we've got to get out, right now!"

Vesuvius stumbled onto a cluster of children between ages nine and twelve. She took a knee in front of them and counted heads. "Is this everyone? Are you all here?"

A little girl clutched her ratty, stuffed bear. Tears streamed down her dirt-streaked face, and she shook her head, pointing into the next room. The mangled body of a teenager laid across the body of the adult worker who had been working as the children's supervisor.

"Is everybody else here?"

Another child nodded.

She took her by the hand. "Everybody follow me. I'm here to help, but we've got to hurry—let's go as fast as we can out the back. I'll keep you safe." Vesuvius stood and rushed down the hall at what she assumed was a brisk pace for a child.

Vesuvius glanced at a clock on the wall. She gritted her teeth and urged them forward. "Come on—let's go, let's go!"

They crashed through the door and hurried out the back, keeping a building between them and the monster at the front door. Green vines and appendages flailed in the distance, revealing the growing enormity of the mutate on the other side of the building, only dwarfed by the tall spire that rose above the orphanage. "Keep going! Run… run as fast as you can!"

30

Guy rushed through the uppermost sections of the top floor looking for any and all structural supports to apply the sticky, explosive material. He looked at his timer and then spared a glance through the window.

The creature had grown easily above two stories already. The rest of the Dozen encircled it and moved while shooting, taking turns baiting the creature which lashed out and stomped after them like a confused child. It got half a step faster and bumbled less with each passing moment. In a short span, it would be fast enough and skilled enough to wipe out those who harassed it.

Guy placed the last charge and synced their detonators. He checked his timer again—with only thirty seconds left, he wouldn't make it out of the building by normal means before they went off. He scaled the last segment of steps and burst out through the roof access. The spire still towered tall above him with its massive monument perched at its top like some kind of religious symbol.

Yanking the grapple gun Nibbs had given from his backpack, he fired at the rooftop on the other side of the road and looped his gun around a length of steel rebar to tie it off on the statue's base. Guy ran towards the edge of the building and snatched the cord, riding it like a zip-line.

The creature roared as it spotted him flash overhead. Guy slipped through the plant monster's flailing arms as the building erupted behind him. Flames shot into the sky and flash-boiled structural supports; the top two levels of the orphanage exploded, raining debris and fire into the streets below and onto the enemy.

Dekker and his crew ran for cover. The monster roared, and the building's internal structure moaned as the spire and monument shifted at the buckle point.

Jeeran's spear-wielding statue tipped into a new angle and then plummeted from its perch. It aimed for the creature that had once been Zarbeth and rushed to attack, bid by gravity.

They collided with a sickening thud and Jeeran's spear pierced through the thing, pinning it to the ground and crushing it below the incredible weight of the Krenzin figure.

The hunk of steel Guy's grapple gun had been tied to was connected to the base of Jeeran's statue. He hadn't had enough time to reach the other side of the building before the change of momentum reversed his course. The thing yanked him downward and Guy plummeted backwards and towards the crushed creature on a rerouted escape route.

Howling surprisedly, Guy rode the steep descent all the way down and crashed into the body of the botanical beast. He slapped against its side like a bird off a windscreen and rolled off the thing, bruised but scrambling away and out of harm's reach.

Finally, he turned to look at it. It had a surprisingly humanoid face with a kind of intelligence behind its darkening eyes—it wore a mixture of confusion and pain on its scarred face.

Guy returned to his friends' side in the sudden, violent stillness that followed the explosion. Vesuvius and a collection of children appeared around a corner nearly a block away when someone shouted from the assembled PFAR protesters, "You… you killed it! It was a life and deserved to live!"

Dekker turned to look at the rioters, incredulous.

The Investigators felt keenly aware of the camera crew zooming in on them to record every facial tick and nuance of their reactions.

An anti-Investigator chant arose from the PFAR horde.

Suddenly, the creature flailed in one final, frenzied act. Zarbeth's colossus shrugged the statue off as it bent to its feet, ripping half its torso away as Jeeran's spear dislodged as poorly as a gut-swallowed fish hook.

It turned and fixed the collection of Investigators, the media crew and DoCS agents, and the PFAR mob with a murderous gaze. Before it could finish the first step of its renewed attack, a blast of impossibly brilliant energy blasted from Dekker as he leveled his Reliquary at it.

A fierce energy beam rippled with crackles of lightning; it burned through the green titan, charring it to ash and eradicating it from existence. Dekker's laser-like beam washed the creature in destructive energy and he angled the weapon downward, blasting the plant colossus into the crater, forming a crucible that incinerated its every molecule and melted away half of Jeeran's visage.

The Reliquary beam burned so bright that when it finally dissipated, it seemed to have stolen the daylight from all around them. By comparison, it left the world darker in its afterglow.

An awed, stark silence renewed. This time, nobody dared utter a peep.

31

Barely more than a day had passed since the debacle at the Reef City square. The sheer amount of paperwork required of Director Lilee nearly made her go cross-eyed and threatened to give her carpel tunnel from signature pages. A short trip was a very welcomed respite.

She arrived at the house on the address. A servant escorted her out the back and towards a grove of trees; Lilee recognized her from her previous visit with Acantha. The tall ring of beech trees concealed whatever laid beyond though a telltale shimmer of dancing light behind the veil indicated a pyre within the center.

Five women emerged from the trees, dressed in yellow robes identical to Acantha's. Their faces remained hidden beneath their hoods, but Lilee felt certain she was among them.

They took her by the hand and led her within the grove. She wanted to ask questions—to find out more about what these women stood for, but they exuded such power that the Acting Director of the Division of Confidential Secrets fell silent under their thrall.

Lilee still knew nothing else about Dodona. Nothing showed up in any of the searches that she managed in the waning moments of free time between stacks of reports, requisitions, and other forms. She followed her guides to the burning stacks of cord-wood.

A nearby wicker effigy of a man wore a robe. He watched from afar like some kind of regal scarecrow.

An old woman in mustard robes sat upon a simple chair in front of the leaping flames. Her chest heaved, and she slouched steeply. Deep bags below her eyes had filled purple; whatever illness plagued her had deeply run its course.

The healthy women gathered tightly around Lilee as their sickly sister stood and disrobed. Just below her sternum, a burnished piece of wood puckered from her skin. She laid aside her ceremonial garb and grimaced as she clutched the wooden knob and slowly pulled a spike free from her body. What pierced her skin looked like a hardened seed pod.

Lilee grimaced at the sight, but could not tear her eyes away, either.

With a wet slurking sound, the woman removed it from its place just below her ribcage; she dropped it as she collapsed. Acantha retrieved it and pulled back her hood while the other four picked up the husk of the old woman and heaved her through the air. She landed unconscious atop the pyre built in her honor.

"Madame Voight carried this seed for nearly two hundred years."

Lilee raised her brows.

“Joining with an Arbolean carries certain inherent perks. Are you ready to become a sister?”

Lilee looked around. She glanced at the male effigy as the others draped Voight’s robes over her. “I have so many questions,” she said as she turned back to Acantha.

Too late. She gasped as the old woman plunged the sharp, woody stake into her. It pierced the skin and implanted within her, sliding behind her sternum and disappearing with surprisingly little pain.

Inside, her voice reverberated a scream between her ears, but no sound came from the woman’s mouth. She did not ask the burning questions. Lilee did not understand, and yet she knew so much all at once. A presence awakened within her and she experienced a state that could only be called communion as she bonded with the alien presence from beyond the reaches of space and felt it's will flow through her. She was no longer Lilee; she had become something else… so much more.

32

Oh how Acantha must've raged when she learned of Zarbeth's failure. Leviathan sent his thoughts towards his master who he knew would appreciate it as he languished in the human dungeon on the south-most continent, the barren District 8.

This had been Austicon's plan all along, he felt certain of it. He would have asked Austicon, but the master was not currently listening for Leviathan's voice. Austicon was a member of Dodona, the Left Hand they called him, and for centuries he and the Yellow Women had vied against each other and alongside one another depending on the circumstances… both sides always looked for ways to harm the other or use them for their own means. Their relationship was more complicated than an uneasy alliance or estranged family.

The loyal servant rose from the new, secret Druze stronghold where he'd been operating from and departed for the secure facility where he kept the broken Doctor Meng. His terrorists had been ordered to abandon the compound and resume their daily lives immediately following the Reef City incident. Only the lab remained at the previous site and he planned to move it as soon as the next seed had completed.

Leviathan arrived and descended the stairwell, letting his footfalls echo through the block columns to announce his arrival. He'd noticed how skittish Meng was around him and hoped to set his mind at ease. Scared prey was too often dangerous.

After punching in an access code, the door slid open. Meng stood on uneasy feet with eyes shifting back and forth. He'd sprouted hair all over his unkempt face and looked more like an animal than a man.

The doctor twitched and mumbled as if arguing with himself-he'd kept his own company within the stark silence of the lab. The cloned Arbolean seed that had begun all the chaos laid on the table next to the genetic printer which whirred and cycled through the operations, nearing twenty percent completion.

Leviathan entered and walked a slow, nonthreatening loop through the room to keep the man at ease. He could feel the scientist's tension. Parts of the doctor's mind had come back together and other parts burned hotter than ever with mental friction, like an engine running at red-line capacity with broken bolts grinding inside the pistons.

He held out his hands, signaling the man-beast to calm down. Leviathan reached out for those parts of Meng's mind that seemed to have healed. He concentrated his astral senses on the man's recent memories. The mental voyage was like walking on thin ice; the fragile mind cracked and groaned as he rested the weight of his presence upon it.

Leviathan stopped walking, quit searching, and merely existed in the moment, observing the doctor's transient thoughts. They bubbled to the surface as Meng remembered his plan with the psychic hitchhiker spying on them. Meng re-lived what he had done days ago in Leviathan's secluded lab.

The scientist replicated the clone experiment and recreated the seed child to create an exact genetic replica. He mixed into the gene sequence some form of arcane mathematics that bewildered the psychic—some formula that only Meng knew and understood—the Meng who lived before his mental breakdown. Now, it only translated as gibberish, but a gibberish that functioned well enough to recreate the process.

The scientist had his own designs on the seed as his fragile mind succumbed to the Grrz insanity. The ice beneath Leviathan's feet sagged and groaned as he understood Meng's motives. *Meng wanted the whole of the human race to die—to feel that same emptiness that had hollowed him out post-Galilee*.

Leviathan felt his footing give way as his psychic hold on the target failed. Before plunging though and out of the dream-fast he spotted a distant memory floating in the void as if Meng had intentionally tried to keep it away from Leviathan's purview, untethered and left to wander.

It presented like a faded reflection in a mirror, but still Leviathan found it. Meng created another seed already—before Leviathan had taken him—and he'd left it in the lab on Galilee.

Leviathan dropped out of the man's mind and locked gazes with the scientist whose mind had healed more and proved stronger than the psychic had given him credit for.

Both knew that only *Meng* had the knowledge necessary to clone a viable seed. Quade had paid with his life on Galilee to unlock that secret for him.

The doctor shuddered, keenly aware that the psychic had gleaned much insight from his mind. Before Leviathan could get any closer, Meng sprang into action.

His fingers flew across the keypad in a flurry and he deleted the gene-prints necessary to complete the cloning process, aborting the new seed child in the process. In one fluid motion, Meng used a scalpel to open a wound across his chest and grabbed the seed meant to replace the one Acantha took.

"I've already awakened the seed—just as I did before you gave the last one away to that Yellow Woman."

Leviathan rushed across the room, but didn't reach the scientist in time. *What have you done?*

Meng plunged the seed inside his own abdomen. "Something new is coming!"

Green vines and foliage spilled out from the wound on Meng's torso. He looked down at the trail of greenery leaking from his body like a pregnant mother might gaze at her kicking child.

Leviathan drew his sword and swung, intent on taking the insane doctor out of the problematic equation. In the breadth of his last second before Leviathan removed his head, the psychic broke down Meng's mental barriers.

As Meng's life flashed before his own eyes, all his plans were laid bare to the blade-wielding clairvoyant. Meng had watched the feeds of the plant creature and understood each of its mechanisms. In the absence of the hive-mind, he intended to join this alien creature and complete the mission it had failed at: to remake this world in *his own image.* Then, he would *be* the planet. Meng would no longer be afraid or alone—perhaps whatever remained of the Grrz would come to planet Meng and he would rejoin the hive-mind as planet Grrz!

Meng's neck split and his head flew from its shoulders. His body toppled to the ground, but still the seed continued to germinate. Leviathan had hoped that death would halt the process.

He needed to locate that last seed and this new, unexpected problem complicated things. A second ago, he had three potential seeds; now he had none.

Austicon was currently silent, but Leviathan knew that his master desired two outcomes. He wanted the Shivans to have the seed… and he also wanted Dodona to have its prize. Leviathan scowled behind his dark mask and grabbed the blooming body of the fallen scientist. He dragged him to the cryo-chamber and flung the flowering corpse within before activating the flash freezer.

He composed two brief messages. One to Acantha regarding the mutating scientist who he'd just preserved in stasis and another to Gr'Narl, the Shivan pirate captain. The Yellow Women could collect the body at their leisure and he promised the pirates a follow-up message once he'd learned the status of the remaining seed. Until Austicon gave him a new mission, Leviathan felt the seed was his new task.

The media feed still played in the corner of the room, broadcasting the corporate marketing segment which caught his ear. He recognized the fingerprints of Dodona on the story of corporate takeover and espionage. The remnant of Jagaracorps sold a huge number of assets to recover from the losses suffered recently. Negative publicity regarding their activity on

Galilee nearly sunk the mega-company. One of those assets, the moon of Osix, was snapped up by Halabella Corps at a discount.

At least to Leviathan, their plans seemed obvious. Dodona had set things into motion well before Zarbeth's failure.

Leviathan exited the laboratory and left it behind him. He had no intention of returning.

The Dozen sat around the mess hall as a group, watching the scathing media indictment of their team via the news feeds. Most of them wore scowls. The PFAR movement which steered most of the newscasters did not treat the Investigators fairly.

Mostly, the crew booed and hissed at the screens. Guy and a few others had invented a drinking game based on the media's renewed hatred of the Dozen; those participants had gotten pretty hammered despite it being so early in the broadcast exposé.

Already irked that he hadn't gotten the genome sample necessary for unlocking the arcane map, Dekker looked up to the figure darkening their doorway. Director Lilee stood in the entry. Her presence aggravated his mood; they hadn't finished licking their wounds.

She approached wearing a scowl on her face.

"I'm guessing that lifetime, irrevocable pass you were offering isn't going to be good anytime soon?"

Lilee shook her head.

"You know we did what we had to," Dekker insisted.

The Director crossed her arms. "The fact is, *you blew up an orphanage… live on the news!*"

"Nobody died in the explosion," Vesuvius sauntered over, meeting the wily woman's gaze with a rival one. "We saved lives."

"You're lucky that enough people believe that," Lilee hissed. "But not everybody is convinced."

Dekker rolled his eyes. It was pretty clear that the MEA planned to hang the Dozen out to dry in the winds of political sentiment and popular opinion. "So no price break and we've got to pay our taxes like everyone else. I guess it was worth a shot," he tried his best to find a silver lining.

Lilee extended a hand and offered him a folded sheet of paper.

Vesuvius stared at it like it could be venomous. She frowned as Dekker took it; she would not have accepted it.

His eyes nearly bulged from his head. "Is—is this a bill? *How dare you stick this on us?* We can't afford this kind of cash!"

Lilee shrugged. "I guess you can always fight it in court."

"This is outrageous!"

Vesuvius peeked at it. Her eyebrows nearly leapt off her face. She turned and snatched up the nearest napkin she could find and scribbled a bill of her own and threw it at Director Lilee. "Oh yeah? Well then here's our bill for services that you contracted us for!"

The paper fluttered onto the DoCS worker's shoulder where it clung for her life. She glanced at it with a sneer. "It might not be official. This isn't signed and dated."

Fully flustered and about erupt volcanically, Vesuvius snatched the paper and scribbled a signature and date. "There! Are you happy now?"

Dekker took her by the shoulders so that she wouldn't attack the woman.

Director Lilee clucked and shook her head. She picked up the paper and pen as she grinned. "Whatever. I'll send someone by from collections soon enough."

She turned on her heels and left the group behind.

"Oh hey!" Guy said, turning from the media feed. He nearly drooled on himself and pointed to the holo-feed projecting an image of Director Lilee. "Isn't that the lady from the news? That probly' means we drink gain. Right?" He reached for his glass, missed, and promptly passed out.

34

Barricades and quarantine tape cordoned off the area. Director Lilee ducked beneath the barrier and entered the hot zone. Unlike the handful of others allowed within the area, she did not wear any protective gear.

The acting leader of the Division of Confidential Secrets knew what the rest of the public did not: there was no threat of contamination or infection from the Arbolean colossus. Rumors to the contrary came from her office in an effort to keep people as far away from the area as possible.

She shook off a few of the odd looks from the science teams as if to say *I'll be fine*. They'd already planned to end the official quarantine that evening.

Lilee walked through the destroyed zone with wide eyes. She had been here when the chaos happened and the Dozen fought the thing that had once been Zarbeth, who she now knew was a Krenzin courier sent by Acantha. Her new membership in Dodona privileged her with all manner of secrets… and also burdens.

She scaled the stairs and entered the ruined orphanage. The entire face of the building on the street side had been ripped away and Lilee stepped hesitantly on the floor of the second level, testing its uncertain structural integrity.

From her vantage she surveyed the greater scene below, looking for any hints at the thing her sisters in yellow had sent her after. The crater below had only recently stopped smoldering and a researcher in a shiny enviro-suit gingerly descended into the pit carrying a case for taking samples. He walked carefully on the uneven footing.

Lilee narrowed her eyes and exited the building. If anywhere, she assumed the crater would be the location of the item she sought. Dodona desperately wanted the seed returned to them. They intended to groom their own colossus—one unlike anything else before it.

Scientists milled about in the distance, taking readings and verifying the safety of the location. Two others had already removed their suits, confident of the area's safety.

As she approached the crater, Lilee shoved away thoughts of research teams like this one who had met terrible fates on Phobos 12. She stood on the lip of the caldera and focused on the task at hand.

Lilee picked her way down the slope, past twisted chunks of steel and broken block frozen in place by the melted asphalt. The scientist in the basin looked up at her with dazzled eyes.

He beckoned to her and Lilee caught his name badge, *Kwambai*. She'd personally vetted every one of the scientists on the forensics team.

Doctor Earl Kwambai was the foremost human expert on galactic botany.

With an audience, Kwambai prattled on, working through his excitement. “Plants operate according to a certain set of biological rules. Hand me that sample jar?”

Lilee leaned over Kwambai’s open equipment case. She grabbed a container and handed it to the botanist who didn’t seem to notice she wore no protective gear.

“There are some plants that seem to defy the rules that govern the flora native to earth, or any of the Sol system, for that matter,” he continued, taking a forceps out of his waistband. “I’ve been collecting extensive research on the topic, ever since I first ran across some cryptic references to an intelligent plant species from beyond Sol.”

“And you think this thing was one of them?”

Kwambai nodded eagerly. “I do. I’ve been compiling my notes and preparing to write a paper on the topic but I never had a biological reference to cite… until now.”

With a grin, Kwambai removed a small tendril of green material nestled amongst the ashes. He deposited it in the sample jar and snapped the lid tight.

Before Kwambai could move, Lilee grabbed him by the back of the head and yanked him to the ground, smashing his head against a jagged pile of rubble; a length of rebar impaled Kwambai's face-shield and skull. He immediately fell still with blood and fog occluding the thin hazmat helmet. Shock froze on his face.

Lilee snatched the container and slid it into her pocket. "Some secrets must remain hidden until we are ready tell them," the Director whispered.

She glanced around to make sure the scene was still private and that Kwambai's heart had indeed stopped. Finally, she ran up the slope and yelled for help. "Somebody come quick—Doctor Kwambai slipped and fell on the rocks!"

35

Ezekiel sat upon the Divine Machine which existed apart from time and dimensional reality. From his perch he watched the Great Engine stitch the cosmic weave into the tapestry of the multi-verse.

The contraption which let him step between the cosmic wheel and the realities it churned out slouched upon his back. He cinched its buckles for comfort and freed the medallion he wore about his neck so that it swung freely.

Rogue threads weaved into potentially dangerous, variant patterns. The weave clouded, losing its organized and ordered pattern. One line in particular seemed to bleed, hemorrhaging reality, and the one nearest it weaved its own design, artistic and Avant Garde, but not like the other, threatening the integrity of the machine with its very existence.

Ezekiel glanced sidelong at the busted mechanisms that should have pruned the problematic channel. It had been Osmadiel's duty to run the apparatus, but he'd destroyed the mechanisms when he fell along with the Watchers and other Operators during the Gardener Rebellion: when Asmodeus abandoned his post and rallied many of his fellows against the Machinist.

Walking across the machine and onto the platform, Ezekiel toed through the wreckage of the pruning apparatus. Little appeared salvageable. He glanced back up to the rogue lines of reality, unsure if he should, or could interfere.

He paused and momentarily wondered if he had done this before. Ezekiel knew he had made many trips to the Great Engine, traveling through time and space, and that not all of his tasks had proven successful—but in each case, the mission had been the same: protect the machine… do the jobs that the absent Operators had been commissioned to do. His mind, however, was cloudy. A haze seemed to obfuscate his fate and how he fit into the system.

Ezekiel grimaced, understanding what that meant. The likely cause was that he'd died on this mission—probably many times over. He blasted a hot breath through his nose; his own mortality did not change the fact of his calling or mission.

He looked back to the fabric of reality as it stitched across the cosmos. The dangerous line had the markings of the Fallen Ones all over it. Whether Asmodeus, Dione, or any other, Ezekiel did not know, but he understood that the damage could not be fixed from outside the pattern. He could only rectify it from within.

Standing at the busted excising instruments he looked forward through reality, searching for the cause and potential solution. A mercenary lost the woman he loved and destroyed the cosmos with power stolen from the batteries of the Divine Engines.

Ezekiel bent low and picked up one of the busted implements that channeled such energy in order to snip those stray reality threads. "This is it," he observed. "This is the thing that destroyed the universe." Ezekiel had seen it in the hands of the man who annihilated reality. He knew how chaotic pieces of the Great Engine could become when inserted into the reality it created.

He looked back through the system that had once been Osmadiel's post. The controls had been linked to the Operator since before the dawn of time, and he still managed some control over them. The grinning face of Osmadiel blocked the screen, and the Watcher locked his gaze on the prophet-turned time traveler.

His eyes practically burned through the blindfold and spoke wordless volumes of what dwelled within the chained creature's heart. *You cannot stop us! The Fallen Legion will never bow.*

Ezekiel turned just as Osmadiel's tools sprang to life. Barely operational, they had lost most of their functionality, but remained deadly enough to any human caught unawares. Like an animatronic scorpion tail, the actuator that moved and focused the cosmic pruner in Ezekiel's hands lashed out.

It struck Ezekiel in the chest, tearing a gaping hole in his torso. Energy super-heated its tip burning his organs as the mechanical arm ripped free a chunk of flesh. Skin and muscle hung in rags, exposing his bones to whatever atmosphere Osmadiel's platform contained.

Ezekiel staggered backwards, certain the wound was lethal. Before the arm could attack again and finish him, he snatched the controls affixed to his belt. The burnished, cylindrical contraption strapped to his body had been given to him by Ezekiel from another time-line.

With an arcane grating noise and a puff of ozone, the machine released a blip of smoke and the cosmic wheel turned at the prophet's behest. The machine flung him through time and space—sending him to the only person he could think to contact under such dire circumstances… the man from Anathoth.

In the seconds before he expired, only Ezekiel could set in motion the necessary events to protect the Divine Machine and cut off the dangerous time-line that threatened the whole of reality. The rogue stitches of the Avant Garde line would have to protect itself.

The End.

Special Offer:

Thank you so much for checking out my ebook collection! As a special bonus for you, I'd like to invite you download FIVE ebooks for free as a part of my Starter Library.

To get your free Starter Library, simply visit this link:

http://eepurl.com/gcd1vX

Enter your email address and then collect your books as they are sent to you. It's that simple!

FREE STARTER BOOK LIBRARY

About the author:

Christopher D. Schmitz is the traditionally published and self-published author of both fiction and nonfiction. When he is not writing or working with teenagers he might be found at comic conventions as a panelist or guest. He has been featured on television, podcasts, and every other medium he can get into. He runs a blog for indie authors.

Always interested in stories, media such as comic books, movies, 80s cartoons, and books called to him at a young age—especially sci-fi and fantasy. He lives in rural Minnesota with his family where he drinks unsafe amounts of coffee. The caffeine shakes keep the cold from killing them.

Schmitz also holds a Master's Degree and freelances for local newspapers. He is available for speaking engagements, interviews, etc. via the contact form and links on his website or via social media.

Dear reader,

Thank you for reading my book. If you enjoyed it or find anything helpful within its pages won't you please take a moment to leave me a review at your favorite retailer? Sharing this title with your friends on social media and requesting it via your local library will also help immensely. Discoverability is the lifeblood of success for authors and we can't continue writing without help!

I also hope you will keep tabs on me by joining my mailing list. You can get free books and other updates by signing up for that list at: www.AuthorChristopherDSchmitz.com.

Thanks for reading and sharing!

Christopher D Schmitz

Discover Fiction Titles by Christopher D Schmitz

The Last Black Eye of Antigo Vale
Burning the God of Thunder
Piano of the Damned
Shadows of a Superhero
The TGSPGoSSP 2-Part Trilogy
Father of the Esurient Child
Dekker's Dozen: A Waxing Arbolean Moon
Dekker's Dozen: Weeds of Eden
Dekker's Dozen: Spawn of Ganymede
Dekker's Dozen: The Seed Child of Sippar Sulcus
Dekker's Dozen: The Armageddon Seeds
Dekker's Dozen: The Last Watchmen
Wolf of the Tesseract
Wolves of the Tesseract: Taking of the Prime
Wolves of the Tesseract: Through the Darque Gates of Koth
The Kakos Realm: Grinden Proselyte
The Kakos Realm: Rise of the Dragon Impervious
The Kakos Realm: Death Upon the Fields of Splendor
Anthologies No.1

Discover NonFiction Titles by Christopher D Schmitz

The Indie Author's Bible
Why Your Pastor Left
John in the John
Gospels in the John

Please Visit
http://www.authorchristopherdschmitz.com
Sign-up on the mailing list for exclusives and extras

other ways to connect with me:
Follow me on Twitter:
https://twitter.com/cylonbagpiper

Follow me on Goodreads:
www.goodreads.com/author/show/129258.Christopher_Schmitz

Like/Friend me on Facebook:
https://www.facebook.com/authorchristopherdschmitz

Subscribe to my blog:
https://authorchristopherdschmitz.wordpress.com

Favorite me at Smashwords:
www.smashwords.com/profile/view/authorchristopherdschmitz

CPSIA information can be obtained
at www.ICGtesting.com
Printed in the USA
BVHW040305070623
665472BV00001B/31

9 781641 532402